VILLAINS

(KALAZAD – BOOK 2)

Also by K.L. Mitchell

Kalazad
The Road to Kalazad

VILLAINS

(KALAZAD – BOOK 2)

K.L. MITCHELL

Desert Palm Press

Villains
(Kalazad – Book 2)

By K.L. Mitchell

©2022 K.L.Mitchell

ISBN: (book) 9781954213432
ISBN (epub): 9781954213449

This is a work of fiction - names, characters, places, and incidents are the product of the author's imagination or are used fictitiously. Any resemblance to actual persons living or dead, businesses, events or locales is entirely coincidental. All rights reserved.

No part of this publication may be reproduced, distributed, or transmitted in any form or by any means, including photocopying, recording, or other electronic or mechanical methods, without the prior written permission of the publisher, except in the case of brief quotations embodied in critical reviews and certain other noncommercial uses permitted by copyright law.

For permission requests, write to the publisher at lee@desertpalmpress.com or "Attention: Permissions Coordinator," at

Desert Palm Press
1961 Main Street, Suite 220
Watsonville, California 95076
www.desertpalmpress.com

Editor: CK King
Cover Design: Rachel George

Printed in the United States of America
First Edition September2022

Dedication

Here's to the villains, the scallywags, rascals and ne'er-do-wells. They are the inciters of action, the complicators of plot, without whom a story is a dull and lifeless thing. They are the cradle of heroes, the reason for happy endings. In all their thousand guises, they teach us that monsters exist, yes, but they may be overcome.

It is to them, therefore, that this volume is respectfully dedicated.

Chapter One

LISTEN, THIS IS THE hell of unfinished stories.

Here are the crippled tales and sagas with no end, the two-part trilogies. The tragedies of time, writer's block, and circumstance. They are the stories once begun, but never ended.

In a Victorian drawing room, a detective stands paralyzed over a body, waiting for an insight which never comes.

Two princes languish in an ogre's cave, waiting for rescue by their younger brother who has decided to stay home and rule the kingdom himself.

In a windowless brick house, a lone pig chokes down another energy drink, rubs his eyes, and goes back to scanning a wall of security monitors in search of a wolf long since dead of trichinosis.

They all float here, nebulous in the never-never land between the pages. Fantasy, tragedy, drama, romance, all are frozen in time, spinning in eternal limbo, groping blindly for un-listening ears, and all desire one thing.

An ending.

Just lately, there seems to be a lot more of them.

* * * *

Once upon a time, there was a little girl who lived with her mother in a cabin by the woods. She had a lovely red riding cloak, which she wore all the time. For this reason, she was known as Little Red Riding Hood.

One day, when she was five, her mother sent her through the woods to deliver a basket of goodies to her grandmother, who was feeling poorly. "Be careful," said the mother. "For there is a big, bad wolf in the forest, and he eats little girls. So never stray from the trail and hurry back as quickly as you can."

Little Red Riding Hood did as she was told, skipping through the woods and never giving a moment's thought to the big bad wolf, or to wandering off the narrow trail, which snaked through the heart of the forest. Nor did she give a thought to the fact that her mother, being fully aware that a man-eating wolf was on the prowl, nevertheless sent her five-year-old child into the woods alone while she stayed at home. Little Red Riding Hood didn't think about a lot of things.

While she was strolling along through the woods, she heard a curious sound, rather like a windstorm. It came on suddenly and stopped almost as soon as it had started. The wind had a hollow sort of quality to it, and what might have been a muffled yip at the end. Little Red Riding Hood waited for a moment by the edge of the trail, but there was no more wind, only silence. Off she went, hoppity-skip down the trail to Grandma's house, which smelled like feet. She dropped off the goodies, left as quickly as she could, and never gave the incident another thought. Ever.

Eventually, she grew up and settled down with an itinerant woodcutter some twenty years her senior. Grandma choked on a bone in her gruel and was discovered a few weeks later. The riding hood, once outgrown by its owner, got demoted to dust cloths.

And nobody ever saw the big bad wolf again.

* * * *

The rains of the morning had moved away west, and the sun was drying out the road as the centauress, Iyarra, loped unhurriedly along. On her back, Revka munched a midmorning apple and fussed with her hair.

"How's it going back there?" Iyarra glanced over her shoulder.

Revka worked another burr free and flicked it away into the woods. "Think I've almost got 'em out of my hair, at least. Pretty sure there's one in my boot, plus a couple of other places I won't mention. I swear, those things get *everywhere*."

Iyarra reached back a chestnut-brown hand and patted her girlfriend. "Sorry about that. Guess we missed 'em because it was so dark when we made camp."

"Mm," Revka grumped. "Well, we wouldn't have had that problem at an inn, that's all I'm saying. I know you prefer sleeping outdoors, but I kinda got used to having a bed, you know?"

Iyarra laughed. "I know, I know, but look at it this way; at least I don't have that farmer chasing after me anymore. Total release from indentures and we can do what we want."

"Well, sure." Revka fidgeted with her hair, which turned out to have another burr in it after all. "But I wish I could have come up with something better than, 'Here, take all of our money, just please go away.' Not exactly my greatest plan ever."

"Well, it worked didn't it?" Iyarra giggled and reached back to give Revka's leg a squeeze. "And I have heard you say that the simplest plans are often the best. Besides, we'd just got finished stopping a war, so maybe it was best to stick to something simple."

That was true. After they'd trekked halfway across the continent and back again to stop a mad duke from building an army of magic soldiers, Revka had definitely needed a week or two to clear her head. Revka and Iyarra had returned the magic book stolen by the duke to the monks, who were very grateful, of course, but as the monks were notoriously short on material wealth, the girls had to settle for some provisions and a promise of shelter any time they felt like climbing up the mountain trail to the monastery again.

Revka frowned at the memory. "You'd think that that would have at least been good for some kind of reward, though, wouldn't you? I mean, I'm not asking for a knighthood, but maybe a medal or two, royal commendation. Sack of cash. You know."

"Oh, me too." Iyarra maneuvered around a dead badger in the road. "But you know what they said."

"Yeah, yeah." Revka rolled her eyes. "Them and their 'Delicate political situation.'" Her voice took on a sarcastic lilt. "'The general feeling is that everyone is better off just pretending nothing happened.' Real convenient. Means they don't have to reward us or anything."

"Well, you can kind of see what they mean. I'm sure the king has got enough to worry about without word getting out about how close things came."

"Eh, maybe, but I bet the king didn't wake up this morning with burrs on his butt."

Iyarra stifled a laugh. "Revka!"

"Not that he'd have to pick them off himself," Revka added. "I bet he's got someone for that. It's probably a special job with a title and everything."

Iyarra covered her mouth, desperately trying to suppress a giggle.

Old leather armor creaked as Revka sat up. "Oh, Lord, can't you just see it? The king ringing a little bell for a servant. What is it, Your Majesty? A great crisis has come upon our land, the king says." Revka sat bolt upright, one hand draped over her chest, while she spoke in a high nasal tone. "A burr has been visited upon Our posterior. Send for the Royal Burr Picker at once!

"Suddenly, a flourish of trumpets! And there he is, the Pluckmaster General! Resplendent in his spiky jodhpurs, holding high his ceremonial golden tongs—"

"Uhm, Revka?"

"The king bends over, somewhere a drum begins to roll—"

"Revka..."

"The Archbishop douses the afflicted area with holy water just as the—"

"Revka!"

"What?"

"Royal guards."

Revka blinked. "What? What about them?"

Iyarra tilted her head forward. "Royal guards. Coming this way."

Indeed they were. Four of them marched down the road in the opposite direction the two girls were going. Revka & Iyarra kept quiet as the guards went by, their faces carefully blank. It wasn't until the guards were around the corner and out of sight that the two dared look each other in the eye. Almost immediately, they began to laugh, and kept it up until other travelers on the road began to look at them strangely.

Iyarra smiled back at her girlfriend. "Feeling better, I take it?"

Revka grinned. "Yeah, I suppose." She leaned forward, giving Iyarra a quick hug. "So, what now?"

The centauress shrugged. "I don't know. I thought maybe we'd head south ahead of the winter, maybe find somewhere warm this year, if you like."

Revka pursed her lips. "Okay, we can do that. I know you're no fan of the snow and cold. Maybe we can hit a beach somewhere. Or..." She trailed off.

Iyarra waited a moment, but nothing was forthcoming. "Or what?"

Revka didn't reply. She just nudged the centauress and pointed. A family was passing them in a farm cart. One of the children wore a rough, cheaply made tunic upon which was emblazoned the words:

> I hath bene to Ye Enchanted Foreste,
> as may be vouchsafed
> by these words upon my shyrte.

Revka turned to Iyarra. She smiled.
"Fancy a vacation?"

* * * *

Opinions differ as to the exact nature of the Enchanted Forest. There are some who say it is the site of an ancient magical accident. There are others who claim the area is under a curse of some kind. And there are those who say that there is nothing unusual at all at work, simply the brain's natural predilection for seeing patterns where none exist, like buying a blue cart and then suddenly seeing them everywhere. There are even those who staunchly believe that the whole thing is a put-on, cooked up to bring in the tourist money.

But the fact of the matter is, the Enchanted Forest has earned a reputation over the years for generating more yarns, tall tales, and epic fables per acre than any other spot in the world. Animals walk and talk, there are magic swords and rings all over the place, and wishes are granted in the most ironic way possible, all as a matter of course. A few years previous, a boy traded the family cow for a bag of beans, which turned out to be perfectly ordinary and not magic in any way. It was the talk of the forest for months afterward.

Unsurprisingly, once word got around, the forest became a popular tourist destination. People of all sorts flocked there. Wandering troubadours came in search of fresh material. Fair (or at least reasonable in good light) maidens came looking for princes or princesses. There was also a steady stream of swineherds, woodcutters, and would-be adventurers, all hoping to get caught up in some of that fairy-tale magic.

Lots of families visited the Enchanted Forest as well. And this was odd because, when you get right down to it, most fairy tales aren't really what anyone would call family friendly. Oh, they often involve children, and there's usually an important lesson to be learned, but the tales were never really *nice*. Get past the bowdlerized versions and later editions with tacked-on happy endings, down to the bone where the oldest stories live, and they are filled with blood and teeth and gore. Lessons learned are brutal, and even the good guys can be pretty sketchy. Even when the woodchopper *does* come, you can expect to spend a little time in a wolf's stomach.

Fairy tales aren't nice. Fairy tales are *nasty*.

* * * *

Revka and Iyarra took the trade road south, following the sweep of the Icarine Mountains down the eastern edge of the continent until they faded into the landscape. Now they were in hill country, with wide rolling vistas stretching off as far as one could see. The trees had been cut back an arrow's shot from the road to keep bandits at bay. Beyond that point, the woods lurked thick and deep, dark even on the sunniest day. The Enchanted Forest was a bit farther south, then a couple of days off the main route. Not a bad journey at all, really.

That evening, the girls stopped at a roadside inn, where they traded a couple of hours' work in the kitchen for a hot meal and a round of ale. A group of travelers were seated before the fireplace, drinking and swapping stories.

"We found the old man in the cave." The speaker was a big fellow, solidly built and grizzled, with lank, brown hair hanging over a rough, leather eyepatch. "I said to him, 'We seek the Tiger's Eye, old man, and we hear you know where it is.' He came up to me, see, and he said, 'You would seek the Tiger's Eye, would you?' and I said, 'Yes, I just said that.'"

"So then he said, 'Oh foolish one, if you would truly seek out that most sacred of gems, know that you must travel to the top of Mount Stonespire, there to pluck a single, perfect specimen of the silver rose that grows only at the peak. This you must take to the blasted wilderness of Yeng, where lives the tattered king in his windowless castle. If he is pleased, he will whisper the password to the Iron Gate of Groth, past which you must climb the ten thousand steps to the lair of the Bloodstone Dragon and answer his seven riddles. Only then, oh rash mortal, will you be allowed to enter the inner sanctum and free the Tiger's Eye from its prison of a thousand years.'" The man paused to take a long draw on his ale.

"So we did that," he continued. "And on the way home, we—"

Revka raised her hand. "Sorry, wait. What?"

The man looked up. "Hm?"

"What do you mean, did that? Did what?"

"Oh, uhm. All of it, you know. All the bits."

"Uh-huh." Revka bit her lip, her hands tracing shapes in the air for a moment. "You wouldn't care to, I don't know, elaborate on that a little bit?"

"Elaborate?"

"Sure. Like that bit with the dragon and the seven riddles. What was that like?"

The man seemed puzzled by the question. He furrowed his brow in thought, mulling it over. After a long moment he looked up at the listening group. "It was hard," he said.

"Hard."

"Mm-hm."

Revka looked around the gathered listeners. This answer did not seem to be going over particularly well. She briefly considered the possibility of pushing for more detail and tried to work out the odds of getting anything further. They weren't encouraging. She threw her hands up. "OK. Well, I guess it would be, wouldn't it? Anyway, you were saying?"

"Ar." The man took another drink. "So anyway, on the way home…"

* * * *

That night, the innkeeper let the two share an empty stall in the back stable. They watched the clouds drift in front of the stars for a while, then drowsiness overtook them and they fell asleep. Iyarra briefly considered asking Revka what she thought of the fellow's story, but she didn't seem particularly concerned, and Iyarra didn't want to sound silly. It was probably just a human thing. Well, it would be a strange world if they were all alike, wouldn't it?

* * * *

The next morning found them on the road again. They fell in with some other travelers who were going their way, and passed a pleasant day strolling down the road and swapping gossip. They turned off the main road about midafternoon and made their way along the slightly smaller road that led to the Enchanted Forest.

That night, the group set camp by the side of the road, circling their tents around a central fire. There was the usual eating and quaffing, and Iyarra and Revka managed to locate some wild potatoes which cooked up nicely.

A little apart from the fire sat a young man, dressed more colorfully than the other travelers. He had a lute in his lap and was plucking idly. Revka watched him for a while, then wandered over and plopped down next to him. "Evening."

The bard acknowledged that it was, indeed, evening.

She extended her hand. "My name's Revka. What's yours?"

"Darel."

Revka gave him a friendly smile. "Well, I'm pleased to meet you, Darel. You any good with that thing?" She poked at the lute, making its owner wince.

"Well, I like to think so," he said. "Good enough that I don't starve, I suppose."

Revka nodded. "Like to play us something? Trade you a roasted potato for a song." She dropped the spud on the ground in front of him, causing an immediate growling noise in his stomach. She grinned. "That a yes?"

Darel coughed. "Well, in fact, I was working on something new. Just today. It's still a bit rough, but perhaps you'd give me your opinion?"

"Oh, sure." She turned her head and called over to Iyarra. "Wouldn't we, 'Yarra?"

"Wouldn't we what?" Iyarra strolled over.

"Like to hear his new song."

Iyarra's ears pricked. "Oh? Oh, yes. Please." She settled down next to Revka and gave the bard her full attention.

He cleared his throat and plucked experimentally at the lute strings, twitching them into tune. "All right," he said. "Here it is."

> *There once was a king and mighty was he,*
> *He dreamed of power and glory,*
> *Then one day he tripped down the stairs and he died,*
> *So it's not a very good story.*

Iyarra and Revka glanced at each other, but neither said anything. The bard continued.

> *Once there was a fisherman, lived by the sea,*
> *He wished that he wasn't so poor-y,*
> *But he was, and he stayed that way all his life,*
> *So it's not a very good story.*

> *In a magical kingdom,*
> *Was a magical princess,*
> *In a magical castle,*
> *With a magic doorway,*
> *But they lost the key,*
> *And they never ever found it,*
> *So outside the castle they all had to stay.*
> *So they sat around and stared at each other all day.*

> *There once was a monster who lived in a cave,*
> *He was creepy and eerie and gory,*

Villains

But no one came by and eventually he left,
So it's not a very good story.

There once was a prince and he went on a quest,
For a sword most ancient and hoary,
And he found it the very first place that he looked,
So it's not a very good story.

Once a beautiful maiden,
Made a wish on a star,
That she'd meet a handsome prince,
And then they'd be wed.
But time moved on,
So she settled for a cobbler,
They had six children and a cat instead,
And she lived to be eighty, then she died in bed.

Now, I think we've gone far enough,
This premise is starting to bore me,
So I'll stop.

No sooner had the words left his lips than the lute was slung across his back. He stood up and scooped up the potato in one movement, then strode off into the darkness.

For a moment, the girls didn't say anything. Revka looked up at Iyarra, then back at the spot where the bard had been. She pursed her lips.

"Well," she said. "Huh."

Chapter Two

ONCE UPON A TIME, there was a very poor miller. Now, when I say poor, I don't mean he lacked money. In fact, he had plenty. I mean poor as in he wasn't very good at milling. He tended to cut corners, and thin out the flour with alum, chalk, and certain other things it's best not to get into. This allowed him to undercut the other millers in town, so that in time, he was the only one left. Whereupon he raised his prices, used even more junk ingredients, became immensely rich, and got a knighthood.

One day, while schmoozing at court, he was boasting to the king about his daughter. "Not only is she the most beautiful girl in the kingdom," he declared. "But she is also the most talented. Why, she could even spin straw into gold if she wanted to! Top up my flagon again, will you, boy? That's the way, keep it coming."

The king knew that the miller had a tendency to talk a lot of rubbish. Nevertheless, the drunken old fool's words intrigued him. After all, you never knew. Besides, there's just something about the prospect of large quantities of gold that tends to short-circuit the critical thinking portions of the brain. Therefore, he had the miller's daughter sent for and taken to a room in the castle with a bale of straw and a spinning wheel. "If you do not spin every bit of this straw into gold by morning," he told the girl, "you will surely be put to death."

"But why?" she exclaimed, throwing herself at his feet.

"Because I am a king," he replied. "And we don't like to be messed around with." And then he was gone.

The girl, who didn't even know how to use a spinning wheel, sat and wept all through the night. She wept so long and so loud, she didn't even hear the windstorm that picked up around midnight, nor did she see the little dwarf that went flying past the window, screaming for help as the wind carried him away.

The next morning, of course, there wasn't a bit of gold to be had. The miller's daughter threw herself upon the king's mercy. In the end he relented, choosing only to cut off the father's head instead. Shortly thereafter, the daughter was persuaded to sell the mill for pennies on the dollar to a company secretly owned by the king, which had pretty much been his plan all along. He then jacked the prices up even more *and started cutting straw into the flour, along with all the other stuff, and thus achieved his dream of turning straw into gold after all.*

The daughter, meanwhile, sold her story to the popular press and became something of a minor celebrity. She spent most of the rest of her life going on lecture tours and selling souvenir woodcuts and miniature spinning wheels (makes the perfect gift). It was not an ideal life, to be sure, but as she was fond of saying, it sure beat working.

Sometime later, a servant of the king was walking through the woods. He found a little cabin, just the right size for a dwarf. The place had clearly been abandoned for a long time, so he contented himself with nicking a few items and clearing off.

And they all lived happily ever after. More or less.

* * * *

It was the next day, and the girls were getting pretty close to the Enchanted Forest. There were a fair number of travelers still going the same way, but a surprising number heading away. At first, Iyarra just assumed it was end-of-summer traffic, but she couldn't help but notice the faces of those who passed by. They tended to be vexed, irritated, and downright sour, even more so than your typical family that's just spent two weeks in proximity to each other, all day, every day. In short, there was definitely a bit of an atmosphere.

Over lunch at a roadside tavern, the girls eavesdropped on conversations among the returning visitors. What they heard was surprising, to put it mildly.

"I call it a disgrace," one woman declared, gnawing on a hunk of bread with cheese. "The whole place has gone absolutely downhill."

"It's not how it was when I was a kid," agreed another woman across the table. "Back then, the place was more...well, *magical*, you know? It really had something back then. Now it's just..." She waved a hand vaguely.

"Oh, I know what you mean," replied the other one. "It's all so tawdry and cheap, and hardly anything of interest. You'd think they'd be able to keep it up, for all everything costs."

"Oh, yes. It's gone up, don't think I haven't noticed." The older woman cut off a hunk of cheese. "Damned cheeky, in my opinion. Charging more and giving less. Well, I've had it. Next year it's us for the elven city, you mark my words."

Revka regarded the women. Things certainly didn't sound promising. She'd never been to the Enchanted Forest herself, but had always heard it was a good place for a bit of adventure and fun. Of course, it was possible these ladies were just indulging in a bit of old-fashioned "Everything Was Better In My Day." Still...

She excused herself and headed to the bar for a refill. At a table near the bar sat a couple with three children in tow. The whole family looked sullen, and they were barely picking at their food. The father glowered at his plate, while the mother, clearly feeling outnumbered, struck out for something to say.

"Well, the weather was nice, at least," she ventured. "Not too hot or too cool. We picked the right time to come, I'd say."

"Mmf," grunted the father.

"The Enchanted Forest sucks." This from the eldest boy. He was around eleven or twelve, if Revka had to judge. Right at the age where they can be just amazingly difficult to be around. "It's for babies."

"You're not supposed to say sucks," answered a younger girl. "And I'm not a baby."

"Yeah, you are," the elder brother replied. "Baby."

"Mo—ommm!"

"Cuthbert, don't make fun of your sister."

"I wasn't doin' nothin'."

"Listen to your mother, boy."

"I wanted to see the mummers!" cried the youngest child. He was three or so, and already had a permanent scowl etched onto his features. He hadn't stopped kicking the table leg since Revka had stepped up to the bar. "Enchanted forests are boring."

The mother leaned forward. "Well, I tell you what," she said brightly. "When we get home, the very next time some mummers come through, we'll go and see them. How does that sound?"

"Wanna see mummers *now*!"

"Don't yell at your mother."

"Gods, this family sucks."

"You're not supposed to say sucks. Mom, he said sucks."

"Shut up!"

"You shut up!'

"Make me, you baby!"

"MOMMMMM!"

"Wanna see the mummers!"

"THAT DOES IT!" The father's fist slammed onto the table, causing his plate to jump. "I only get two weeks out of the year to have a little peace and quiet and vacation with my family. All I've heard is constant complaining since we got here! Now, we've got two days' journey home, and I am *not* going to put up with this anymore! You all start enjoying yourselves, or by the gods, I will give a hiding to each and every one of you!"

There was a long, shocked pause. The mother cleared her throat. "Uhm, who knows any good songs?"

Revka just shook her head. She got her refill and headed back to the table, plopping down next to Iyarra, who gave her a nudge. "What's up?" said Revka.

The centauress leaned down. "Is it just me," she said. "Or do people coming back from the forest seem less than pleased?"

"Not just you, no." Revka told her about the family. They compared notes and looked around the bustling tavern. Once you knew what to look for, it was easy to see. The people on their way to the forest all had a look of anticipation. The ones on the way back, on the other hand, looked universally disappointed. Revka frowned, taking it in.

"What do you think?" she said. "I'm beginning to think it might be a washout."

"Could be." Iyarra shrugged. "But I'm still kind of curious about it. Even if it isn't as good as it apparently once was. Besides, we're nearly there. We can pop our heads in and have a look. If it's no good, we have plenty of time to go somewhere else before the cold weather sets in."

Revka shrugged. "Okay." She took a swig of her drink. "Might as well go ahead, right?"

"Exactly." Iyarra gave her girlfriend a reassuring smile. "Besides," she said. "How bad could it be?"

* * * *

How bad could it be?

At the ninety-third annual conference of the Royal Society for Tactical Linguistics, that particular phrase was voted the third most terror-inducing combination of words in any language, just behind "The boss wants to see you," and "Hey, watch this."

Research theologians have theorized that, along with the well-known household gods of raising bread, changing milk to butter and so on, there are also gods of irony and foreshadowing. These perverse creatures lurk in the shadows, just waiting for someone to put temptation their way by way of a comment liable to come back and bite them later.

Some years ago, an order was established to appease these theoretical creatures by means of prayer and sacrifice, in hopes of establishing, once and for all, whether they did exist, and if so, how they may be mollified. Sadly, their findings were inconclusive, as the day after the brothers moved into their mountaintop retreat, it was destroyed by an earthquake, a volcano, a landslide, another earthquake, and a herd of frightened water buffalo. Applications for a second group are now gratefully being accepted.

* * * *

As the girls were talking, something was moving through the dark heart of the Enchanted Forest. The presence had no form to speak of, nothing by which it could be marked, except by the particularly sensitive. Call it an influence, perhaps. Or a drive.

A hunger.

It pauses in its tracks and spreads itself thin. If it had a nose, it would sniff the air. There is something, yes, something *familiar*. Not far off at all. It knows this well.

The...thing heads off in a new direction. It is moving faster now.

How bad could it be?

It could be very bad indeed.

* * * *

After lunch, they hit the trail again. There was still some company along the road, but it might not have been Revka's imagination that the crowd had thinned somewhat. Possibly, word had gotten around.

It was around late afternoon that the group trickled into Hervesville, one of the small villages which existed primarily to service the tourist trade. A quick survey of the inns made it clear they were in for another night under the stars. Revka snagged a complimentary map and studied it, looking for somewhere they could camp out.

"Saltwater taffy?" she muttered to herself. "Why do these places always have saltwater taffy?"

"Beats me," Iyarra said. "It's not as if we're even near the ocean or anything."

"Exactly!" Revka scanned the map. "But there's, like, three of them here. Anyway..." she muttered to herself, sweeping her eyes back and forth. "Okay. It looks like we're going to have to go ahead into the woods. I'm sure there's a clearing or something."

In fact there were several, but not many you would want to spend the night in. The first one they hit had a small cottage made of gingerbread. Unfortunately, it had been out in the elements for a good while and it was going downhill fast. Patches of mold were springing up all over, and the house was leaning in on itself beneath a swarm of flies. Revka raised her hand to knock on the mushy-looking gingerbread door, then thought better of it. She grabbed a fallen tree branch and rapped gently on the door. "Uhm, hello?"

The door fell in on itself in a pile of soggy confectionery. The smell that rushed out at them was...indescribable. Revka was nearly bowled over. Poor Iyarra, whose nose was particularly sensitive, had to go be sick behind a tree. The stench was almost physical. Revka briefly considered peeking inside to see if there was anything of interest, but quickly realized that there couldn't be anything in there she'd want to know about.

The next clearing along was much nicer. There was a house there as well, though made of more usual building materials. It was very nice actually, freshly painted and situated next to a carefully tended garden. It was clear the place was being looked after. Revka brightened. Maybe they could bum a meal or something. She licked her hand and wiped a bit of the road schmutz off her face. "Come on," she said. "Let's see who's home."

Iyarra hesitated. "I don't know," she said. "Something smells off."

"Oh?" Revka looked over her shoulder at the centauress. "Like what kind of off?"

Iyarra sniffed the air some more. "Uhm, not *bad* off, just off-off, if you see what I mean."

"Okay..." Revka nodded. She knew enough to trust Iyarra's sense of smell. Still, it was such a nice house. If it didn't actually feel *bad* it was probably all right. Still...

"Wait here." She strode up to the door and knocked. "Good evening, sir or madam of the house, I was wonder—oh my goodness. I do beg your pardon." A large shape loomed in the doorway, glowering down at her.

"What do you want?" it growled.

"Er, I, uh..." Revka shrank back.

"If you're selling something," it rumbled, "we don't want any." The shape was silhouetted against the light of the house, making it difficult to see details, but it was definitely very big. And hairy. And cross.

"Actually," Revka said. "I think we may in fact have the wrong house. Terribly sorry."

"Yeah," the shape glowered. "I think you do, too."

"Papa!" the voice came from inside the house. "Who is it? Your porridge is getting cold."

"Coming, dear." He fixed Revka with one last look, then shut the door in her face.

Iyarra watched Revka come back from the house. "Bears?" she asked.

Revka shrugged. "Bears."

* * * *

The third clearing led to a wide bluff that tapered quickly upward. At the very top, at the end of a winding trail, a tall black castle loomed against the twilight. Clouds hovered in the otherwise clear sky above it, almost as if anchored in place. It was a tangled, jumbled, heap of a place, towers and buttresses jutting out in odd directions and not a single right angle in sight. The two stood at the base of the path, regarding it with suspicion.

"I don't know," said Revka. "What do you think?"

Iyarra wrinkled her nose. "I think I'd rather take my chances with the bears," she said.

Just then, the massive doors to the castle flew open. Out marched a hunched little man in a hooded smock, towing a rough wooden cart behind him. He stomped down the path, muttering to himself as he went.

"Excuse me," said Revka as the little man approached them. "Sorry, but whose castle is this?"

The man stopped dead in his tracks. He looked up at them, as if only just seeing them for the first time. "Eh?"

"The castle. Who lives there?"

He snorted. "Nobody, now." He waved a hand back at it. "Thirty year I've been there, man and hunchback. Went into town this morning to pick up some groceries, when I get back, nothing. No marster, no bats, no snakes, even the cobwebs were gone. I was *months* on those bloody things. Checked from top to bottom I did, the whole place silent as a...as a..."

"Tomb?"

"Oh, much quieter than that." He shrugged. "I thought the marster was having one of his little jokes, or maybe one of his experiments had gone a teensy bit wrong. He did like to fiddle about with things, so he did, but it's as if he was never there."

"Golly," said Iyarra.

"It's bloody gentrification, that's what it is." He slapped the rim of the cart. "Everything's going upscale. These bloody tourists coming in, building retirement homes. All the prices have been going up, too. You know they've been on to us about the lawn? It's a castle! It's *supposed* to look like that!" He spat. "Well, I'm off. Not going to sit around, waiting for them to drive me off as well. I've got a cousin in the capitol, does nose jobs. I'll get on with him."

"Oh," said Revka. "Well, that's...good?"

"You just watch," he scowled, waving a hand back at the castle. "In a week it'll be a wine bar or a theme restaurant. That's if they don't knock it down. Probably put up some condominiums." Rarely had a word been pronounced with such vitriol. "Well, I'm not hangin' around. I suggest you don't either. Now, if you'll excuse me..." He grasped the cart poles again. "Good evening to you."

The two watched him storm off along the trail leading into the woods. After a moment, they headed off down the trail themselves. Behind them, the castle settled a little more into the earth with a rattle of falling stone. A tower near the back wall buckled, then collapsed in on itself. Above, the clouds began to dissipate, and fade away.

Chapter Three

THE NEXT MORNING CAME, and they were back on the road. The trail was worn with neglect through this part of the woods and bore every sign of having been abandoned for quite some time. As she strolled along beside the centauress, Revka began to suspect that they may have traveled a bit too far afield in their search for somewhere to bed down. There were occasional signs of life. They'd pass the odd souvenir stall or abandoned fudge shoppe. The forest had begun the work of reclaiming this area, and everything was overgrown with vines and weeds. Iyarra shuddered.

Revka patted her side. "You okay up there?"

Iyarra shook her head. "There's just something about a place like this, you know? Abandoned places always give me the creeps." She poked a hoof at an old wooden sign next to a stump that had once invited visitors to get their picture taken with *A Real Live Gnome*. This caused a bit of blue card to fall off the side of the sign and into the weeds below. Revka fished it out.

"What's it say?" Iyarra craned her head to see.

"Back in five minutes."

Iyarra harrumphed and looked back at the stump. "I think that might not be the case."

"Yeah." Revka flipped the card back onto the stump, and they traveled on.

* * * *

A little farther down the road, they came to a place set off a bit from the road. At first glance, it looked like another abandoned property. The yard around the tumbledown shack was piled with junk. Once you looked closer though, it became apparent that the place was being looked after. The grass was trimmed down and free of weeds. The "junk" consisted of plaster statuettes of goblins and toadstools and multi-limbed gods. There were colored-stone peacocks and garden gnomes mooning ceramic frogs. Some of the pieces even had splashes of fresh paint on them here and there.

An old-fashioned machine sat by the side of the road with a wooden dummy of a fortune teller inside. The paint on her head and shoulders was fading away to expose the old wood underneath. Her inert hands lay on either side of a fogged-up crystal ball. A faded banner across the top invited passersby to *Explore the Mysteries of the Universe* and *Find Fame - Fortune - Romance* for only a copper. Revka grinned and gave Iyarra a nudge.

"Hey 'Yarra, you ever see one of these things in action?"

Iyarra shook her head. "No. I mean I've seen them around from time to time. It just spits out a card, right?"

"No, no, it's really neat. Hang on, I'll show you." Revka fished in her coin purse for a copper and dropped it into the slot.

The machine came to life. A dim, hesitant light flickered behind the painted glass eyes of the fortune teller, and her hands began jerky movements around the crystal ball. The tune, from somewhere in the depths of the machine, would have been mysterious and evocative were it not being plunked out on an old cylinder in desperate need of oiling. After a few seconds, the extravaganza shuddered to a halt, and a card dropped into a waiting hopper. Revka scooped it up.

Iyarra peered over her shoulder. "What's it say?"

"Machine broken, collect fortune inside. Huh."

They turned and looked at the shack. Someone had gotten a good deal on paint. The walls, the door, and the crazy paving leading up to it were all painted with more colors than Revka even knew the names for. Each individual roof tile was hand-painted in various colors and patterns. The shack seemed to lean in on itself, crushed under the weight of the signs that covered the front facade.

SOOVENEERS
MAPS
WATER CLOSET
LADY IF HE WON'T STOP HERE HIT HIM ON HEAD WITH SHOE

"What do you reckon? Should we?" Revka looked over at Iyarra.

Iyarra wrinkled her nose. "Well, it smells inhabited, just barely. Bit musty, though, if you want my opinion. I think the paint may be the only thing holding it together. What do you think?"

Revka eyed the building critically, then shrugged. "Come on," she said. "May as well get our money's worth."

The two made their way inside. Once they were in, their eyes needed a moment to adjust to the darkness, and another, somewhat longer moment to make sure that they were really seeing what they thought they were seeing.

It wasn't the fact that the place was packed from floor to ceiling with shelves and stacks of brightly colored junk; or the dozen or so cages hanging from the ceiling in which a riot of birds chattered, screeched, and crapped more or less constantly; or the lines of fairy lights draped along the shelves and across the ceiling. In fact, it was the lights *and* the junk *and* the birds combining in a perfect sensory storm. It was a scene that would make even the most eccentric, top-hatted candy maker want to go for a nice quiet lie down in a dark room. Revka closed her eyes for a second, but when she opened them again, it was all still there. She cleared her throat, waving the card vaguely. "Uhm, excuse me? Anyone here? I think your machine outside is broken."

"Coming!" A bolt of red cloth behind the back counter began to bob its way around to them. As it came around the corner, it turned out to be attached to a short, elderly woman. She was plump, and had a face that was basically one big wrinkle. She hobbled toward the two with a gnarled walking stick, her hair (around which the red cloth was wrapped) bobbing above her and nearly doubling her height.

She clapped her hands together as she approached the two girls. "Oh, I *am* sorry! I have been meaning to get that thing out there fixed. Don't you worry about a thing. Ol' Mother Vieille will have your fortune told for you right this minute." She took the card out of Revka's hand and stuffed it away in her hair wrap.

She took Revka's hand, turning it this way and that. She pursed her lips, hummed a little to herself, then dropped the hand. "All right, dear," she said to Iyarra. "Let's have yours now."

Iyarra leaned down enough for the old woman to fold her hands around the mare's. She gave the new hand a moment of careful attention, then straightened up. "My, oh, my," she said. "Are you two ever in for a *time!*"

"I don't know," said Revka. "Are we?"

"Oh, indeed, indeed." A faraway look entered the old woman's eyes. "Such things you will do, and such things you will see. Many strangements and wonders. Yes. You will see an impossible creature and a two-faced truth teller, and you will learn what makes a hero. Yes, indeed."

Revka and Iyarra exchanged glances. "Are you sure?"

"Oh, absolutely. You can trust Mother Vieille. You've got quite a road to travel, but it will take you where you need to be. Just don't expect to take the direct route. Oh, and beware of happy endings."

"What?"

The old woman patted their hands. "Now then, off you go. Don't want to miss out on your future, do you girls? I mean, then where would you be?" She laughed and bundled them off toward the door. "You mind what I said about those happy endings, now, you hear me? Don't be strangers!" The door slammed.

* * * *

"Well," said Revka, as they proceeded down the road. "What was all *that* about?"

Iyarra shrugged. "Beats me," she said. "Maybe it's like in those stories. You know, where the hero meets a mysterious stranger who sends them off on a noble quest, or something."

"Oh," Revka snorted. "One of *those*."

"What did you think she meant about beware of happy endings? Aren't they supposed to be good?"

Revka waved an arm dismissively. "Heck if I know. One thing's for sure: if we get out of here without any major weirdness, that'll be about as happy an ending as I could hope for."

"Yeah."

Mother Vieille waited until they were gone 'round the bend in the road, then hobbled back out into the yard. She moved behind the fortune-telling machine and tweaked something, just out of sight.

The fortune teller's eyes lit up. A mechanical rattle shuddered through the machine, and a card dropped into the hopper. The old woman picked it up.

YOUR LUCKY STONE IS TOPAZ. YOU ARE A TERRIBLE LIAR.

Mother Vieille barked a short, sharp laugh. "Maybe so, but I had to tell them somethin'. Anyway, that ought to get them on the right track."

Rattle, rattle, rattle, clunk.

A SMILE IS THE BEST UMBRELLA. DO YOU THINK IT WILL WORK?

The old lady shrugged. "I hope so. If it don't, we're all gonna be in it."

* * * *

Once upon a time, there was a beautiful princess who lived all alone in a big castle with her father, the court advisers, seven chefs, seventy-three servants, three platoons of guards, and a small army of courtiers, diplomats, bureaucrats, and assorted hangers-on. Her skin was white as snow, her lips were as red as blood, and her hair was as black as ebony. Actually, it was all kind of creepy and made her look like a mime. Still, she was a princess, so everyone just called her Snow White and kept their opinions to themselves.

Her mother had died in childbirth—Snow White's childbirth, not her mother's—so her father married a queen from a neighboring kingdom. She, too, was very beautiful, but she was very cold-hearted and terribly envious of her stepdaughter. The queen constantly critiqued the girl's hair, wardrobe, and manners, and would make lots of little, passive-aggressive remarks whenever she could.

Despite the ill treatment, Snow White grew up happy and more beautiful every year. The queen, whose looks relied on three hours of intense preparation every morning, began to feel her own charms fading. She changed strategy and started picking out the girl's outfits for her. She encouraged her to cultivate an "interesting" personality and not concern herself so much with her appearance. She tried introducing the girl to pasta, but somehow, the princess only became more appealing and didn't gain an ounce.

Things were getting desperate from the queen's point of view. When her magic mirror told her she was no longer number one in the royal hot-or-not stakes, she decided it was time for action.

The next day found the palace in chaos. Sometime in the night, the queen had up and disappeared. The king, who had been off hunting, sent out search party after search party, to no avail. He despaired of ever seeing her again and decided that perhaps he wasn't the marrying kind after all. He got a low-slung racing carriage with a convertible top, dyed the gray out of his hair, and started picking up ladies-in-waiting half his age. In time, Snow White discovered the wonders of hair bleach and spray-on tanning. She completely revamped her look and changed her name to Candi. She died at age fifty due to complications during plastic surgery.

Everyone else lived happily ever after, except for a small group of dwarfs out in the nearby woods, who ran a mining operation until their sheer lack of hygiene overtook them and their cottage fell in on them.

Villains

* * * *

Iyarra picked her way along the overgrown trail that wound its way through the forest. On her back, Revka continued to try and make sense of the map. "Okay," she said. "I think we want to take a right at the next fork. That should take us past the giant pumpkin patch, then we follow that along until we get to the enchanted glade. Another right, and we should be somewhere we can get a decent bite."

Iyarra nodded. "Right, pumpkins, glade, right again. Got it." She plodded along, keeping an eye out for giant vegetables. "Say, Revka?"

"Mm?"

"Why do they call it the enchanted glade?"

"It doesn't say." Revka peered at the map. "Maybe there's lots of magic there or something. I suppose we'll find out."

A fork in the road appeared, and Iyarra reassured herself with a nod and took the right fork. "Was just wondering. I don't think I've ever looked at something and said, Gee, that's enchanting. You know what I mean?"

"Oh, sure." Revka carefully folded the map. "Not that this place is likely to stand up to it. The whole forest just feels run down. I wonder what happened."

"Good question." The pumpkin patch was coming into view. The pumpkins were giant, as advertised. Several of them were large enough for a person to hollow out and live in, if they didn't mind the smell. In fact, now that she looked at them..."Oh, good grief."

Revka saw it too. "Wow," she said. "Look at that. Windows and a chimney and everything."

"Bizarre."

"Definitely."

"Nice curtains, though."

They moved on.

After a while, the produce began to diversify a bit. There were giant cucumbers, giant squash, tomatoes as big as a head. And then, on the other side of the patch...

The beanstalk stood by itself, just next to a small, run-down cottage. Like a typical example of its kind, it was bright green, with a stem about the thickness of one's finger. Also typically, it was covered in long, tapering leaves. Bean pods hung here and there, ripe and ready to eat.

The stalk was also going straight up into the air, where it disappeared into a bank of clouds. This was not typical.

The two girls stared in silence for a moment, squinting upward in a vain attempt to spot the top. "What on earth," asked Revka, "is holding this thing up?"

"Magic." A young man stepped around from the back of the cottage. He was dressed all in green, including a peaked cap from which hung a lone, bedraggled feather. He leaned against the cottage wall, waving a hand at the beanstalk. "Been that way ever since my grandad was a kid. Three generations of beanstalk climbers, we were. You'd go up, burgle some unsuspecting giant, climb back down again, and be on solid ground in time for dinner. It was a great life, if you weren't afraid of heights."

"What, *real* giants?" Revka quirked an eyebrow at him.

"Oh, sure." The lad shrugged. "Used to be bunches of them. These days...I don't know, they just seem to have disappeared. It's like you can't make a living anymore."

"Breaking and entering, you mean."

"Well, *technically*, sure. I always thought of it as more, sort of harvesting, you know? Like farming except without the sowing part. You plant beans in the ground, and reap a harvest of giant treasure, singing harps, that sort of thing. But now? I'm down to the last golden egg, and no more giants. I've been reduced to putting on climbing exhibitions to make ends meet. That, and a steady diet of beans. Did you know there are over three dozen ways to cook beans?"

"No, I—"

"I *counted* them."

"No, wait," said Iyarra. "I think I heard about this. Some of the farmers I used to work for. There was a hen or a goose or something, and then the giant smelled him, and followed him down the beanstalk. Only he slipped, didn't he?"

"Slipped?" The young man glanced off to one side. "Uhm, sure. Yeah. That's what happened. He slipped." He pointed off to a large clearing nearby. "You can see where he landed."

The girls looked. Sure enough, with a little imagination, you could easily see the spot as being in the shape of a very large, very unlucky man. Revka whistled.

"Took ages to clean up," the boy added.

"Just imagine the smell." Revka nudged Iyarra, who wrinkled her nose.

"*Revka!*"

"Sorry about that, but look!" Revka waved a hand at the stalk. "You honestly expect me to believe that some giant climbed down this little scrawny thing? I mean, I'm amazed it can even bear its *own* weight, let alone a giant. Hell, it probably couldn't even hold you!"

"Don't believe me? All right." The young man's jaw set in an expression of grim determination. "You see that bit up there? Where there's a bell tied to that leaf?" He pointed to a spot about ten meters up. "I can get up there, ring the bell, and be back down before you count to one hundred."

"Oh, that's not neccess—"

"Watch me." He grabbed hold of the beanstalk with both hands and tugged. There was a sound like a base note being plucked and a worrisome slithering noise from above. The young man gaped, staring slack-jawed up at the stalk, until Revka, with great presence of mind, cannoned into him and knocked him out of the way.

As they watched, the spot where he had been standing was quickly covered in beanstalk. Coil after coil came down in a cascade that was nearly up to Revka's chest by the time it stopped. One little forlorn end landed with a plop, and a bean pod, knocked loose by the fall, rolled to their feet.

The young man went white. He reached out for the fallen stalk, clutching desperately at its remains. He grabbed hold of the end and tried to straighten it out. No luck. Iyarra nudged Revka and nodded her head toward the road.

They crept away quietly, following the road around the corner. Behind them, the young man kept throwing the end of the beanstalk up in the air, back up toward the clouds.

* * * *

A little while later, the two were proceeding down the trail when they came to a sign. A rough-looking specimen, the placard's paint was faded from years out in the weather.

To the Enchanted Glade

An arrow pointed to a barely-there trail that wandered into the woods. Iyarra peered into the shadows. "Enchanted Glade, isn't that where we're supposed to go?"

Revka unfolded her map and squinted at the tiny text. "Well, yes, but...it doesn't look like we're supposed to go off on a side road. In fact,

I'm not sure if there's a side road here at all." She traced her finger along the trail, muttering to herself. "No, let's see...we did that, passed that part, followed it straight along...yeah, this road should take us straight there."

"But the sign says *that* way."

"Yeah." Revka glanced down the path. It didn't seem particularly well-traveled. She nudged the sign with her toe, but it was dug into the ground pretty deep and had obviously been there for a while.

Well okay, maybe the road had been changed. Cheaply printed giveaway maps tended to not be the most reliable things in the world, she did know that. Generally, they'd print up a bunch and keep putting them out until every last one was gone. You could burn the place down and they wouldn't replace the maps while they still had a few left.

All right, then.

She folded the map and nodded to Iyarra. "We follow the sign."

The path led them, very quickly, into the depths of the woods. The going was easy enough, but they were surrounded on all sides by untamed nature. Revka got the feeling they were seeing parts of the forest tourists generally didn't get to see—at least, not more than once. Iyarra followed right behind her, her head on a constant swivel as the wilderness closed itself in around them. Old stories whispered their admonitions in Revka's mind. *Don't go near the woods. Stay on the trail. Beware the big bad wolf.* She shuddered.

Revka was just on the cusp of calling a halt and suggesting they go back the way they'd come when a large clearing appeared up ahead. She let out a sigh of relief at the sight of plentiful sunlight and grass. The Enchanted Glade, that would be it. She moved forward again, faster now, ready to get out of the dark and claustrophobic woods. Iyarra trotted behind her, the two bursting out into the glade almost at a run.

Suddenly, they were not alone. The clearing was full, end to end, with the vilest conglomeration of fiends that either girl had ever seen. There were witches and masked men with choppers. There were sneering princes in black, and beautiful women whose eyes bespoke cold menace. Among the many creatures were wolves, some on haunches and some upright, even one in a battered old top hat. Trolls and trickster sprites mingled with hellish monstrosities. Toward the back, obscured by the tree shade, larger creatures lurked, their features mercifully obscured.

Revka and Iyarra turned in unison back to the path, but found it gone. They looked around. There was no way out. They moved closer together, their bodies tensing up. Revka slipped a hand down to her sword and gave it a tug. Nothing. Something was holding it, keeping her from pulling her blade free of its scabbard.

The dire assembly stood and watched them, not saying a word.

"Oh, hell," Revka muttered.

Chapter Four

THERE WAS A LONG, terrible silence. The lightly rustling autumn breeze died away. Even the ever-present birds ceased their singing, waiting to see what would happen next.

From the motley assembly, an old crone hobbled forward. She was bent almost double, clad in a shabby, hooded cloak that might once have been black. A few strands of shock-white hair clung to her scalp, and what could be seen of her face was covered in wrinkles, moles, and liver spots. In the crook of one arm, she carried a basket with a cloth draped over the top. In the other hand, a gnarled old walking stick.

A dirty brown rag was tied over the crone's eyes. Revka was never comfortable with not being able to see someone's eyes, and this was somehow even worse than usual. There was something about the way the rag draped over the woman's face that suggested Revka wouldn't want to see what lay underneath.

The crone shuffled her way forward until she stood about midway between the girls and the group. She moved her stick to the other hand and rummaged in her basket. She pulled out a round, red apple that caught the light in a way Revka didn't quite like. It seemed to glisten, somehow, in a way that apples don't usually do. Still, it didn't seem to be a weapon. Revka relaxed her grip on the sword's pommel but stayed alert.

The old woman lifted the fruit to her mouth and took a bite. She tilted her head upward, munching thoughtfully. A stray rivulet of juice trickled down the side of her chin and onto the hair of a wart, where it caught a momentary glint of sunlight. Then, she spoke.

> *"Born of mountain and of plain,*
> *Single heart in body twain.*
> *More than seen there is to see,*
> *Not heroes, but heroic be."*

There was a snort from the front of the crowd. "*Them?*" one of the wolves sneered, its voice a deep wet growl. "You *can't* be serious."

"Hush your mouth." A dripping green thing, roughly the shape of a person, waved its arm in the wolf's general direction. "Old Mother Bedlam knows her business. If she says 'tis them, then I believe her."

There was a low susurration of agreement. Toward the edge of the gathering, a decaying specimen shuffled forward. It was a man, one who had not-so-recently met his end. Possibly in some sort of threshing machine accident, by the look of him. He shambled forward, one leg trailing behind the other, until the two girls could see the white of his single remaining eye.

"*Heeeellllp usssss,*" he said.

Revka blinked. This was not what she had expected. "Eh? Wait, us? Help you?"

The creature nodded vigorously, reaching out a decaying hand for her. "*Youuu! Helllp ussss! Pleaasse…?*"

Revka recoiled. "But…how? I don't…"

"Do pardon my lamented friend." Another man stepped forward. He was tall and lean, and richly clothed in red and black silk. His whisper-thin mustache matched his sly, beady-looking eyes. He spoke with the cultured crisp of the upper classes and a side order of sneer. "He really hasn't been the same since he, ah, passed on."

He bowed. "What he is trying to say, what we are all trying to say, is that we are in dire need of assistance. We believe you, dear ladies, are just the ones to render it." The man finished with a sweep of his arm, taking in the whole direful assembly.

Revka raised a hand. "Look, if this is about money, you might as well—"

The man laughed a sinister sort of laugh, a just-when-you-thought-you-were-finally-safe kind of chuckle. "No, no, not at all. Nothing like that. I shall explain." He struck a dramatic pose. "You see before you the last of a dying breed. Once we roamed these woods, happy and free, going about our business in accordance with our time-honored ways."

Revka made a face. "What, like cursing people? Eating them, that sort of thing?"

"Time-honored ways. But lately, we find ourselves under attack. Us! *Victims!* Unable even to defend ourselves! Unable even to survive! You see us now as a ragtag, a scattering of vagabonds. The strong have become weak, the powerful powerless. Something is plucking us from the very heart of this place, and we know not what or why." He steepled his long, lean fingers. "The fact is, we are dying."

"Dying!" the others chorused.

"As we die, so too does this place. For we are knitted into its very bones, the very fabric of these woods. Surely, you will have seen that things here are not as they should be?"

Iyarra and Revka exchanged glances. "Well," said Iyarra. "I did think the place was looking a bit shabby."

"That's true." Revka nodded. "Something is definitely wrong, we could see that, but listen, who are you, exactly?"

"We are…" The man hesitated. "Well, there's really no way to get around it, is there? Very well. In short, we are the reason for heroes. We are the obstacle, the antagonist, the awful example, and the dread warning. In a word, dear ladies, we are villains."

* * * *

Elsewhere in the forest, *something* was suddenly all attention. It hadn't heard the words exchanged, not even with its nice, new ears, but there was a…yes, a magnetism of sorts. It could feel the drawing force and sense that it was big. And it was waiting.

The thing changed direction, still moving awkwardly on its brand new legs, and began to run.

* * * *

"Villains?" Revka took an involuntary step back. Admittedly, they certainly looked the part, but still.

He bowed. "Indeed, dear lady. Be not afraid. As` I say, we are in dire need of assistance, and would not dream of, er, inconveniencing you in any way."

Iyarra looked doubtful. Revka pulled herself together and folded her arms. "So, uh, Mister Villain, what exactly is going on here, anyway? And what are we meant to do about it?"

"Ssstoppp themmm," the dead man spoke again. The stench of old graves washed over the two with every word, and Revka had to hold her breath to keep from being ill.

"You see, dear ladies," the aristocratic man said. "This place is a…oh, how shall I put it? It is a place where new energy flows into the world. Energy is created, or rather summoned, through stories. Think of stories as the water that turns the mill wheel, which brings life force into the world. Lately, someone is hunting us down, erasing us."

Revka tilted her head. "You mean, you're being killed off?"

There was a snort. It was the wolf who had spoken earlier. "Not killed! No! We know about being killed! That's part of it. This isn't like that. This is…" His growl dropped an octave. "…cheating."

The tall man nodded. Revka was prepared to bet he was a grand vizier, or possibly a sorcerer or something. He certainly had the look down. "Quite true. Sometimes we win, sometimes we lose, but that's all in accordance with the narrative flow. It is to be expected, but that is not what is happening here. We are being *removed,* as if we never existed."

"I hear you." Revka coughed. "But I'm not sure I see where the problem is. I mean, you're bad guys. Presumably, getting rid of you would be a good thing, right?"

"No, no, *NO!*" He loomed over them, great and terrible. Clouds of darkness poured into the sky from all directions, and lightning crashed in deep shadows around the clearing. The two women stumbled back. He strode toward them, his voice sharp with bile and fury. "Listen to me! Without us, stories do not happen! There is no way to continue the flow of new energy into the world! No villains, no stories. No stories, no life. No life, no anything. No good or evil or anything in between. Nothing but emptiness, forever!"

He stopped and kneaded his temples. "I do not have time to deliver a full lecture on the subject. Suffice to say, if you do not help us, if you do not find what is hunting us down and stop it, then that which separates man from dumb animals will drain away to nothing. The age of thinking creatures shall come to an end. Men will live, but they will not thrive. They shall be as beasts, empty vessels with nothing to fill them, the spark forever gone from their minds. Now do you see?" His voice grew old and tired. "You must have heroes, and you must have villains. That is how it is. Now, will you help us?"

In the silence that followed, the only sound was the quiet mastication of the one they called Mother Bedlam. She smeared a dirty sleeve across her mouth, turned her blind face to the two girls, and spoke.

> "Winter and summer, night and day.
> Dark and light forever sway.
> Let one be lost, the other fails.
> Restore the balance, restore the tales.
>
> Speed you deep into our wood.
> Find the evil in seed of good.
> Into your hands we rest our fate.
> It comes! Flee now, or it's too late!"

Turbulent and chaotic activity sprung loose amid screams and roars that mingled with the wind, which came from nowhere and was building up already to a howling gale. The villains scattered in all directions. Even the slower ones showed a remarkable turn of speed. Before they knew it, Revka and Iyarra had the clearing all to themselves.

The wind blew itself out. The clouds dissipated, letting the sunlight push its way back. Somewhere, a bird began to sing.

Revka gazed over the empty scene of sylvan calm, which moments before held a conclave of nightmares. She shook her head and reached up to pat Iyarra on the withers.

"Well," she said. "So much for a relaxing vacation."

Chapter Five

THE GIRLS MADE THEIR way back down the trail toward the road. "Well," said Revka, breaking the silence as usual. "I have to admit, I didn't see *that* coming."

Iyarra nodded. "True," she said. "Not the sort of thing you would expect to see on your vacation." She hesitated. "Uhm…"

"What?"

"Revka, do you think they were telling the truth? About stories and life and all that?"

It just so happened that Revka had been mulling that over herself. "Well…I'm not sure. I mean, on the one hand, these are literally bad guys we're talking about, so you know they've got to be good at lying to people, right? So maybe it's just that, but…well, it didn't feel like a lie. Not to me, anyway. What do you think?"

"They certainly weren't faking it with the fear," Iyarra said. "I could smell it coming off them. And some of those things don't look like they scare easily. I think, probably, things must be pretty desperate for them to get together like that, let alone asking a couple of total strangers for help."

"Hmm. Good point, good point. So, a bunch of baddies are scared they're getting wiped out, and apparently this is a bad thing."

"And we're supposed to stop it."

"And we're supposed to stop it, right." Revka plucked a leaf from a tree as they went by and twiddled it between her fingers. "So what the heck do we do?"

Iyarra pushed a low branch out of her way. "I don't know. Maybe we could ask for help?"

"From whom?"

"Well, maybe we can find some more of the locals. Ask around, see if they've seen or heard anything unusual."

"That makes sense. When we get back to the main road, we'll head toward the more touristy areas. Bound to be someone there we can talk to." She faltered. "Uhm…"

"What's wrong?"

"Speaking of the main road," said Revka. "Shouldn't we have gotten back to it by now? I'm pretty sure the trail wasn't this long before."

"I think you're right," said Iyarra. "And what's more, I'm sure it's curving around more than it did. The way in was a straight shot. I think we must have taken the wrong path."

"I don't think so." Revka's eyes narrowed, peering back at the way they'd come. "We were standing right at the entrance to the clearing, remember? The paths must join together at some point. Probably we missed it on our way out and wound up on this one instead."

"Or they moved the path to get us there."

"Really?"

Iyarra shrugged. "Just a thought."

"Hmm." Revka stopped and leaned against a tree. She looked back and forth over the trail, carefully inspecting both directions. "Maybe," she admitted. "I mean, we know they can do magic already. Some of them, anyhow. Though I think it's more likely we just got lost."

"So what do we do now?"

Revka tapped her fingers on the tree. "I don't feel much like backtracking," she said. "Let's just go ahead and follow the trail. It's got to lead somewhere, right?"

"I suppose that's right." Iyarra shrugged. "I just hope it's somewhere we can forage some lunch, that's all."

The walk was actually quite enjoyable. The deep, dark woods had given way to pleasant greenery, with plenty of sunlight pushing its way through the canopy. Colors seemed richer here, brighter somehow. Birds flitted from tree to tree, keeping up a constant stream of chirrups and twitters that somehow managed not to become irritating. All in all, it was downright congenial.

Revka turned to Iyarra. "You know," she said. "This place isn't bad once you get past the twinkly fairy stuff. I could see us settling down here one day. You know, once we've made our fortune and all that."

"It is pretty, yes," Iyarra agreed. "Though honestly, I'd like something a little more wide open. Running space, you know. Besides, I think you have to be in a story to live here."

"Oh, that's not a problem," said Revka. "We've got lots of stories. Most of them are even true. Well, mostly true."

"I think there's a little more to it than that. I think they have to be well-known stories."

"You think?"

"Well, I can't really see people flocking to meet two women who once had to escape from a dungeon via the sewers and needed two weeks to get rid of the smell."

"Well, not *that* story, obviously. Maybe I could tell *The Centauress Who Once Ate Somebody's Hat*."

"Look, I said I was sorry."

"Okay, well how about—"

"Of course, I could always share *The Amazing Novelty Wrestling Act*. I bet that story's got around a bit."

"I'm sure it has." Revka shuddered. "All things being equal, I'd just as soon not be remembered for that, if at all possible."

"It was memorable."

"Well, yes, but—"

"Especially after those pigs got out and started to stampede through the city. I never did see so much—"

"Okay, okay! You've made your point." Revka made a face at the centauress. "Anyhow, you're probably right. We're probably not the much-beloved, family classic types, are we? Probably not suitable examples for the youngsters."

"I think we more likely come under dire warnings." Iyarra grinned. "You know, do your lessons or you'll end up like those two."

Revka laughed. "OK, that's legitimately scary." She nudged Iyarra. "Say, maybe that can be our new thing. We could rent ourselves out to parents of unruly children. Spend a few days around us, any kid would straighten out, right?"

"Or go sailing over the edge of no return."

"No, think about it!" Revka's grin was huge. "I can just see little Cuthbert running back home to momma. 'Oh Momma, I'm so sorry I didn't clean my room! I promise I'll be good from now on, just keep those two maniacs away!'"

Iyarra giggled. "Oh, come on."

"Mommy, look, these are the most immature people I've ever met, and I'm seven! They're crazy! Crazy, I tell ya!"

"Oh, stop!"

"*Crazy!*" Revka's hand darted to the lower part of Iyarra's tummy, where the woman half met the horse half. She tickled her fingers over the fine hairs that marked the join. The effect was immediate. Iyarra's eyes went wide, and she squealed. "Oh, no—*no!*"

"I gotcha!" Revka kept it up, an evil grin on her face. "Here comes the evil tickle monster! You're in trouble now!"

Iyarra cantered in place, trying, without success, to bat Revka's hands away. Her equine ears flushed a dark red, and she squealed as her girlfriend set off her ticklish spot. "Stopitstopitstopit! Ohhh, I'm going to get you for this!" She broke down into peals of helpless laughter, so loud that they almost didn't hear the screaming.

Revka pulled her hand back. "'Yarra?"

"W-what?" Iyarra sagged a little, panting.

"That...wasn't you, was it?"

"No."

"Oh, hell." Revka grabbed Iyarra's saddle and swung herself into position. "Let's go!"

Iyarra shook her head, collecting herself. "Right," she said. "Hang on."

The centauress broke into a canter, belting down the trail at speed. Fortunately, the path seemed to lead straight toward the source of the scream. Revka held on tight, pressing herself down to avoid the occasional errant branch that whipped by.

They heard a second scream, closer. Iyarra flattened her ears back against her head and leaned into a full gallop. Behind her, Revka held on with one hand while checking her weapons. Whatever spell had held her sword in its scabbard before was gone. Good. She licked her dry lips and hung on.

A moment later, they burst into a clearing. In the middle was a small, well-kept cottage with chintzy curtains in the windows and flower beds on either side of the door. Just in front of the dwelling, a woman in rag curls and a low-cut dress had been tied to a pole in the ground. She was being menaced by a man who had apparently splurged on the complete Ne'er Do Well Deluxe Starter Kit. He wore a black cape and a black stovepipe hat, and twirled his long, thin mustache between his fingers as he cackled evilly. The sword he held in his hand was a bit of a giveaway, too.

"And now, my dear," he sneered. "I grow tired of our little game. What is your answer, mm? Speak up!"

"Never!" The woman declaimed. "Never, do you hear? No, no, a thousand times no!"

"Don't beat around the bush," he replied. "If you're not interested, just say so."

Iyarra galloped up to the two and came to a halt. Revka slid off the centauress's back and pulled out her sword. "All right," she said. "First thing's first." She pointed to the woman. "You. What's going on here? What's the story?"

"Oh, thank heavens!" The woman nodded toward the stranger in black. "This fiend has threatened to burn my house down if I refuse to marry him!"

Revka glared at the guy. "Do *what*, now?"

He snarled. "Stay back, you two! This doesn't concern you." He turned his attention back to the rag-curls woman. "And now, my pretty one, I shall give you one last chance! What say you?"

"Okay, hold it." Revka waved her sword in the direction of the man. "First of all, Mister..."

"Silas," he said.

"Okay, Silas. What are you so hell-bent on getting married for? And why her?"

Silas shuffled his feet. "Well, it's not so much her," he said. "I'm just trying to get a fair hearing. You've no idea how hard it is for a nice guy to get any action these days."

"A *nice guy!?*" Iyarra boggled. "You were going to burn her house down!"

"Well, I let her out of it first, didn't I?"

Iyarra facepalmed, muttering to herself. Revka shook her head. "Look, Mister, I hate to be the one to break it to you, but if you have to tie a woman up and threaten to set fire to her house to get her attention, it's just not going to work out. I mean, you have to have some kind of basis to build on, you know? Like, why waste your energy on someone who's clearly not interested?"

The woman spoke up. "I'm heir to a small fortune."

There was a moment while the penny dropped. "Ah," said Revka. "I see." She turned to the Silas character again. "OK, look. It's not going to work, buster. You might as well give up now. I tell you what; if you drop that sword, untie her and get out of here, then my colleague and I won't hunt you down. What do you say? Best offer you're going to get today."

The villain sneered. "Oh, I really don't think so. Do you two honestly think you can stop me? You forget, I have all the cards." He whipped his sword away from them and brought it to the woman's neck, hovering it a whisker's length away. "Now," he said. "I believe you will be going. Right now, in fact. Yes, and you'll stay away, too. Because if I see either of you again, so help me, I shall be forced to employ rather more...old-fashioned means of persuasion. I'm sure you take my meaning, yes? Now, be off with you."

"Now look, Mister, just a minute—"

"No more minutes!" He brought the very tip of the sword against the woman's skin, pushing slightly. The woman closed her eyes, too scared to tremble. "I told you to leave."

"All right, all right." Revka made a show of slowly putting her sword back into its sheath. "We're leaving. No need to hurt anyone. Besides, it's too late now. It's already coming."

Iyarra opened her mouth, then stopped. The wind was picking up, and quickly. It was just like the wind back at the clearing, when the others had fled. She took a step back from the tableau.

Silas narrowed his eyes. "What are you talking about? What's coming? Don't try to pull one over on me, I'm warning you." He paused to grip his hat against the wind, which had suddenly stirred up. "I'm no country bumpkin to be fooled by transparent deceptions like that."

Revka moved back, keeping pace with Iyarra. "You had your chance," she said. "You could have walked away." She slipped a hand through one of Iyarra's saddle straps. The wind was getting stronger. In a moment, it would be hard to be heard above it.

"Answer me! Or so help me, I'll—" Silas barked with annoyance as the wind snatched his hat out of his hand and blew it into the far trees. "Curses!" He swung the sword back at the two women. "I don't know what you two are up to, but if this is your doing, I'll—oh dear Gods, what is THA—"

The wind howled around them, sending leaves and branches flying. Revka half expected to be blown right off her feet, but somehow it didn't seem to touch her. It was almost as if the worst part of the storm was routing itself neatly around them.

Silas wasn't so lucky. The wind hit him full in the face, knocking him back like he'd been launched from a catapult. He flew toward the trees, heading right for a large sycamore. He never made it. It seemed as if he was falling down a deep pit, his form dwindling beyond sight far beyond the meager distance of the clearing. It made their eyes water to watch him.

The wind stopped so quickly that the howl was still echoing in their ears as the air went completely still. Revka watched a lone leaf drift its way unhurriedly to the grass. It landed right where the man had been.

The two women exchanged glances. "Wow," said Revka. "That was disturbing."

"Those villains weren't kidding." Iyarra's eyes were wide. "What do you suppose that was?"

"That's a toughie. It's probably some kind of—"

"Excuse me?"

Revka looked up. "Mm?"

The rag-curls woman coughed. "I don't want to be a bother," she said. "But do you think you could untie me?"

"Oh! Right!" Revka hurried over and began to work at the ropes. "Sorry about that! Just got a little distracted."

Iyarra nodded. "It's not every day we see someone get blown away like that."

"Of course, we're new here," Revka added. "For all we know, this happens every day." She pulled the last bit of the knot free and began unwinding the rope from around the woman. "By the way, I'm Revka, and this is Iyarra. And you are?"

The woman didn't answer right away. She seemed more interested in staring at the patch of ground where the man had been. When the last bit of rope had been pulled away, she stumbled away from the pole. Revka gave her a helping hand and checked her over carefully. Sometimes people tended to shut down a bit after a bad experience. Heaven knew they'd seen it before. "Uhm, Miss? Can you tell me your name?"

The woman stopped. A puzzled frown crept its way onto her face and settled in like it intended to stay awhile. "It's...er, how odd. I don't seem to..." She lifted her hands, turning them this way and that, as if she'd never seen them before.

"Uh, Miss...?"

"Hello!" A smile snapped onto rag-curl's face with disconcerting speed. "I must tend to my garden," she said. She skipped—*skipped,* for heaven's sake—into the cottage, then emerged a moment later with a watering can. She began to tend to the flowers.

Revka furrowed her brow, feeling rather out of her depth. She'd seen people react to traumatic events in any number of ways: relief, laughter, rage. Crying was a popular one. She'd once seen a woman react to losing a child by hauling its cradle into the yard and chopping it into a thousand pieces, but spontaneous outbreaks of horticulture? That was definitely a new one.

She tried again. "Miss? Excuse me, Miss? Look, could you put down the watering can for maybe one minute? I promise not to take up too much of your time." The lady ignored her, humming a pleasant tune to herself and watering the tulips, or hydrangeas, or whatever they were. Revka didn't know much about flowers, save that Iyarra favored chrysanthemums and violets because they tasted nice. Whatever these were, they were apparently more than enough to keep the woman's attention firmly pulled away from any attempt on Revka's part to strike up a conversation.

"Uhm, Revka?"

"Just a minute." Revka waved a hand in front of the woman's eyes. No reaction. She tried tugging the watering can out of her hands, but the lady's grip on the thing was surprisingly strong. "Okay," Revka muttered. "This is getting weird."

"Revka?"

"I mean, you're seeing this, right? It's like she's switched off or something."

"Revka."

"What?"

"Look at the trees."

Puzzled, Revka turned her attention to a nearby tree. It was...well, it was a tree. Trunk, branches, leaves, the whole bit. Nothing unusual that she could...

As she watched, several leaves curled in on themselves, their green color fading to a dull gray. One by one, they began to drop.

Revka looked around the clearing. Sure enough, it was happening all over. Not all of the leaves were changing. You could easily miss the transformation if you weren't paying attention, but once you noticed, it was everywhere. "Good grief."

Iyarra nodded. "Yeah. It just started about a minute ago when she went in to get the watering can."

Revka nudged a fallen leaf with her toe. "You know what I think?"

"What's that?"

"I think this is that spirit energy or whatever that villain was talking about. I think this place just lost a little bit of life."

"I think you're right."

Revka knelt down next to the woman, who had gone back to her flowers. "And this one," she said. "I'm pretty sure she's gone bye-bye. Nothing to react to, you see. No more villain, so she's basically switched off for the duration."

"Do you think we ought to get her somewhere? Find someone who can help?"

"Yeah, all right." Revka hooked an arm around the woman's. "Come on, lady, we're just going to take a little walk. Gonna go see some people, all right? Up we go." She gave the woman a tug, but she remained immobile. Revka pulled harder. Nothing. She wrapped both arms around the lady and attempted to lift her bodily, but managed only to strain herself and stagger backward. The woman hadn't budged. In fact, it seemed like she hadn't noticed Revka's efforts at all.

Revka lay panting on the grass. "Okay, what's going on?" she groused. "There's no way she weighs that much. Iyarra, come over here, give me a hand with the crazy lady."

Iyarra knelt down and gave the woman a tug. Centaurs were built for strength, and she could easily shift a large man out of the way if she wanted to. She couldn't even get the woman to budge. "It's as if she's anchored to the spot."

Revka pursed her lips. "You think she might be?"

"Could be." Iyarra shrugged. "Beats me how that would work, but I should be able to lift a human that size easily."

Revka leaned against the centauress for a moment, lost in thought. Meanwhile, the woman started in on some light pruning. She seemed utterly unaware of their presence.

"Okay," said Revka. "Let's go."

"Go? Where?"

"I don't know," Revka said. "Somewhere I can sit down and think about this. We're going to need a plan."

Iyarra nodded. "Good idea."

In the quiet of her mind, Revka hoped she could come up with one. At that moment, she had no clue.

* * * *

That night, they camped out in a smaller clearing by a stream. Iyarra was cooking up some stew while Revka took advantage of the water supply to get a little laundry done.

"Revka?"

"Mm-mm?"

"You seem a little preoccupied."

"It's nothing."

"Well, you've been washing the same tunic for like five minutes, now."

Revka looked down. "Oh. Right." She put it down. "Just thinking about this whole mess. Trying to figure out what to do."

"I'd offer some suggestions, but you know I'm no good at plans and stuff."

"Well, I've got nothing. So if something occurs to you, don't be shy."

Iyarra laughed. "Okay, I won't." She moved over to Revka and knelt behind her. "I'm sure you'll think of something," she said. "You always do."

She slipped her arms around Revka. "Remember the time when we had to escape from that cave, and you used that candle to find which way the wind was coming from until we found our way out?"

"Mmm. What about it?"

"Just saying. You're pretty good at coming up with clever plans." Iyarra nuzzled at Revka's neck. "I'm sure you'll come up with something."

"I sure hope so." Revka leaned back. "Because I'm drawing a blank right now."

"What you need," Iyarra said, "is to stop thinking about it. My mother once told me that when she had a particularly difficult problem to solve, she would get as much information as she could. Then, when she'd thought it over so much she was going around in circles, she would make herself go off and do something else. Like mending clothes, or gathering herbs, anything like that, but she wouldn't let herself think about the problem."

"What, not at all?"

"Nope. She said she would just leave it in the back of her head and keep herself occupied for a while. And sure as anything, the answer would just pop into her head."

"Is that so?"

"Mm-hm."

Revka thought it over. "Well, okay," she said, "I guess I'm game. So, what do you suggest?"

"Well..." Iyarra smiled. "The stew is just about ready, so I think we should have some of that. Then I'll give you a hand with the rest of the washing. When all that's done..."

"Yes?"

"Well, it's a nice night, the stars are out, and it's a beautiful moon tonight. I thought perhaps we could, you know, make our own entertainment."

Revka cocked an eyebrow at the centauress. "Oh, you did, did you?"

"Mm-hm."

"Well." Revka set the tunic aside. "I think that just might be a plan right there." She stood and stretched, whereupon her stomach let out a loud gurgle.

"Er, stew first, of course."

"Of course."

Chapter Six

THE NEXT MORNING, THEY hit the trail again, winding their way through the forest. Revka had given up on the map. The fact was, she had no idea where they were. Still, the forest was pleasant and there was a trail to follow. That was good enough for the time being. She still had no idea what to do, but honestly wasn't too worried about it. Iyarra was right; a plan would turn up sooner or later.

"You know," she said. "I've been thinking about that guy we met earlier. You remember, the beanstalk guy?"

"What about him?"

"Well, it was a bit skeevy when you think about it. I mean, he'd just go up there, find the nearest castle, and grab some stuff. Doesn't sound awfully heroic to me."

"Well, the version I heard said that the giant had stolen the treasure from the guy's father in the first place. So it was all right."

Revka looked up at the centauress. "Wait, what?"

Iyarra nodded. "Apparently, the father had a singing harp and this goose that laid golden eggs. The giant stole them, and the family became poor. The son traded a cow for some beans, and he used the beanstalk to climb up and get the treasures back."

For a moment, Revka was uncharacteristically silent. Slowly, carefully, she said, "Are you *quite* sure you've got that right?"

"I believe so, yeah." Iyarra looked back at her girlfriend. "Is something wrong?"

Revka shook her head. "I'm just trying to decide where to begin." She took a deep breath. "Okay, setting aside the whole cow thing, you say these guys had a singing harp? And a goose that laid golden eggs?"

"That's right, yes."

"Were they royalty or something? Because I can't see a bunch of farmers having stuff like that. Not for long, anyway."

"Well, I..." Iyarra furrowed her brow. "Well, come to think of it, I'm not at all sure."

"I mean, you saw that house the guy was living in. That was not a big house. If I had a steady supply of golden eggs coming in, you can bet your boots—"

"Horseshoes."

"Horseshoes, sorry—I wouldn't be living in some dinky cottage. I'd have a nice big home. And a big thick safe to lock that stuff up in."

"That is a point, yeah."

"I mean, how did the giant get hold of these things, anyway? Did they say? It's not like he could sneak up in the middle of the night or something."

"I never heard that part."

"Not surprising. It doesn't make sense."

"Well," said Iyarra. "Maybe the giant just showed up one day and said, 'give me your goose and your magic harp or I'll stomp your house into the ground with you in it.'"

This gave Revka pause. "Okay," she said. "I can see that. The direct approach."

"Right."

"Still, it sounded like he was hitting more than one giant up there. If I understood him properly, that is."

"And?"

"Well, they couldn't all have robbed him, could they? Even if the first one did, and I must say the story sounds extremely iffy, that still doesn't explain the others."

"Dunno."

Revka tapped her teeth. "You know," she said. "I wonder if we haven't got hold of the wrong end of the stick with that guy."

"What do you mean?"

"I mean, what if he wasn't the hero? What if he and his family were the bad guys all along? Like, maybe there's a fairy tale that giants tell each other, you know? I bet when giants put their children to bed at night they read to them about the foolish giant who didn't lock his castle, got his stuff stolen, and died."

Iyarra laughed a little. "I think that's probably a bit unlikely."

"Unlikely compared to what? Mr. Beanstalk being a hero?"

"Okay, I see your point."

"Heck, I'm beginning to think we should see if we can go back and find him, maybe keep an eye on him, see if this wind thing comes for him."

"Do you know how to get back to him?"

Revka frowned. "Okay. That's a good point." She shrugged. "Oh well, just a thought."

They walked on.

After an hour, they came to a broader road, a proper dirt one with carriage ruts dug deep from many trips. Picking a direction at random, they followed the road to an ivy-strewn wall of red brick punctuated by a towering iron gate. The gate was black and imposing, with spikes on top and a giant locking mechanism. It was also hanging open. Revka nudged it with her toe and turned to Iyarra. "What do you think?"

The centauress peered at the wall. Just to the right of the gate, a bronze plaque was half obscured by vines. She tugged them away and showed Revka. "Take a look."

Doctor Heinrich Von Skullensmaschen
Brain surgery, full-contact chiropracty, spleen-venting a specialty.
Closed Wednesdays. Please No Solicitors.

"Skullensmaschen?"

"Must be from Schwarzwald." Revka tapped the gate. "Well, let's give it a look. Might be something useful." She tugged the gate back enough for Iyarra to get through.

They followed the road until it ended at an old, giant mansion, all towers and gables and chipped paint on the wooden slat walls. They worked their way around an ornamental fountain, which now held nothing but dead leaves. They approached the front door, which bore a sign that read *For entrance, please push button* above an arrow. Sure enough, there was a pole coming up out of the ground just a little to the right of the porch, with a small metal box on top. In the middle of the box was a dingy, red button. Revka frowned at a very large stone slab, perfectly square, on the ground in front of the pole.

"You know what I think?" Revka asked.

"What's that?"

"I think this must be some kind of trick. Big old button like that. And that slab? That just screams trap door to me. He probably lures people here and traps them in his dungeons to do evil experiments."

"You think so?"

"Oh, yeah," she said. "Name like that? Gotta be a mad scientist. Probably needs a steady stream of victims. Seen it a million times."

"What, have you?"

"Well, I've heard of it." Revka looked around the long-neglected courtyard and picked up a stick. "Come on," she said.

Villains

Along the stone walkway with the slab, a bit of hedge ran parallel to the front of the house. The hedge encircled a patch of lawn, which had clearly seen better days. Revka threaded herself through a gap in the hedge and moved to a spot just on the other side of the suspicious stone slab. Fortunately, there was a dirt patch here which gave the two a clear place to stand. Revka took the stick and reached across the hedge, jabbing at the button. After the third try, she managed to poke the red button just enough, whereupon a merry little chime sounded. The front door opened, and the trap door concealed under the dirt patch slid aside. The two women dropped like rocks.

In the chamber below, Revka rubbed her aching head. The fall hadn't been too bad, just a quick tumble down a metal chute, but the landing had been a bit rough. Having 400 kilograms of centauress cannon into you certainly doesn't help things. She groaned and pulled herself up to her feet.

Behind her, Iyarra leaned against the wall. She shook out her legs, grumbling to herself in Low Equine. "Well," she said. "At least you were right about the trap door." She tapped a sign on the wall. *Special entrance for der schmart alecks.*

Revka spat and punched the wall, which turned out to be stone. This did nothing to improve her temper. "Okay," she said, rubbing her sore knuckles. "We're dealing with a devious little cuss, here."

She hobbled over to the door and rattled the handle. "Locked," she announced. She began to rummage around the room, looking for something to open it with. The room was primarily for storage, with rusty shelves full of old patient records and other things of that nature. The floor was mostly taken up by the mattress someone had thoughtfully put to catch anyone who fell prey to the trap door. Nothing to be seen in the way of battering rams. Perhaps, if she could scramble back up the metal chute and—

A splintering crash interrupted Revka's musings.

She turned around to see Iyarra shaking some feeling back into her hooves. She caught Revka's eye and shrugged. "Cheap door," she said.

The doorway opened into a large basement area, furnished from end to end with more scientific equipment than either woman had seen in their lives. Large metal boxes with mysterious buttons and levers were tucked into every corner, and thick lengths of cable ran in a crisscross spider web all over the ceiling. One table held a seemingly unending collection of glass bottles, jars, and tubes, through which bubbling, multicolored liquids flowed from one to another.

Revka regarded the glasswork with awe. "Hey 'Yarra, you seeing this?" She pointed. "This green stuff, in the bottle with the fat bottom? Look, it's going up the coily part and dropping into this jar over here. How the heck is it doing that?"

Iyarra shrugged. "No idea," she said. "But I'm fairly certain you shouldn't be tapping that."

"Oh, I'm sure it's fine." Revka flicked the retort with the back of her nail, causing a bit of red fluid to bubble down a bit of zigzag pipe and into a beaker full of blue liquid. With a loud hiss, the liquid immediately turned black and began to foam. The foam quickly spilled over the edge of the beaker and all over the surface of the table. Only then did it subside, but not before a small amount went over the table edge and landed on the floor with a splat.

Revka heard a scuttling noise coming from the floor. A fairly large cockroach came around the corner of the table and beelined for the black foam that was spreading itself languidly over the stone floor. As she watched, the insect poked a questing antenna at the foam, then moved in and began to slurp noisily.

A few seconds later, the cockroach began to thrash around wildly. Coarse green hairs sprouted from its exoskeleton. As they watched, the cockroach grew, doubling and tripling its size in a matter of seconds. It reared up on its hind legs, let out an almighty screech, and charged out of the lab, leaving a perfect cockroach-shaped hole in the wall.

Revka rubbed her chin thoughtfully. Iyarra nudged her in the back. "No."

"No? No what?"

"No to whatever you're thinking."

"I didn't even say anything."

"You didn't have to. Revka, I *know* you. And I'm telling you now; whatever you're thinking, no."

"Okay, okay." Revka gave up and went back to exploring the laboratory. There was all kinds of interesting stuff if you were into levers and buttons. It wasn't easy to keep her hands to herself. Some of the stuff looked excitingly dangerous. She was dying to find out what they did. "Dying to find out," whispered a treacherous inner voice. "That sounds about right." Revka sulked. That was consciences for you. She clasped her hands behind her back and stalked through the maze of machines and equipment-strewn tables, trying to look serious.

Another table in a far corner held a collection of what, from a distance, looked like giant pickle jars. Upon closer examination, they contained strange creatures, and sometimes parts of creatures, all bobbing in a greenish-yellow solution. Iyarra looked nauseated, but Revka moved from one to another with wide-eyed curiosity.

"Hey, 'Yarra!" she cried. "Look at this one!"

Iyarra made a face. "Do I have to?"

"Seriously, look!"

Iyarra risked a peek. Inside one of the smaller jars was a rat. Iyarra looked it over: nose tip, rat head, little rat legs with the bare feet she always found creepy, fat and long rat body, two more legs, and…"Oh."

Revka nodded. "A two-headed rat. Crazy, huh?"

Iyarra crouched a little, peering down at it. "Uh-huh," she said. "One on each end. That's certainly, uhm, unique."

Revka snorted. "I'll say." She tapped the glass. "Wonder how it goes to the bathroom?"

"Oh, *ew*."

"What? It's a legitimate question. I don't see any, y'know, *bits*." She peered closer. "Actually, come to think of it, how would something like that…you know?"

"What?"

"You know…" Revka rubbed the back of her neck. "Make little two-headed rats. I mean, there's none of *those* bits, either." She peered closer. "Unless they've come up with something new."

Iyarra brightened. "So, it's impossible, would you say?"

"Mm?"

"Like an impossible creature? Like that old lady said?"

"Oh yeah." Revka tilted her head at the creature. "I think you may be right." She tapped the glass again. Inside the jar, the impossible (or at least highly unlikely) creature bobbed serenely in its fluid. "How about that."

At the other end of the lab was a small room, roughly double the size of the one they had landed in. It was also much more lavish. Wooden shelves lined the walls, crammed full of books. There were more specimen jars, models of various organs, interesting scientific gewgaws and assorted clutter. A large desk took up most of the back of the room. It, too, was in a state of severe clutter, except right in the middle where there was only a large, open book.

Revka wandered over to the desk and began to rummage through the clutter, looking for anything useful. A word from the open book caught her eye. She blinked and peered closer. A word became a sentence, then a page. Eventually, Iyarra had to cough to get her attention.

"Oh! Sorry." Revka flipped back a page. "Just reading this. Looks like the good doctor was after the same thing we are. Listen to this: *It seems apparent that the entity, whatever it is, has a way to seek out villainy and, for reasons yet unknown, consume it. I have determined to discover the limits of what it can or will seek out. I have equipped two of the mice with the mind control devices, and have directed one to be a thief, the other to be a victim. I shall take them this afternoon to the grassy area behind the house and have them enact a robbery several times, to see if the attention of the mystery entity can be attracted.*

"Let's see, next day, blah, blah, blah...ah, here. *Mice experiment unsuccessful. Mice stole small bag of seed three dozen times under my supervision, no sign of any paranatural activity. Left thief mouse in cage outside overnight, still there in morning. New hypothesis: the villainy in question may need to be tied to a known narrative. The record of disappeared malefactors thus far would appear to support this. Interesting.*"

"Known narrative?"

"I think he means they have to be bad guys in a story, not just random crooks. There's more. *News of two more gone today: another witch and Dr. Von Monstro. It seems he was building another one of his creatures at the time, and apparently the witch was turning someone into a toad. Hypothesis: the entity only comes when a potential victim is in the middle of an act of villainy.* What do you think?"

"Well, it's true we did catch that one guy in the act. Doesn't necessarily mean that's always the case, but I can see that it might be. What else does he say?"

Revka leafed through the text. "Mostly unrelated stuff until...yep, last entry. Listen to this. *I have determined there is only one reliable way to ascertain the nature of the villain snatching phenomenon, and that is to engage the thing directly. This evening, I will make an effort to construct as grotesque and unnatural a creature as time and materials allow. Further, it is my plan to put up all manner of measuring apparatus so that I may gather as much information as possible. I will prevent any attempt at abduction by the simple expedient of securing myself to the building.*

In order that my laboratory may not be unduly damaged, I am setting up a makeshift facility in the greenhouse. This should provide me not only with invaluable data but also first-hand experience with this mysterious force. With any luck, I shall be able to proceed toward its neutralization."

"And?"

"And nothing. That's it. Last entry."

The two exchanged a look. "You thinking what I'm thinking?" asked Iyarra.

"I'm thinking his plan worked. Up to a point, anyway."

"Right."

Revka drummed her fingers on the book. "I think I'd like to see this greenhouse setup of his. Might be something there."

"Why did I know you were going to say that?" Iyarra sighed.

Revka winked at her girlfriend. "You just know me so well, that's all. C'mon."

Finding the greenhouse took a while. The stairs were easy enough to find, but they were rickety and old. Every time Iyarra took a step, the boards creaked loudly. She moved gingerly, holding her breath and taking each slow step one at a time until she reached the top and squeezed her way into the narrow hallway that divided the front of the building from the back. The place had a sort of faded-glory motif going on, with rich carpet and old wood everywhere, lots of art cluttering up the place. Also, there was rather more dust than you would expect. Rather more in the way of cobwebs too, for that matter. Revka got the impression that the place had pretty much looked like this even before the good doctor disappeared.

Out through the kitchen, a door led to the backyard. It was easy to spot the greenhouse; a tall, glass-paned structure set off a little way from the house, next to a small ornamental pond. The fact that nearly every bit of glass in the place had been smashed was a bit of a giveaway.

Revka pushed the door open, poking the broken glass away with her boot to make a clear path. Shelves full of plants and potting supplies had been shoved against the wall, leaving room for a miscellany of nasty-looking machines, a smaller version of the chemical setup they'd seen downstairs, and a tall metal pole that reached up and out through a hatch in the roof. Cables ran everywhere, but most converged in the center of the room, where a circular metal stand held the shattered remains of a large glass tube.

Easing their way through the rubble, the two began to search. Given the level of mess in the place, it was a surprisingly short time before Revka called to Iyarra, "Found him."

"What? You did? I mean, he's still here?" The centauress began to work her way over to where Revka was standing.

The girl waved her off. "I wouldn't if I were you," she said. "It's not pretty."

Iyarra hesitated. "Why? Did the whatever-it-is get to him?"

Revka looked down at the leg still manacled to a large wooden table. "Don't think so," she said. "But he really should have reconsidered doing this in a building made of glass."

"Oh. You mean...?"

"Yup."

"Ew." Iyarra made a face and took a few steps backward.

It is a well-known fact that horses are not generally in favor of walking backward, and this goes just as well with centaurs. The reason—well, one of the reasons—is that it's awfully difficult to maneuver the back half of a horse body while making certain that one isn't about to bump into something, step on a stone, go sailing off a cliff, etc. With patience and care, it can be done, but overall, it's not the kind of thing one would generally want to do, especially when one is standing in a glass-strewn, makeshift laboratory.

Iyarra felt a glass shard poke at her pastern just before it could penetrate her hide. She yelped, drawing instinctively away, and jostled the table next to her. There was a resounding crash...followed by a growl.

"What was that?" Iyarra looked around in a panic. Revka risked a peek in the direction of the noise. Her facial expression didn't change, but she did seem to go a bit pale. "Well?" said Iyarra.

"Iyarra..." And now Revka's voice was low, with a flat calm that only made things worse. "I need you back out of here. Right now, please. Just take a step to the right, and you should have a straight shot out. Please, go now."

"What? Why?"

"Because I'm about to run like hell, and I don't want to run into you when I do."

What came next wasn't a growl, it was a roar. Iyarra backpedaled quickly until she was clear of the greenhouse, with Revka following close at her heels. The two ran full tilt for the kitchen just as the creature came barreling out through the greenhouse door.

The beast was large, almost twice as tall as Revka. The blue creature looked like two arches connected at the top by a squashed melon. On the underside of the middle part was a large mouth with teeth going all the way around. It scuttled toward them on its four legs, bellowing. It followed them across the backyard and began to fight its way through the too-small door.

The two women hurried through the kitchen, across the hall, and into the main room, heading full tilt for the front door. Sounds of crashing timber followed them as the beast pushed its way into the house. Revka hurried to the front door and yanked. Locked. She cursed and began to fight the lock. It turned out to be one of those complicated new ones, probably a custom job. All very well if you weren't in a hurry. She wrenched it open just as the monster forced its way into the living room with them.

The door opened into a small foyer, nothing much more than a coat rack and some galoshes. The outer doors still hung wide open, showing the courtyard. Between them and the door was a giant, green, mutant cockroach in the middle of the room, hissing at them.

Revka groaned. The cockroach had gotten bigger since they'd last seen it. It came up to her waist and, if anything, looked angrier than before. Cockroaches are not the most prepossessing of creatures, even at their best, and this one looked positively vicious.

"Oh, for crying out—" The cockroach leaped and sailed right past them, going flat out for the large blue monster thundering into the main room. The beasts immediately began to fight, leaping around the room and smashing everything in their way in their efforts to destroy each other. Revka tapped Iyarra on the shoulder, beckoning toward the open doorway. "Time to go."

The two ran out the door as quickly as they could. Revka made a slight detour to mash the red button on their way out. The outer doors slammed shut as the two hurried down the driveway. Revka vaulted onto Iyarra's back and patted her flank. "Okay!"

Iyarra took off, galloping full speed until they got back to the iron gate. Between the two of them, they shoved the gate closed until they heard the clunk of the locking mechanism settling into place.

For a moment, they stood still, catching their breaths. The woods were silent except for a couple of birds in a nearby tree. Revka let out a breath. "I think we made it," she said. "Just as long as those two don't come after us."

"I don't think they will." Iyarra pointed. "Look."

In the distance, the roof of the mansion could just be seen over the top of the trees. It began to sway and buckle, and finally disappeared below the tree line. They strained their ears to hear what could have been the far-off sound of smashing rafters.

"Huh, brought the house down." Revka stood with her hands on her hips.

"Seems like." Iyarra seemed a little shocked.

"Think they survived that?"

"Doubt it. Want to go look?"

"Not a chance."

"Don't blame you," said a voice.

The two of them turned around. The source of the voice was a young man with short, sandy hair. He wore simple traveling clothes and a peaked, green cap on his head with a feather in it.

"Hello," he said. "My name is Jack."

Chapter Seven

REVKA PULLED HERSELF TOGETHER. "Hello, Jack. Nice to meet you. I'm Revka, and this is Iyarra."

Iyarra waved. "Hi."

"What brings you here?"

The boy shrugged. "Oh, just out seeking villainy wherever it may be. Doing good deeds, righting wrongs, carving my name upon the face of history. Yourselves?"

Iyarra and Revka exchanged glances. "Oh, er, pretty much the same," Revka said. "As a matter of fact, we were just doing a little investigating in that—well, in the house that was there." She waved vaguely in the direction of the gate. "Mad scientist, you know. Creating all sorts of monsters and whatnot. You should have seen this cockroach. Big, green, hairy sucker."

"Sounds nasty."

"Oh, yeah. Bite your legs off."

"And did you vanquish him? The scientist, I mean?"

Revka half-grinned "Well, actually, he died at the hands of his creations. Well, more like the legs and teeth of his creations. And the tentacles. And then they killed each other just now, and uhm, that's pretty much it."

Iyarra opened her mouth to say something, but caught Revka's eye at the last second and buttoned up. She just nodded. "It was a real mess," she added.

Jack nodded sagely. "Well, it often is in these cases." He prodded the gate with his toe. "Still, it sounds like there's nothing else to do here. I think I'm going to head back into town. Care to come with?"

"You know the way back to town?"

"Sure. It's just down this road a little way. We can be there by sundown, easily."

After glancing at Iyarra, who shrugged, Revka turned to Jack and nodded. "Why not."

* * * *

The sun beat down full on the road, but the day was moving on and beginning to cool a little. The three traveled along, following the wheel ruts, chewing the fat, and comparing notes.

"So we finally got up to the top of the tower, and I'm like, c'mon lady, let's get you out of here. She wouldn't go. Went and threw a fit because we weren't a handsome prince." Revka was in full story mode.

"Really?"

"Yeah, turned out she had planned it all along. The tower, the guards, the witch, everything. Her way of bagging a husband, it seems."

"What did you do?"

Revka shrugged. "What could we do? Turned around and went back down the tower. Not so much as a thanks for the effort. I had half a mind to stick her with a callout fee."

Jack shook his head. "Amazing," he said. "People just don't know how to behave anymore."

"Tell me about it."

"Do you know," he began. "I once caught a man tying up a woman out in the woods? I tried to fight him off, but the woman started yelling at me. It turned out they were a married couple and they were apparently, uhm..." He blushed.

Revka held up a hand. "Say no more," she said. "Seen that kind of thing before. At least nobody got hurt, though, right?" She thought about it. "That didn't want to, anyway."

"Well, no. It's just..." He shook his head. "Heroing isn't what it used to be."

"Definitely."

"So, what was it?" said Iyarra.

She squirmed a little under their combined gazes. "I mean, it's probably common knowledge, but I'm still kind of new at this stuff. As far as I can tell, it's mostly just trudging around in all weather, running endless errands for people who may or may not be grateful, constantly putting yourself in peril, and hoping you can scrounge up something for dinner." She shrugged. "Is that not what it used to be?"

Revka didn't answer right away. She stood a moment, marshaling her thoughts. "Well, okay. Maybe it's *mostly* like that, but in the old days, you could be reliably certain about saving the day pretty often, and not having weird complications. People would be grateful, you know, that kind of thing. And every once in a while, you'd get to totally save the world or something neat like that. Or at least, that's how it is in the old stories."

Jack's face lit up. "Oh, you like hero stories too? I practically grew up reading them! Giant killers and adventurers running around in tombs after ancient treasures and everything. And they're always fighting against impossible odds, but they win in the end and everyone's just like, 'Wow, we can't believe it,' and they're all 'Oh, it's all in a day's work.' Then you ride off into the sunset and onto the next adventure!" He sighed, a dreamy sort of light entering his eyes.

"It's the only life I've ever wanted," he said.

Revka coughed to break the awkward silence that followed. "Really? That's, ah, that's very interesting. Iyarra and I, we just sort of stumbled into it, you might say. We're kind of jobbing adventurers. It's a pretty good life, actually. I have to admit, it isn't much like in the stories, but we find our way along."

"I will admit, adventure has a tendency to find us," Iyarra said. "Even when we're not looking for it. Actually," she added, "*especially* when we're not looking for it. I don't think you can look for adventure, exactly. You just kind of have to go where it can find you."

"Oh, I don't know," said Revka. "I think you can find adventure pretty easily. Just go into a bar and throw a drink at the biggest guy."

"No, Revka. That's excitement. That's different."

"Oh, yeah. Yeah."

Jack looked back and forth between the two women. "I don't think I've ever come across a couple of heroes like you before," he said. "Still, I think this is great. Three wandering heroes, on the road to adventure."

"Or into town." Iyarra noted.

"Okay. Yeah. Into town in the short term, but really toward adventure, right?"

"Probably."

"Fantastic." Jack whipped out his short sword and made a few swishes in the air. All around him, imaginary giants and dragons fell.

Behind him, Revka and Iyarra exchanged a look. Iyarra tilted her head toward Jack, and Revka nodded. She patted the mare on the back.

"We'll talk later," she said.

* * * *

The sun was just beginning to set as they got into town—if you could call one main street with a scattering of buildings on either side a town. It was picturesque, though. The buildings were all done in the architectural style Revka thought of as Early Cuckoo Clock. Other than the gasthaus halfway down the main drag, the main industries seemed to be souvenir wood carvings and novelty jerkins.

A smallish castle perched on a hill anchored the far end of the town, all white stone and gleaming turrets. Iyarra thought of the time they had visited the kingdom of the elves and seen the great castle there. This looked like someone had tried to do the same thing at half scale and a tenth of the budget.

Revka stopped in at the local constable's office to let them know about the incident with Dr. Skullensmaschen, and was pleasantly surprised to find out there had been a long-standing reward in the town for anyone who got rid of him. Fortunately, they weren't long on questions, and Revka had enough sense not to go into *too* much detail. The upshot was that they wouldn't have to worry about money for a while.

The three adventurers found a spot at the long, communal tables that lined the gasthaus and dug in. The place was fairly busy, though very clearly nearing the end of the season, so it was actually pretty manageable. The ale was pretty good, if a tad on the tepid side. The prices were jacked up, but nothing out of the ordinary for tourist-oriented places. Still, the food was good, and there was plenty of it.

"So we chased him all through town to the docks, see," Revka was off and away again. "And he took off down one of the piers. Total rookie mistake, of course. No way back. We chase him all the way to the end. He's about to be trapped and he trips. The hat full of coins goes sailing. I dive and catch it midair. I'm about to go into the drink when Iyarra here catches me."

Jack listened, wide-eyed. "Really?"

"Oh, yeah," said Iyarra. "My arms are still sore."

"Hush, you." Revka grinned. "So anyway, we stagger back to the dock, and there's everyone standing there, watching us. Turns out they thought it was all part of the show. Best purse we ever got."

"That's amazing."

"Yeah." Revka nodded. "And we could have done even better if we had gone for an encore."

"I *told* you," Iyarra said. "That was *not* happening."

Revka just laughed. The sausage tray went by, and she speared herself another one. "Anyway, as I was saying, you have to be versatile. You can't just run around rescuing princesses all the time. I mean, apart from anything else, there's so few of 'em about."

Jack nodded. "That's true. Just can't get them these days."

"Right. So we always make sure we have a few tricks up our sleeves to keep us alive between saving-the-world-type gigs. Usually renting out as hired muscle, but there are other options."

Jack stared into his ale. "I guess I have a lot to learn," he said. "The books never talked about any of this."

"Oh, don't worry about it." Revka gave him a light shoulder punch. "You'll pick it up as you go along. Everybody does."

"Unless they get incinerated first."

"Right. Thanks for that, Iyarra. Very helpful. But yes, it does help if you're a quick study."

Jack looked up. "It seems you two are awfully good at this sort of thing. Uhm…" He looked down for a second. "I don't suppose you would be interested in having someone tag along? I mean, I'm totally a hero, and I know how it is, but it seems like you guys have got a little more experience with this stuff than I do. Besides, heroes banding together is always a good thing, right? And I can pay my own way, and I promise not to be too much of a bother."

The two women exchanged glances. "Could you excuse us a moment?" said Revka.

"What? Oh, sure."

"Thanks. Won't be long."

* * * *

In a quiet corner of the inn, the two hunkered down.

"Well," said Iyarra. "This feels familiar."

"Yeah, tell me about it." Revka shrugged. "So, what do you think?"

"Difficult to say. I mean, he smells all right. Seems sincere, though I'm not sure how much good he'd be in a fight or something."

"True, true. Mind you, I wasn't too different when I was first starting out."

"Oh, same here. I think we all go through that phase."

Revka pursed her lips. "Mind you, if he was around a couple of experienced adventurers, that might speed up the learning process," she said.

"Not to mention keep him alive long enough to learn."

"Fair point, fair point." Revka looked back at the lad. From her vantage point, he seemed a bit frail, maybe a bit vulnerable. She'd never had any inclinations to motherhood, but she had been the eldest of five children, so she'd grown up looking after her younger siblings. Some long-forgotten echo of that stirred in her.

"All right," she said. "I'm game."

* * * *

"Here's the deal," Revka said as they returned. "You can come with us for now. We come across any treasure, it gets split three ways. We've got no room for passengers, so if we get in a fight I want to see you in there swingin'. And when I tell you something is important, trust me, okay? I know what I'm talking about."

Jack practically beamed. "Yes, ma'am!" He actually saluted. "I won't let you down!"

Revka laughed. "Okay, okay. Calm down. It's not like you're joining the royal guards. Now, I suggest we get some rest. We'll head out in the morning after breakfast. Sound good?"

"You bet!" He gulped down the last of his ale. "By the way, what are we looking for?" he asked.

"Bad guys," said Revka. "And I hope to hell we can find one."

* * * *

That evening, Revka and Iyarra camped out beneath the stars. The gasthaus had been a bit pricey for Revka's taste. Anyway, it was a nice night, and she had a feeling they would want some alone time.

"So," said Iyarra as they stretched out together in the dark. "Why didn't you tell him about the thing?"

"The thing?"

"You know, the villain-eating thing. The wind. Or whatever it is."

"Oh. That. Not sure I want to bring him in on that just yet. He's new to this hero stuff, and he may not appreciate the nuance."

"Oh, gotcha. Nuance. Thought it was something like that."

"Well, you have to admit it sounds weird." Revka settled in a bit, getting comfortable. "You don't get heroes running around shouting, 'We must save the bad guys!' Doesn't fit. Besides, I want to see how this guy is in a normal heroish situation before we hit him with something oddball."

"I see what you mean." Iyarra shifted herself a bit. "Well, it will be interesting, anyhow."

Revka propped her head against Iyarra's side. "Anyway, we'll probably run into something or other tomorrow. Get an idea of how much of a hero he actually is."

"Well, as long as he isn't *too* good." Iyarra grinned. "After all, I'd hate to have him come on as a permanent member of the group. It would put a crimp in things, you know?"

"Oh, come on." Revka poked the centauress in the side. "You know better than that."

"Oh? You sure about that?" Iyarra couldn't keep the teasing out of her voice. "I'd hate to think you were being swept off your feet by some pretty boy with blond hair and freckles." She pressed the back of her hand to her forehead, making like she was about to swoon. "Oh, Jack," she sing-songed. "The feather in your hat is so *big!*"

Revka snorted. She sat up and gave Iyarra a squeeze. "Okay, now you're just being silly." She moved to face the centauress and looked her in the eyes. "Nobody takes the place of my girl, *nobody*. You got that?"

Iyarra locked eyes with her. She leaned forward to lick Revka's lips. "Prove it," she whispered.

Revka grinned. She turned and smothered the fire with dirt until it was out. The woods were plunged into darkness.

And the rest of the night just *flew* by.

Chapter Eight

MORNING DAWNED WITH A bit of early autumn chill. The three adventurers set off down the road going out of town. Revka, as usual, had taken the initiative as far as conversation was concerned.

"The point is, you always have to watch your back in a fight. Even if it's a one-on-one sort of deal, you still need to check every few seconds to make sure there aren't any environmental hazards."

"Environmental hazards?"

"Right. Cliffs, spikes, even just basic furniture and stuff around the place. You're fighting someone and you step on a stray beer bottle, that can ruin your day real quick. Plus, there's always the chance of reinforcements showing up. Always have a mental map of the situation and keep it updated."

Jack nodded seriously. "Mental map, keep it updated. Right."

"Actually," said Revka. "The best idea is to have someone along with you, so you can kind of watch each other's back. Now, me and Iyarra, we have our routine down pat. You know why?"

"Why's that?"

"Practice. A few afternoons in a quiet field somewhere can really pay off when the fertilizer hits the windmill."

"Practice. Got it."

By this time, they were well along the road, having left the town far behind. By mutual consent, they took one of the side trails leading off the main road and began to follow it deeper into the forest.

Eventually, they came to a rocky area with boulders and smallish bluffs punctuating the uneven terrain. This was cave country, and many of the rocky inclines had tunnels leading down into their depths.

Most of the entrances were too small for the adventurers to crawl into. However, they eventually came across one that was more than large enough for even Iyarra to enter without ducking. This particular cavern was further distinguished by the fact that someone had dragged a rock out by the entrance and scratched a message on its surface.

PERFECLY SAFE CAV

FREE FUD

"Well," said Iyarra. "I'm convinced."

"Okay," said Revka. "Object lesson. You come across a cave with a sign like that out front. What do you do?"

Jack's brow furrowed. "I...explore the cave?"

"Always bearing in mind what, exactly?"

"Uhm...that it's probably not as safe as it says?"

Revka grinned at Iyarra. "See? He *can* be taught!" She nodded to the boy. "Good job. Things that are safe do not, as a general rule, have signs up telling you how safe they are. An important tip, there. Now, let's go."

The cave went about seven meters in before taking a bend to the right. There, just where the last traces of outside light trickled into darkness, a few turnips had been piled haphazardly on the floor. A rope stretched in front of them, anchored on one side of the passage by a rock.

There was another sign. *FREE FUD.*

Revka chuckled, shaking her head. "Nice."

"What do we do?" Jack peered over Revka's shoulder at the setup.

"OK," said Revka. "First thing with traps, figure out what you're dealing with." She raised a torch and used it to follow the rope. Its other end was secured to a stick, which appeared to be holding up a small mound of rocks.

"Wow," said Iyarra. "That's it?"

"Seems pretty obvious." Revka nodded. "In fact, it seems a little *too* obvious." She peered closer. "Sometimes you get one where it looks like a big, dumb, obvious trap. You trigger it, and that sets off the *real* trap." She studied the setup, then gestured to everyone to step back. "OK, let's see what we get."

Drawing her sword, she moved back a couple of paces to join the others. She leaned forward, hooked the sword under the rope, and tugged sharply upward. The stick fell away, and about a dozen largish stones came tumbling to the ground. Other than that, not a damn thing else happened.

Revka surveyed the scene. "On the other hand, sometimes it really *is* just a really big, dumb, obvious trap after all." She kicked some of the smaller stones away. "Iyarra?"

"On it." The centauress punted the rest into a corner with little apparent effort.

Revka knelt down and inspected the pile of turnips. "Do we want to grab these, since we're here?"

Iyarra shook her head. "Wouldn't recommend it. They're a bit on the stale side."

"You know," said Jack, as they made their way farther into the tunnel. "I swear this place feels familiar."

"Oh yeah? Been here before, have you?" Revka turned to Jack.

The boy shook his head. "No. I mean, I'm almost certain I haven't, but it still feels like I know the place." He shrugged. "Kind of hard to describe."

"Well, caves do all tend to be about the same, in my experience," Revka mused.

"Yeah, dark and cramped." Iyarra shuddered.

"S'alright, Iyarra," Revka said. "We won't be here long. Just having a little field training for the new kid."

The tunnel eventually took them to a larger area, roughly oval in shape and with another passage going out the other side. A threadbare old rug lay right in the middle.

"Oh, come on." Revka just shook her head and pulled the rug away with one tug. Underneath was a very small pit, maybe two meters deep. Someone had put some loose stalagmites at the bottom and had more or less arranged them pointy side up. Anyone falling on them would be more likely to break the brittle formations than be impaled on them.

Jack surveyed the pit trap. "Wow."

"Sad, really." Iyarra shook her head.

"No craftsmanship anymore," Revka said. "Personally, I blame the schools."

They continued on their way down through the cave, keeping their eyes peeled for further surprises. They didn't have long to wait.

"Up ahead," Revka pointed. "See? On the wall." They hurried over to the spot and looked. It was plainly exactly what it looked like, though their minds needed some time to get used to the idea.

Start with the wall. It was your standard cave wall, slick, glistening limestone that billowed and curved from ceiling to floor. On this particular stretch, facing opposite a T junction in the cave, someone had painted three roughly concentric circles using ochre clay. A bullseye, in fact.

Obscuring a great deal of the bullseye was the back half of a common cave troll *(cavernous vulgaris)*, a squat, heavily built creature with stonelike skin and long, bandy arms. Cave trolls were a rare species, not often spotted in the outside world, and clearly they had very recently gotten a bit rarer. This one must have been going extremely fast when he hit the wall.

Below this was the tail end of a giant firework. It was in bad shape.

Revka took in the strange tableau before her. It appeared the troll had been straddling the firework when it hit the wall and had been flattened out in the process. She turned away and began to pace down the T junction until she found what she was looking for. "Here," she called. "Look at this."

There was a ramp, if you could give that name to a semi-organized pile of stones augmented with a few wooden planks. A little way behind the makeshift ramp, she saw a large wooden crate marked *ACME Rocket Company*. Revka nudged it with her toe.

"Well," she said. "I'll give them credit for originality."

Iyarra paced back along the narrow corridor from the ramp. Sure enough, it was a straight shot. "Good grief," she whispered. "Whatever were they thinking?"

Behind them, Jack was leaning against the wall, his face sickly in the flickering torchlight. Revka went over to him and patted his shoulder. "You okay there, guy?"

Jack shook his head. "It's not that," he said. "Well," he corrected himself, "it is *partially* that, but also it's the fact that I could swear I've seen this before."

Revka blinked. "What now?"

Jack nodded. He pushed himself away from the wall and staggered toward the remains. "I...have these dreams, sometimes. Nightmares, really. Of monsters and things. And I remember one, a couple of days ago. There was a cave, just like this. And voices, and I was flying through it, like you do in dreams? And then there was this incredible noise, and I looked, and there was this troll flying toward me on...something. He was screaming, and I was screaming, and there was fire everywhere."

"And then?"

"And then?" He shrugged. "And then I woke up."

Revka let out a low whistle. "Wow."

Iyarra trotted over. "I don't suppose you've been by this place before, and you remembered it from then?"

"No, no, nothing like that." Jack shook his head. "Just the nightmare. It happens sometimes."

"Uh-*huh*." Revka leaned against the cave wall for a moment, lost in thought, then she pushed herself away. "All right," she said. "Let's check around for provisions, anything we can use. Then we head out of here. I don't fancy spending all day here, especially not with that mess hanging off the wall. Any objections?"

* * * *

About half an hour later they were back in daylight, following the winding trail through the cave-infested woods.

"So," said Revka. "About these dreams..."

"The nightmares? What about them?"

"Well, for a start, are they always the same?"

"Mostly." Jack considered the question. "I mean, they do generally involve some kind of creature or bad guy of some kind. I go to attack them, and..." He trailed off, shaking his head. "I can never remember what happens next," he said. "It just sort of fades. You know how dreams are."

"I know what you mean," Iyarra agreed. "I dream that I'm grazing or something, and that my family is with me, but suddenly they aren't, and then they are again, but we're somewhere else, and I'm like different ages at the same time. It's weird."

Revka looked over at Iyarra. "You get that too? Isn't that *strange?* It's like, you're a kid, but also you're an adult. How does that even work?"

"I've found," volunteered Jack, "that if I eat cheese before bed, I get really strange dreams."

"I've heard that," said Iyarra. "Someone once told me that the mad prophets of Balaam would load up on Limburger cheese every night, and that's where they got all their weird visions from."

"Can't stand Limburger," said Revka.

"Camembert's nice."

"I myself," said Jack, "am partial to a bit of Asiago."

"*Asiago!?*" The girls chorused in unison.

"Have you no sense of smell?"

"Good grief!"

"Well, you don't have to smell it," Jack protested. "Just eat it."

"Smells like it's already been eaten."

"Oh, Revka!"

"What, am I wrong? Smells like feet."

"That may be why some people like it."

"Iyarra, ew!"

"What? You're the one who told me about that Mister Hunterson fellow."

"Hunterson?" asked Jack. "Who's he?"

"Oh," said Revka. "Just a guy in the town I grew up in. Had a bit of a thing. Strange fella. Really liked boots and shoes and things. Used to be he would buy your old shoes off you, the older the better. 'Course, nobody was exactly rich up there, so it was nice to get a little extra money once in a while, but in retrospect, I guess it was kind of weird."

"Did anybody know what he was doing with those shoes?"

"Well, not exactly *know*, but I think the adults all kinda suspected it was nothing you'd want an engraving of. I mean, he never actually bothered anyone. Kept to himself. Never did marry. I remember when he passed on, they cleaned out his house, just room after room of shoes. Dad was on the committee to clear the place out. He said it gave him the willies."

"That many shoes, he should have been a cobbler."

Revka shrugged. "Maybe. I don't think he liked working on them so much as...uh, *appreciating* them."

"Wild."

"Yeah. And you know, the thing is, if you had passed him on the street you'd never have guessed."

Jack shrugged. "Just goes to show, I guess."

"Right, right." Revka's brow furrowed. "What were we talking about?"

"Shoes?"

"No, no. Before that."

There was a moment of collective cogitation.

"Cheese?"

"Right...yeah. Cheese."

"That's right," Jack said. "I was just saying that Asiago is pretty good, if you can get past the smell."

"Well, yeah, but that's the real trick, isn't it?"

The trio wandered deeper into the woods, their path, like their conversation, getting further and further off the track. This was unfortunate. Had they stayed on the original conversational path, they might have come to some rather astonishing conclusions and might have saved themselves a good deal of trouble later, but such hindsight is of little use in the real world, being only really useful in fiction as a cheap way of foreshadowing when something terrible is about to happen.

Such as now, for example.

Chapter Nine

THE NIGHT WAS SPENT at camp in the woods. The girls had been sleeping rough long enough that they were quite used to it, but it seemed Jack was still not fully acclimated to life on the trail. He kept tossing and turning in his sleep and muttering under his breath. A couple of times, Iyarra was dragged into a half-awake state by the noise. She tried to listen to what he was saying, but was unable to make out anything coherent.

Still, the next morning found him in good spirits. They had a quick breakfast, courtesy of a nearby pear tree, then picked a direction and headed out. There was no trail this deep in the woods, but they were out of the thickest part and the going was actually pretty easy.

About an hour later, they came upon what had once been a road. It was cut straight and wide, but clearly had not been used in a very long time. A quick survey showed there were distant buildings in one direction, so they headed that way.

They had just come upon the first couple of buildings—ancient, stone farmhouses, by the look of them—when they heard footsteps coming toward them at speed. Revka hastily gestured the other two to get behind a wall. They hunkered down in silence, waiting to see who it was.

It was...well, it was a prince. You could tell by the outfit, all puffed sleeves and silken tights. Real outdoors wear. Plus, there were the obligatory golden curls, the rapier in its scabbard dangling off his belt, and the fact that he was, to put it bluntly, cleaner than pretty much anyone the girls had seen in several days.

He also looked absolutely terrified. This was not part of the standard prince uniform.

Revka hurried out from their hiding place and flagged him down. "Hey, there! Hey! Mister! Prince guy! Whoa! Stop!" She trotted after him, waving until he slowed down and turned to face her. Revka and the others hurried over to join the trembling noble.

"Listen," said Revka. "Are you okay? You look like you've seen a dragon or something."

The man shook his head. "Not a dragon, no," he said. "Th-the castle. I went in, and...*ohhhh, bad!*" He clutched his head, moaning.

"The castle? What castle?"

Villains

The prince pointed. "Up the street," he said. "Can't miss it. I wanted to rescue the princess, but the trial, oh lord, *the trial!*" He staggered a bit, as if pummeled by the memory.

"That bad, huh?" Revka looked skeptically up the street. Sure enough, she could see the towers of an old stone castle peeking up, just above the treetops. "Got a princess needs rescuing, you say? I kinda thought that was your guys' specialty? I mean, you *are* a prince, right?"

"Oh, yes. Yes." He held out a hand. "Prince Reginald of Saxe-Selmeria. You may kiss the ring if you like. And I had every intention of helping her, but the trial…I just…I couldn't…oh, it was just too horrible!" He broke down into sobs.

The three looked at each other. Finally, Revka broke the silence. "Look," she said, as kindly as she could. "We can see you're busy, so we'll just leave you be. Come on, you two." She turned around and started heading toward the castle.

Jack looked back and forth between the prince and the two women, then bustled after them. "Are we actually going to rescue a princess? I mean like, an *actual* princess?"

Revka shrugged. "Well, we're going to try to. As for an actual princess, I guess we'll just have to find out when we get there." She kicked a stone, sending it skittering down the remains of the road.

"I suppose." There seemed to be something weighing on the boy's mind. "Only…"

"What?"

"Well, I mean, is it allowed? Us rescuing a princess, I mean. I thought that was only for princes. That's how it is in all the books."

"Oh, well, obviously they get first crack," said Revka, the instant expert. "When you're in a princess-rescuing type situation, you always defer to any princes in the vicinity, but if there aren't any, then it's basically open season."

"For heroes, anyway," added Iyarra.

"Right. It's princes, then heroes, then miscellaneous. And we're heroes, so that means it's our turn," Revka asserted.

"Really?" Jack's eyes widened at the prospect.

"Yup."

Iyarra spoke up. "I always thought we were miscellaneous. I'm sure you said so before."

"Well, we are a *bit*, but at the moment we're technically heroes."

"And Jack? Is he miscellaneous?"

"Oh, no," said Jack. "I'm not religious at all."

"What?"

* * * *

It was a short hike down what had once been the main street to the typical, old-fashioned castle, a rough stone building surrounded by a wall and a moat that was nearly choked with weeds. The drawbridge groaned under Revka's weight as she crossed, so much that Iyarra insisted on waiting until the others were across before she tried it herself. A cobblestone courtyard that had clearly seen better decades lay beyond. There was also a heap of clothes piled on a bench. It appeared to be snoring.

Revka tilted her head, peering at the heap. On closer examination, it proved to be a very old man in a suit of clothes far too big for him. Some decades before, there had been something of a fashion in royal courts for bright colors, pantaloons, capes, ruffles, and brocade, the end result looking like an explosion in a carpet factory. These days, the fashion was tending toward white and silver. Apparently, out in this neck of the woods, no one had gotten the memo. The old man had clearly been wearing this outfit since it first came into fashion. He would probably be buried in it. It was quite possible he already had been.

Revka waved a cautious hand. "Scuse me? Sir? Pardon?"

After a rattling and a wet snort, the old man stirred. He looked up at the three with an eye like an underdone egg and sighed. "Ah. More."

"Uhm, yeah. Hi." Revka gave him her best smile. "We heard there's a princess needs rescuing?"

The old man jerked a thumb in the direction of the main tower. "Up the stairs. All the way to the solarium. I've been up twice today, so you can find it yourselves."

"Great. Fine." Revka fidgeted for a moment. "Only..."

"Mm?"

"Only we heard something about a trial. Apparently it's a really bad one?"

"Oh, *that*." The old man shook his head, setting off a minor avalanche of dandruff. "Yes, there is a bit of one. It's nothing difficult, really. You just have to kiss her."

"Kiss her? That's it?"

"That is, as you say, it."

"So, what's the problem? This doesn't sound like the kind of thing that would send people running from the room, if you don't mind my saying so. Unless she's, uh...?" Revka waved a hand.

"Oh, no. She's quite beautiful." He sighed. "I suppose I'd better tell you the story. The fact is, she's asleep. Has been for twenty years, ever since she touched that damn spinning wheel."

Revka nodded sagely. "I had a friend like that once," she said. "Try and get her to do any work around the house and she'd act like the world was coming to an end."

The old man waved a hand. "No, no. It's not like that. It was a curse, you see. An evil fairy put it on her. When she reached her sixteenth birthday, she pricked her finger on the spindle and dropped like a stone. Of course, they tried everything to wake her, but nothing ever worked. A few years ago, a diviner came through. Said that only true love's kiss could break the spell."

Revka put her hands on her hips, nodding and trying to look knowledgeable. "Oh yeah," she said. "You're gonna get that."

"So we put the word out. There were still a few people around at the time. Since then, there's been a steady stream of princes and such coming through. Alas, none of them have ever been able to do it. Search me why."

"I assume you've tried it yourself?"

"Me? Goodness gracious, no. I'm just a minor noble. Besides, it has to be true love's kiss, you know. I mean, she is my princess, so naturally, I worship the very ground she walks on—"

"Sleeps on."

"Sleeps on, yes, but...well, it just wouldn't be right, that's all. No, I'm afraid it's out of the question. Has to be a hero, preferably a prince of course, and it has to be true love. I'm afraid there's just no other way."

"Fine." Revka eyed the tower speculatively. "Up the stairs, you say?"

The old man nodded. "Right up to the top. Can't miss it."

"Okay, thanks for your help." Revka sauntered over to the tower and had a peek in. The place was empty except for the spiral staircase that wound its way upward. The three adventurers regarded it for a moment.

"Uhm, I don't think this is going to work for me." Iyarra took a step back.

"Why?" asked Jack. "Are you afraid of heights?"

"No. Well, a bit, but mostly I'm just not very good at stairs."

"What do you mean, not good at stairs? They're stairs."

"Put it this way," Revka explained. "Imagine having to work your way up a winding staircase with four hooves and almost no room to maneuver."

"And possibly no place to turn around," Iyarra added.

"Oh," said Jack. "Right. I see what you mean."

"Exactly. So Iyarra, do you want to stay down here, guard our flank?"

Iyarra nodded. "Please."

Revka smiled at her, then turned to Jack. "All right, hero boy," she said. "Let's go meet the princess."

* * * *

In truth, the trip wasn't that bad. The steps were wide and wound gently around the central support of the tower. To a modern eye, it was about the size of a three-story building. As the two trooped up the stairs, they discussed next moves.

"So, I just go in there and kiss her, huh?"

"That would appear to be the plan, yes."

"OK, but how about the true love part? How's that supposed to work?"

"Well, I guess in theory, you take one look at her and just...bam. Like that. Music swells, birds sing, little fat kids with arrows fly around, blah, blah, blah."

"Wait. Does it actually work like that?"

Revka chuckled. "Never been in love, huh kid?" She shook her head. "No. No violins, but sometimes, if you're lucky, you'll meet someone and it's like this little light goes on, you know? Like, aha! This person, right here. And you just...well, you just *know*."

"Sounds amazing."

"Oh, it is."

"Has to be better than little fat kids with arrows."

They walked on in silence for a moment.

"Revka?"

"Hm?"

"What if it doesn't work?"

"How do you mean?"

"I mean, it's supposed to be a true love's kiss, right? Well, what if I just sort of like her? Or if I'm like, eh. Can I still wake her then? What if she wakes up and it turns out we don't like each other? I don't have to marry her, do I? I mean, that always happens in the stories, but I don't know if I'm ready to settle down."

Revka chuckled. "Calm down, fella. There's no rush. For what it's worth, though, I think if you *are* the right person, it's supposed to just kinda work out. Actually, not being a prince, you probably aren't going to wake her anyhow."

"So...why are we doing this?"

Revka stopped. She turned to Jack and looked him in the eye. "Because we're heroes, and that's what we do. I've read some of those stories like you talk about, and they always make it seem like being a hero is all nobly riding off to save the day and everyone being so grateful, but let me tell you, it's a lot of hard work and very little reward.

"If you're in this for the glory, take my advice. Pack it in right this minute. Seriously, just go home and, I dunno, open a hat store or something. Because being a hero ain't about glory. It's about doing what has to be done, even when it feels like you don't have a chance. You still gotta give it a shot, if only so you can live with yourself. You understand what I'm saying?"

Jack nodded slowly. "I...I think so, yes. You're saying that even if we don't think we'll succeed, someone has to step up. Right?"

Revka nodded. "You got it."

"Even if we fail?"

"Even if we fail. Heck, sometimes failing is important too, you know. Sometimes there's no way to succeed at something until enough people fail. True story."

"Well," said Jack, as they resumed the climb. "I suppose I see what you mean. I guess I can regard this as hero practice. At the very least, I can say I gave it a shot, right?"

"That's it." Revka slapped him on the back. "Come on. We're almost there."

The solarium was a large room taking up the entirety of the top of the tower. Windows opened all the way around it and allowed the sun in from any angle. Originally the family's inner sanctum, the place had been left to neglect. Elegant, old wood furniture lay heaped with dust and clutter, and once-rich tapestries—those that hadn't collapsed into little heaps on the floor—barely clung to the walls. The smell of must and neglect was everywhere.

In the middle of the room was a large bed, one of the grand, four-poster variety that Revka had only ever seen in picture books. Laid out on the bed, the princess was fair and trim. Her golden hair had grown long enough to reach her waist. She lay perfectly still, only the faintest movement of her chest showing that there was any life at all.

Jack pushed aside a bit of cobweb and peered closer. He moved toward the bed, on the lookout for anything suspicious. Revka followed along behind, keeping an eye on the boy and generally ogling the decor. The situation sure looked straightforward enough. Walk in, kiss princess, happily ever after. She stepped up to Jack and patted him lightly on the back.

"Off you go," she said.

Jack stepped forward until he was next to the bed. He poked at her arm a couple of times, but there was no response. He braced himself and took a deep breath. Suddenly, he turned green and collapsed to the floor.

* * * *

Iyarra, who had pretty much run out of small talk with the ancient caretaker, waited quietly in the courtyard. At last, the sound of footsteps descending from the tower could be heard, and she hurried over to greet her friends. Revka was supporting Jack, who was upright but looked like he really wished he wasn't. The two women guided him to one of the few stone benches not completely overgrown with ivy, and Revka went over to the old man.

"Well," she said. "I think we have some good news."

The caretaker looked up in surprise. "Good news? You don't mean you've awakened her?"

Revka shook her head. "No, not that," she said. "But I think we may have an idea why it's taking so long."

"Well, by all means, tell me, please."

"Okay." Revka sat down next to him and gathered her thoughts. "Tell me, Mister, ahh..."

"Hambles. Lord Hambles."

"I see. Well, y'lordship, how long is it she's been up there?"

"About twenty years, by my reckoning."

"Twenty years. Right, right. A long time. And you're the only one here, I take it?"

"I'm afraid so. After their majesties passed away, everyone else moved on, you know. I'm the last one."

"I see. So, when was the last time the princess had a bath? Or, you know, even a decent wash?"

"*Ohhhh*," said Iyarra.

Jack didn't comment, but turned an even deeper shade of green.

"A bath? Well, I suppose the servants looked after that in the old days. As I said, I'm the only one left now, and well, of course, I couldn't possibly do it."

Iyarra nodded. "I see," she said. "You don't feel it would be appropriate for you to bathe her since you're a man and she's a girl."

"What? No." The man blinked in surprise. "I mean it wouldn't be appropriate because that's *servants'* work. I'm a courtier. I don't do menial work. For heaven's sake, I don't even know where they kept the soap."

"Yeah. Obviously." Revka sighed. "And I assume that also goes for the last time she was given clean clothes? Or sheets?"

"Well, I could hardly be expected—"

"Or had that chamber pot cleaned out? I had a look at it. It's *fuzzy*."

"Well, er…"

"Look, all I'm saying is, your prince types are…well, they got standards, you know? They like things to be a certain way. And I think that the odds of one of them falling in love with her are really going to improve if they can get within kissing distance without gagging." Behind her, there was the sound of Jack being ill into a hedge.

"You, er, you really think so?"

Revka nodded. She patted the old fellow on the knee. "Listen," she said. "There a village hereabouts?"

He nodded. "Well, yes. Just an hour down the road. Why?"

"Well," she smiled. "Why don't you trot along down there and find some capable lady with a strong stomach to come up and look after the poor girl? I'm sure someone would be willing to take on the job."

The old man nodded, then a cloud of doubt crossed his personal horizon. "Er," he said. "What if she wants paying?"

"Mister," said Revka. "You find someone willing to clean that girl up, believe me, *pay her*."

"Well, if you're sure…?"

She gave him a smile. "Trust me," she said.

*　*　*　*

The next day, His Lordship took a trip into the nearby village and managed to find someone to come and have a look at the princess. She went with him to the castle, took one look, and immediately sent back to town for reinforcements. In the end, it took a small army of villagers to set things right, but they were able to get the girl into a presentable state, and even cleaned up the courtyard and surroundings a bit.

After that, things really began to pick up. The word got out, and tourists began to arrive. The castle became one of the standard stops for anyone out to "do" the Enchanted Forest, to the point where there was often a line snaking right out of the courtyard. By the slow but inexorable alchemy which governs these things, the town rearranged itself into a tourist spot, with new inns sprouting up around shops selling souvenir models of the castle, small jars of "lucky" lip balm, and souvenir tunics reading:

I Kiss'd ye Sleepinge Princesse
& All I Got Was
This Godsblasted Shyrte.

Of course, none of the new crowd were seriously trying to wake her. Most of them were just there to try their luck, or for bragging rights, or because the average person really needs very little in the way of motivation when it comes to kissing a pretty girl. Inevitably, there were a few who tried to take advantage of the situation, but one of the townswomen was always present. A few chamber pots to heads put a stop to that very quickly.

Inevitably, the day of rescue came. A handsome prince came from a kingdom up north and was utterly smitten the moment he laid eyes on her. The townsfolk, seeing their meal ticket vanish into thin air, panicked. Worse, the princess found out what had happened, and how she'd spent the last several years being kissed by every strange commoner who managed to find their way up the stairs. She flew into a rage, announced that she was joining a convent, and took off.

In the end, it was decided to carry on as before. A group of local girls took turns in place of the erstwhile princess. The castle is still open to visitors six days a week, midmorning to sunset, holidays excluded. Two gold a try, and no tongues, please. They still have the chamber pot and they're not afraid to use it.

Chapter Ten

THE NEXT DAY DAWNED dark and cloudy, with distant grumblings of thunder and the sort of I-can-do-this-all-day patter of rain that dribbled its way down through layers of leaves until it splatted softly onto the dirt.

The three travelers walked together, more or less sheltered from the weather by keeping well under the trees. The girls had slipped on their oilskin cloaks. The light but persistent drumming of the raindrops on their hoods was almost hypnotic as they walked along. Jack, not having any wet-weather gear, stuck to his traveling togs.

"Say," said Jack. "You know lightning?"

Revka tilted her head in Jack's direction. "Uhm, yes," she said. "What about it?"

"You ever see anyone get struck by lightning?"

"Me? No. How about you, Iyarra?"

The horsewoman shook her head. "Not me," she said. "I've heard of it."

"Guy back home had it happen once. Was out plowing in the field. It came on to rain, and he ran for shelter under the nearest tree. Next thing he knew, it was two days later. Got him just like that. Said he didn't even hear the thunder."

"Gosh."

"Yeah. And the weirdest part? After it happened, metal would stick to him. Forks, spoons, all that. Lasted for weeks."

"I could see where that would be handy."

"Well, yeah, but he couldn't go near knives."

"When it was raining out on the plains," said Iyarra, "we would always try to find somewhere with a tree or two. We'd camp near them. Papa says lightning is lazy, so it always goes for the tallest thing."

"I once heard," said Jack, "that lightning never strikes the same place twice."

The girls mulled this over for a moment. "How?" said Revka.

"How? How what?"

"I mean, how does it know? The lightning, I mean. Is it just like, oh, I can't go there. I hit that place last year. Or something?"

Jack's brow furrowed. "I...actually, I don't know. How *would* that work?"

"Well," said Iyarra. "Maybe it's an act of Zodd."

Zodd was one of the more controversial deities in the pantheon. Officially a thunder god, he was also regarded, in some circles, as a dispenser of holy justice. In the more fundamentalist areas of the kingdom, victims of lightning strikes were regarded as abominations unto Zodd, or one of the many other gods on whose behalf he acted. Since, as of last count, this included nineteen holy men, one hundred and forty-eight buildings, fifty-seven knights in armor, and one very surprised sheep, there was some controversy as to how much actual justice was being meted out. The priesthood class tended to take the view that judgment of the gods is ineffable, therefore it was best not to question it under any circumstances. And incidentally, they could do with some new vestments and maybe some nice tapestries for the nave, thank you very much. A few people expressed doubts with this hypothesis, but not very loudly and never during a thunderstorm.

Somewhere in the upper branches, a pool of water that had been collecting on some leaves reached critical mass and came down all at once, landing mostly down the back of Jack's tunic. There ensued an entertaining few minutes as the boy danced around, swearing and trying to shake the water out.

"You know," said Revka once the show was over. "You really ought to get some sort of raingear if you're going to be living out on the road like this. Gotta be prepared for all kinds of weather."

"Well, the books never said anything about rain." Jack tramped along beside the two women, squishing a bit as he walked. "It's usually just one of those...what do you call them, the handkerchief on the end of a stick?"

"Bindles?"

"Probably. Yeah. I figured a couple changes of clothes, some clean underwear, a few sandwiches...nobody said anything about rain gear. Or soap." he added ruefully.

Revka fished in Iyarra's saddlebags. "Well, the thing to remember," she said, "is that the people who come up with those stories are generally writing them inside a nice warm house. They're not what you'd call too worried about the particulars." She pulled out a peach. "Want one? They're pretty fresh."

"Thanks."

She tossed it over and grabbed another. "'Yarra? Peach?"

"Not just now, thanks."

"Okay." Revka took a bite and continued down the trail, pontificating. "Anyhow, as I was saying, you gotta be prepared. When I first set out, I just had a rucksack full of things like fire fuel and extra arrows and a facecloth…"

"And the earplugs," added Iyarra. "Don't forget those."

"Right. The earplugs. Point is, I overpacked. I tried to think of everything I might run into out in the world and made sure I was ready for it. Turns out, the first thing I really ran into was nearly breaking my back hauling that stuff. Fortunately, over time, you learn what the really important stuff is, so I was able to shuck a lot of excess baggage on the way. Efficiency, fella. That's important."

"Gosh."

"And yet," said Iyarra quietly. "Three of my saddlebags are all your stuff."

"Well okay, but it's mostly essentials."

"Including all of your 'lucky' rocks?"

"Well, I…"

"Lucky rocks? What's so lucky about them?"

"They get a free ride everywhere we go." Iyarra grinned.

Revka made a face. "Very funny. Look, I just think they're neat, that's all."

"Anyway," said Jack. "I get what you're saying. Don't under-pack, but don't overpack either."

"Right. It's best to start with more than you think you'll need and winnow it down as you go."

"Or get a horse," Iyarra added.

"Or get a horse. Right."

* * * *

It wasn't long after that the rain began to taper off. By noon, there was even a little bit of sunlight poking through the clouds here and there. They took lunch in a small clearing, and Revka suggested they get in a little combat practice.

"All right." She scanned the clearing and selected a nearby oak. "Right. Let's say this tree here is a troll. He's got a—" She fished around in the undergrowth for a moment, then picked up a thick, fallen branch. "—a club, and he's menacing you. Show me what you can do."

Jack nodded. He dropped his bag and began to dig through its contents. The two women exchanged glances, but watched in silence as he went through his belongings. Finally, with a cry of triumph, he held up a dagger that, in terms of menace, was basically one step above a letter opener. "Found it!" He held the knife over his head in both hands, screamed, and charged.

Revka rolled her eyes. She leaned against the tree, swinging the branch back and forth as the boy approached. Just as he got within range, she leaned forward and whacked him on the shoulder with the branch. He yelped and fell over, the dagger flying from his hands and pinwheeling into the soft grass. "Ow!" he yelped. "What was *that* for!?"

"That," said Revka, "was the troll whacking your brains out before you could get near him with that little pig sticker of yours." She helped him up. "First rule of combat, make sure your weapons and tactics fit the situation. A big ol' troll with a club is never going to let you get close enough to stick him, even if *you could* get a knife through troll hide, which I'm frankly going to guess you can't. You have to think strategically. Iyarra, faced with a troll with a club, what do you do?"

"Personally? I run away."

Revka saw the look on Jack's face. "No, no, that's a perfectly legitimate tactic. If you can avoid a fight, sometimes that's the best thing to do. Trolls are strong, but they're slow. You can take advantage of that. Get them chasing after you and you can start whittling them down from a distance. Now, you got any distance weapons?"

"Uhm..." Jack cast an uneasy eye back toward the belongings he'd scattered out of his bundle.

"Guessing that's a no. Which reminds me, rule number two. If you are in a situation where you may need to fight, have your weapons ready to hand. No monster is going to stand there and wait while you toss your laundry around looking for a knife. Incidentally, throwing knives are okay for an opening shot, but you really want one of these." She went over to Iyarra's saddlebags and pulled out her crossbow. "Ever shot one of these before?"

Jack shook his head. "Good grief, a crossbow? No, I've never used one of those. Is it safe?"

"Well, no," said Revka. "But that's kind of the point." She walked over to Jack. "Now, before I let you try this thing out, we're going to have a little safety lecture. First off, you see this thing right here? This is the safety catch. You—"

"What, this thing right here?"

There was the zip-thwack of a crossbow bolt flying through the air and burying itself in the dirt. Revka sighed.

"All right," she said. "Rule number three..."

* * * *

A few hours later, the three came to a small stream trickling its way lazily between the trees. Revka gave Jack a grin. "OK, guy. Time for a little wood lore. You're lost in the woods, no trail or anything, but you come upon a stream. What do you do?"

Jack thought it over. "Don't pee in it?"

"No! Well okay, yes, but that's not what I'm talking about." She turned to Iyarra. "Go ahead, 'Yarra. You tell him."

Iyarra shrugged. "Search me. That's what I was going to guess, too."

"Oh, for..." Revka shook her head. "I *mean* that you can follow running water. Sooner or later, it will take you to civilization. You've always got to have ready access to water, am I right? So, we follow the stream."

"Oh! Right!" Jack gave a credible impression of someone committing something to memory.

"Come on." Revka turned and began to follow the course of the stream, the others tagging along behind.

It was about an hour or so later that the stream crossed a couple of paths. Revka called a halt. "OK," she said. "Two different paths." She pointed. "This one looks larger, but this one follows the stream more closely." She frowned. "Bit tricky, this."

"Maybe split up and follow each down a little way?" Jack suggested.

Revka shook her head. "Bad idea," she said. "Best to stick together." She did skulk down the wider path, however, trying to get a feel for it.

Iyarra shuffled over to the other one and had a look-see. It was just a path, as far as she could tell. She was just about to turn and head back when a glint of light caught her eye. "Guys?" she said. "I think there's some money here."

Sure enough, a gold coin was just lying on the ground where it had apparently been dropped. Revka scooped it up and tucked it into her purse. "Good catch," she said. "That'll come in hand—" She stopped, narrowed her eyes, and crouch-walked forward a few steps.

"There's another one," she said.

She scooped up the second one and looked around to see if—ah. A third one, just a few paces away. And if she looked beyond that...

"A trail?" Iyarra stepped up behind Revka.

Revka shrugged. "Maybe somebody's purse sprang a leak."

"It seems awfully regular." Iyarra frowned.

"Maybe it was intentional," said Jack.

He smiled nervously as the two women turned to him in surprise. "I mean, I'm admittedly pretty new at all this and everything, but maybe someone is trying to lure us. Okay, probably not *us* us, but they're trying to get someone to follow this trail. I mean, you know, possibly?"

The women looked at each other. Revka nodded. "You know," she said, "I think you just might be onto something. Any ideas on who would do that, or why?"

"Search me," Jack said. "I just think it makes more sense than a leaky purse."

"Okay." Revka squinted her eyes. Now that she knew what to look for, she could see a few more in the distance, marking out a very definite little path through the forest. "Let's assume it's a trap. We'll go alongside the path, and everyone keep an eye out for surprises. Could be an ambush or something. Eyes sharp, got it?"

Iyarra put up her hand. "We are still collecting the coins, though, right?"

"Well, yeah. That goes without saying."

* * * *

After about a quarter of an hour, they came to a place where the trail opened up into a clearing. Motioning the others to stay put and keep quiet, Revka snuck into the underbrush and worked her way forward until she could get a good look.

It was a smaller clearing than the one where the trail had begun, but even so, it was unusually large for this part of the forest. Probably someone had cleared it out at some point in the distant past. The forest was beginning to take it back. A few saplings competed for the scant traces of sunlight that pushed through the gap in the canopy. There were flowers here and there, a few moss-covered rocks, and a wooden dummy in a red cloak, propped up against a pole.

Revka watched the figure for a minute, but it just sat there as motionless as, well, as a lump of wood. She wondered if there might be some sort of enchantment on it, but that was pretty unlikely. Maybe someone's practice target? No visible nicks or holes, so they must be a pretty bad shot. She gave up and crept back to the others.

"A red cloak?" Jack furrowed his brow. "That's...odd."

Iyarra nodded. "Just that, and nothing else?"

"That's all I saw. I mean, the place looks safe enough. Come check it out if you want to."

The three of them filed into the clearing. Sure enough, it was just a wooden dummy with a cheap, red cloak draped over it. Someone had painted a face on the dummy. It seemed awfully happy to be in the middle of nowhere.

Iyarra poked at it with a hoof. "Well, it's got me stumped," she said. "Looks a little like a scarecrow, if there were any sort of crops around here."

Jack paced around the dummy, an odd look on his face. "Red cloak," he kept muttering to himself. "Red cloak. Why does that sound so familiar?"

Revka shrugged. "Well, it doesn't seem to be dangerous, and it isn't much help either, so I suggest we move on. There another way out of here?"

It wasn't long before they found the telltale trail of coins leading them down another path to a second clearing. This one had a dummy of a fat man sitting under a tree. This figure had been dressed in merchant's clothes and had several bags with gold signs on them. The three stood over the display, eyeing it critically.

"All right," said Revka. "Someone's messing around here." She dropped onto the grass in front of the dummy and grabbed one of the bags.

"I'm not sure you should be doing that, Revka," Iyarra said.

"It's all right," Revka said. "I'm just checking something." She untied the string around the top and tugged the sack open. "Uh-huh. Thought so. Have a look."

Iyarra and Jack craned their necks. There was no money, just some wadded-up rags.

Revka retied the bag and tossed it back with the others. She looked up at Jack and Iyarra. "Well, do either of you have an idea? It's got me stumped."

Iyarra pursed her lips. "Well," she said. "Maybe this used to be a bandit camp. And maybe this is what they used to train the new bandits. Er, or something."

Revka scratched her chin. "Possibly," she said. "Possibly. But that doesn't explain the coins."

"You know what?" said Jack. "I think it's supposed to be some kind of trap."

"A trap? What kind?"

"Well," he said, "think about it. We were lured here with money, right? And first we get a representation of a girl all alone in the woods, right? And then we get this guy here who's supposed to be a merchant, I guess. Don't you see?"

"See what?"

Iyarra let out a little gasp. "Oh, I *see!*" She raised an eyebrow at Jack. "You think so?"

"Seems likely, doesn't it?"

"Well, yes, but why would anybody want to?"

"Uhm..."

"Well, that's the real question."

"Scuse me..."

"I mean, it makes as much sense as anything, sure, but—"

"*What* makes as much sense as anything?" Revka had had enough.

"Villain traps," said Iyarra.

"Villain traps? You mean like, someone's trying to trap bad guys?"

Jack nodded. "I mean, I'll be the first to admit it's an odd idea, but it fits the facts, don't you think?"

Iyarra nodded. "The trail of money, the fake victims. Maybe this is the work of the—" She glanced over at Jack. "Er, of what we're looking for."

Jack looked up at the centauress. "What *are* you looking for, anyway?"

Revka turned to Iyarra. "What do you think?" she asked. "Should we tell him?"

"He'll have to know eventually." Iyarra shrugged.

"Know what?"

"Okay." Revka shifted her weight, so she was facing the boy. "This is going to sound very strange, but stay with us on this."

"O...kay?"

"The fact is, we're kind of on a mission. Someone's been kidnapping all the bad guys around here, and we have to find out who, and why."

"And stop them."

"Right. And stop them. Iyarra and I think there's some kind of supernatural whatsit running around in these woods that's snatching them away. We saw it happen once, actually. There's this big—"

"Wait," said Jack. "Do you mean to tell me we're trying to *save* the bad guys?"

"Well, not *save*, I mean not quite. Okay. Maybe yes we are, but it's not like that."

Iyarra nodded. "You see, there was this old lady..."

"But I thought we were trying to defeat the bad guys!" Jack looked back and forth between the others. "I mean, it's what heroes do! We are heroes, right?"

"Well, I don't know about heroes, not exactly, but—"

Jack's eyes narrowed. "You're trying to protect the bad guys," he whispered. "But that means you..."

"Hold on, now. Let me explain."

"Oh, you've explained *quite enough*." And now there was an echo to his voice, sharp and baleful. "I understand now. You *tricked* me!" His eyes took on a yellow-green cast. Around them, the wind picked up, rustling the branches on the trees. "You're just like them. Well, you won't get away with it."

The two women glanced at each other. The wind was blowing hard now. Revka tugged herself onto Iyarra's back and hung on tight. "GO!" she shouted.

They were so deep into the forest that there was nowhere to go. There was just the clearing, surrounded on all sides by the deep snarl of primal forest. Iyarra cantered in place, searching frantically for somewhere to escape to.

The wind was roaring. Revka clung to Iyarra as hard as she could. The noise was deafening. Out of the corner of her eye, she could see Jack emerge from the foliage, his body...no, that couldn't be right. She looked, and yes, he was floating just half his height off the ground, his limbs moving like some twisted marionette. The glow from his eyes was nearly blinding. His mouth was moving, but the words—if they *were* words—came from somewhere else.

"*Ra! Iya-to nassi botala-ya! Motala gabasi toya!*"

Iyarra whinnied in terror. Her hooves began to lift off the ground. Any second now...

The noise crescendoed, a terror-filled mix of howling wind and guttural syllables from whatever was speaking through Jack's mouth. Revka felt Iyarra's hooves slip, felt gravity shift. The world twisted...

Everything went black.

Chapter Eleven

THERE WAS A GUT-PLUNGING sensation like falling in several directions at once. Revka felt her consciousness drifting away, fading into nothingness. She couldn't even scream.

Suddenly, pain clenched tightly around her left ankle. Consciousness and sensation returned in a rush, as did the ground, which Revka hit face first with considerable force.

Suddenly, the clearing was full of gray-hooded figures. They surrounded the two women, shouting instructions to each other. Revka dragged herself up on one elbow and looked around in a daze. The wind had gone, and so had Jack. There were just the two of them and the dozen or so figures who surrounded them. Several had weapons. None looked particularly friendly.

Revka tried a grin. "Hi," she said. "You're not going to believe this, but—"

A spear jabbed her in the small of the back. "Up," it said.

Revka hauled herself up to her feet, endeavoring all the while to look as harmless as possible.

The spear jabbed again. "Forward."

Revka exchanged glances with Iyarra. The centauress had two spears pointing at her, the bearers keeping a wary distance. Revka's eyes narrowed. Now that she came to look, there was a distinct undercurrent of fear coming from these guys. Revka and Iyarra were more than used to people with weapons ordering them around, but it seemed like this bunch were genuinely scared of them.

Could she possibly scare them away? It was an intriguing thought. Of course, the thing about people who are scared is you never know what they'll do. And when scared people have weapons that are already hovering inches from you, spooking them is probably not the best idea.

She sighed, put her hands up where her captors could see them, and started walking.

* * * *

It was only about ten minutes before they came to a rather large clearing in the forest. Here, their captors had set up camp. There were several horse-drawn wagons, a few canopies and smaller tents, and a large fire pit in the middle. In fact, a fairly typical nomadic camp.

There was also, for some reason, a large wooden desk at the entrance to the clearing.

Manning the desk was a tiny old woman with a face like the back end of a lemon. That kind of face didn't happen by accident; it was clearly the result of spending an hour each morning sucking persimmons and practicing in front of a mirror. Revka had once heard that it takes more muscles to frown than to smile. This person had clearly decided to put in the extra effort.

The woman peered at them through giant, bug-eye spectacles. "Name," she snipped.

"Uh, hi, I'm—"

"*Shhhhhhh!*" Almost as one, the hooded fingers brought their fingers to their lips, or at least to where their lips should be under those cowls. The old woman pointed indignantly to a sign on one side of the desk that read in large, unfriendly words, *QUIET, PLEASE*.

Okay...Revka mentally shrugged and tried again. "Revka," she whispered.

The old woman cupped an ear. "Eh?"

Oh, lord. "Revka," she tried again. "Rev-ka."

The old woman snorted and jotted something down. She turned to Iyarra.

"Iy—I mean, Iyarra," she stammered.

The old woman handed over two little cardboard oblongs. "In you go." She jerked a thumb over her shoulder. The spear prodded Revka again.

They were led to a tent, somewhat larger than the others and off a little ways from the central fire. Inside, three figures in gray looked up from their conversation.

"We caught these two at the northwest trap, ma'am," said one of their escorts. "There was a third, but he got away."

"I see." The one in the middle, a stately older woman with spectacles and short, bobbed gray hair stepped forward. She must have been about fiftyish, the gray of her hair offsetting the dark brown of her skin. She carried the unmistakable air of being in charge. She looked them over in a businesslike manner. "Hmm. Interesting. Yet they appear to be normal travelers. Tell me, Brother Bartholomew, are you quite sure these are the ones we are looking for?"

"You should have seen it, ma'am," said the figure who had spoken before. "The other one started chanting, and his eyes started to glow. Then there was this wind that came out of nowhere and almost swept these two away. We were barely able to snare them."

"Interesting. And the third?"

"Well, as I said, he got away. One moment we were hanging on to the ropes to keep these two from disappearing, the next he and the wind were gone. We've got scouts trying to track him, but nothing so far. He can't have gotten too far, though."

"*Ha!*" said a voice.

The old woman ignored it. "Very well. Do let me know if you find him." She turned to the two women. "Well now. You don't appear to be particularly villainous. Ne'er do wells almost certainly, but not *quite* the quarry we are looking for. Care to account for yourselves?"

"Probably just tourists." There was that voice again.

"*Uhm,*" Revka whispered...

"You may speak freely in the tents," the woman said. "The rule of silence is only for the common areas."

"Oh." Revka cleared her throat. "Well, I am Revka, and this is my associate, Iyarra."

"Hi."

"We were just traveling through the woods, seeking adventure, and we found this trail of coins. Your work, I'm guessing?"

The old woman nodded.

"Right. So we came across those dummies. I guess they were the traps he mentioned. There was a bit of an argument and stuff happened, but look, what were those things about, anyway?"

"They were..." The woman hesitated a moment. "Well, they were bait. To trap villains. It's a bit complicated."

Revka smiled just a bit. "Really? Anything to do with the bad guys around here disappearing and no one knows why?"

A surprised murmur traveled around the tent. Bingo.

The older woman held up a hand, causing the others to fall silent. "As a matter of fact," she said, "you are correct. That is exactly what this is about, but may I ask how you know about this?"

"Well," said Revka. "There's a bit of a tale to that."

* * * *

It took a while to tell it all. Revka in full story mode had a tendency to embellish as she went along, but under the circumstances she stuck pretty close to the facts. Still, with the three asking her to repeat certain parts, or getting clarification on particular details, it was fairly slow going. Occasionally, the mystery voice would throw in with some unhelpful comment. If anyone else heard it, they gave no sign.

"And when I got back up, Jack was gone, and your guys here had all these spears and things pointed at us and...well, you know the rest."

"I see." The older woman looked down. She tapped her pencil thoughtfully and looked over her notes. "Quite the remarkable tale." She turned to the others. "Thoughts?"

"I believe them. I mean, if you do. Do you? I mean, if you don't that's all right. I don't mind, honestly." The speaker was a youngish woman, frizzy-haired and with an impressive collection of twitches and facial tics that had been going on pretty much since they'd walked in. She spoke in a kind of flustered, singsong voice, such as might be used by a kindergarten teacher trying to talk someone off a ledge.

The third figure was a tall, lean man with scraggly black hair and a face that put Revka in mind of a horse that had just seen something it disapproved of. He was a gratt, one of the irrevocably pedantic, gray-green humanoids whose faces, by some odd accident of nature, were cast in a perpetual frown. This one could have won prizes. He cast an eye over the two of them, arms folded. "Oh, I believe them," he said. "If only because I find it difficult to believe anyone could make up such a completely ludicrous story."

"You would know," said the voice.

"All right," said Revka. "Am I the only one hearing that? Iyarra? Anyone?"

Iyarra nodded. "It sounds like him," she said, pointing at the third figure. "But he's not moving his lips. I watched."

The older woman coughed. "I think, perhaps, introductions are in order. I am Sister Agata, head of our little group." She indicated the younger woman. "This is Sister Peasley. And this is Brother Sudgen."

"Hello."

"How d'you do?"

"Well, now that that's over," said Brother Sudgen. "I wonder if—"

"Oh, no," said the voice. "You're not getting away that easily."

"Look, I really don't think—"

"Oh, we *knew* that! But you'd better show them now, while I'm still being nice!"

Sister Agata put a hand on Sudgen's shoulder. "I think you had better. Get it out of the way and all that. Go on."

"Oh, very well." Brother Sudgen shook his shoulder out from under Agata's hand and turned around with bad grace.

The girls boggled. Revka tilted her head, not quite able to believe what she saw, but there, on the back of Sudgen's head was...Sudgen.

Or rather, his face. An identical copy of the original glared back at them, except inasmuch as it carried an even more cantankerous expression. "Well?" it said. "Not much to look at, is it?"

Sister Peasley leaned over. "W-we call him Brother Sudgen Two," she explained. She twitched a little.

Revka sought for something to say. "Er, it's not, I mean..." She faltered. "Uhm, how...?"

Sudgen turned back around. "A curse," he said. "Bit of a misunderstanding several years ago. Take a tip from me—never date a witch."

"*Misunderstanding!?*" Sudgen Two hooted. "She caught him in flagrante delicto with a barmaid! Said that since he was already two-faced, she'd make sure at least one of them always told the truth. And presto, here I am."

"I'm afraid it's so," said Sister Agata. "Sudgen Two has a rather bad case of Belkin's Syndrome. We've tried everything and haven't been able to get rid of it."

"Yes," said Brother Sudgen. "Or the syndrome."

"*Ha!*"

"You get used to it."

Belkin's Syndrome, named after the thirteenth Lord Belkin, who infamously struggled with it all his life, is the uncontrollable compulsion to tell the truth at all times. This is done constantly, whether anyone asks the speaker to or not, and with no regard to the feelings of those present, or whether it might be a good time to keep one's mouth shut. Other symptoms include irritability, constant sore throats, and having very few friends. Curiously, medical historians revisiting Lord Belkin's case now believe he may not have had the eponymous syndrome at all, but in fact, may have just been an asshole. Inquiries are continuing.

"So," said Revka in what Iyarra often noted as her let's-change-the-topic-right-now voice. "You said that you are the leader."

Sister Agata nodded. "More or less, yes. Technically, I am the senior librarian, so really, I'm more of a first among equals. We are The Withdrawn."

"The who?"

"Withdrawn. Out of circulation." She swept her arms out. "Everyone here is a former librarian who left their post, either voluntarily or otherwise."

"What, all of you?"

"Oh, yes. I was the librarian for one of the noble houses of Molina until the new earl decided it would be more aesthetically pleasing if we organized the books by color." She nodded toward the two-faced man. "Brother Sudgen here, you can, of course, work out for yourself. As for Sister Peasley…"

At the sound of her name, the younger woman flinched a little. Sister Agata patted her soothingly. "Sister Peasley used to be a children's librarian," she explained. "Poor dear. Once had four school groups show up at once. Nerves haven't been the same since. Have one of your pills, Sister. You'll be all right in no time."

"Wait," said Iyarra. "You mean you're all just librarians? Living out in the woods?"

"Oh, we are more than that. We serve as a traveling library, moving from town to town, bringing the books where they are otherwise not to be found. We hunt down and secure books lost to time and the minds of men. And when the structural narrativity of the universe is compromised—"

"Beg pardon?"

"When the stories are going wrong, we intervene. As you surmised earlier, we've been trying to work out this villain problem for several days now."

Revka let out a low whistle. "All that? I just thought you guys, I dunno, reshelved books and told people to be quiet and all that."

Sister Agata smiled. "Oh, librarians do much more than that. And we…well, we're not what you'd call typical librarians, in any case. Come with me." She beckoned them toward the tent flap, holding up an admonitory finger. "In the tents we can speak," she said, "but outside we observe the rule of silence during hours of daylight. Now, follow me."

They exited the tent and stepped out into the camp proper. A few gray-robed figures stood guard. Most of the rest were either reading, carrying, or otherwise occupied with books. Sister Agata pointed to one nearby. "Brother Simeon," she whispered, "caught a patron bending the spine back on a book and attempted to do the same to the poor man."

Revka winced. "Ow," she whispered.

"Double ow," grimaced Iyarra.

The old woman pointed to another. "Sister Wilding. Resigned after three people in a row came to her asking for, quote, 'a book, I don't remember the title, but it had a brown cover, and it was about a guy who goes on a trip,' unquote."

"Oh, dear."

"Exactly." A huge, hulking brute of a man lumbered by. "Brother Conan," whispered the elder librarian. "He once had someone come in with a book thirty years overdue."

"Gosh."

"What did he do?"

The old woman shook her head. "I don't think I ought to tell you," she whispered. "But if he ever sets foot in Molina again, the price on his head could buy a small city."

Revka coughed. "Quite the—" She remembered herself and switched to a whisper. "Quite the bunch you've got here. And you think that you can figure out what this whole villain thing is all about and put a stop to it?"

"I think if we don't, no one else will." She smiled at the two women, leading them back into the tent. "So, you've seen our little band," she said. "What do you think?"

Revka searched for something to say and eventually settled for, "Well, they're certainly unique."

Sister Agata chuckled. "I suppose that will have to do. It seems to me that, since we are concerned in the same struggle, it would be wise if we joined forces."

"What do you have in mind?"

"I propose to take you on with us. You will travel with us and learn our ways. Where two groups have thus far failed, perhaps our combined efforts will succeed. That is, if my colleagues agree? Sister Peasley?"

"Oh! Uhm, I think whatever you say will be perfectly all right?"

"Brother Sudgen?"

"I suppose so." He shrugged. "We couldn't possibly be doing any worse."

Sister Agata cupped her hands together. "Splendid," she said. "Then it is decided. That is, if you are willing?"

Revka looked up at Iyarra, who gave a little shrug.

"Well, yes, we're willing," said Revka. "But the thing is, we're not exactly librarian material, you know?"

Iyarra nodded. "I'm not...*super* good at reading," she said.

Sister Agata smiled. "Don't worry about that, dears. We will train you in our arts. I suggest you take the night to think it over before you make up your minds. In the meantime, feel free to roam around the camp, and of course, avail yourself of the books. You did get your cards?"

"Pardon?"

"Your library cards. Sister Wizen should have given you some as you came in."

"Oh, those!" Revka realized she was still holding hers in her hand. She glanced down and read.

TRAVELING LIBRARY
Member Name: ~~Refka~~ Revka
If lost please return

"Your library cards," the sister explained. "They mean you can borrow any of the books you like while you are here. Very important. Don't lose them."

"Oh," said Revka. "Fine." She tucked it into her belt pouch.

"Now then," said Sister Agata, "I have some things to do. Feel free to explore the camp today. We'll discuss things further tomorrow." She patted Revka on the shoulder. "Don't worry. I expect we'll make proper warrior librarians out of you in no time."

"Oh," said Revka. "Lucky old us."

* * * *

"I know what you're thinking," whispered Iyarra as they walked around the camp.

Revka's wandering mind scrambled back to the present. "Mm? What? What am I thinking?"

"That Brother Sudgen. He's the second sign."

"What, now?"

"You know. The second thingummy. The two-faced truth teller. That lady back at the house, remember?"

Revka shrugged. "Could be a coincidence."

Iyarra raised an eyebrow. "Coincidence? How many people with two faces do you think are out there, exactly?"

"All right, all right." Revka kicked a pebble. "So we're on the right track, anyhow."

"Looks like it."

"Great."

"Shhh!" scolded a passing robe.

"Sorry. Great. Still can't figure out what she meant by, 'Beware of happy endings.' Do you have any idea what she meant by that?"

"Not a clue, sorry."

"Well, I guess we'll have to find out when we get there. And I'm really not looking forward to it."

Chapter Twelve

THE NEXT MORNING, THE girls were brought before Sister Agata in her tent. "Good morning." She gestured to the soft, woven mats before her. "Please, be seated."

Peasley and Sudgen filed in and sat on either side of the older woman. "Now that you've had time to sleep on it," she said, "I would like to formally invite you to join us. Not as full members of our order, of course," she added quickly. "But as allies. You would travel with us, share our resources and so on, until the present emergency is resolved."

"Yes," said Sudgen Two. "We can do more damage that way."

"The point being," Sister Agata continued, "that we here are essentially the only ones who fully understand the import of what is happening, and also the only ones who are in any position to do anything about it."

Iyarra raised a hand. "What about guards? Surely there are some in the towns nearby?"

Brother Sudgen shook his head. "I'm afraid not. The guards around here, they are...well, fairy-tale guards, if you see what I mean. Have you ever read a fairy tale in which guards were even remotely competent?"

"Well, now that you mention it..."

"Exactly. Whereas you two are clearly no strangers to a good fight, and we...well, we know how stories work. That gives us a considerable advantage."

"Not to mention the fact that—" started Sudgen Two.

Sister Agata cleared her throat. It wasn't loud, or particularly expressive; just the muffled thump of a boulder being dropped into the path of the conversation.

Sudgen Two shut up.

"If you are going to fight by our side," she said, "you must first learn our ways. I know neither of you has been called to the Shelf Life, but I think you'll find our skills extremely useful. We will, therefore, take a few days to acquaint you with some of the more practical aspects of our calling. Less to do with, as you say, stamping books and so on. I think you will find them quite interesting. While with us, you will have food and a place to sleep. I ask only that you follow our rules, do as you are bid, and do not interfere in the business of the library. I trust this is agreeable?"

Revka looked at Iyarra, who nodded. "All right," she said. "I suppose we're in."

Sister Agata smiled. "Very good," she said. "We shall begin your training after breakfast. Please, join Sister Muri in the clearing to the east when you are ready."

* * * *

When the centauress and woman filed into the clearing after breakfast, it appeared to be empty. Revka looked around and coughed. "Uhm, hello?" she said. "Anybody here?"

"Ah, you're here." A short, younger woman had apparently materialized between them. She gave them a shy little smile and stepped forward, turning to face them. "My name is Sister Muri," she said. "And, ah, Sister Agata has asked me to instruct you in silence."

Iyarra nodded. "Oh, we know about the whispering rule already. I'm sorry if we've forgotten a couple of times, but we're getting better, I promise."

The young woman waved a hand. Her soft, hesitant voice lilted nearly every sentence into a question. "No, you don't quite understand. You see, uhm, when you're a librarian? And you learn all these different skills as part of being one? Well, you can sort of take them and turn them into survival skills. Uhm. Like silence. It's like, it's not just talking quietly. You can, ah, sort of..." She waved a hand vaguely. "*Become* quiet? Like, embody it? But I think we'll start off with just moving quietly. Uhm. If that's all right."

The rest of the morning was spent in what Sister Muri called the, uhm, art of silence. Revka had always reckoned she was no slouch when it came to sneaking around, but the younger librarian made her seem like a one-man band fighting his way through a turkey farm. Revka got the impression that Sister Muri was naturally inconspicuous to begin with, but she had really refined this tendency into an impressive amount of skill. They spent the better part of the morning crawling back and forth through a stretch of forest practically littered with dried leaves, loose twigs, and low-hanging branches, until even Iyarra could move through the undergrowth without loudly announcing her presence with every hoof step.

"Okay. Now, ah, you've both done very well," said Sister Muri after lunch. "And I think we're ready for the next part? It's kind of tricky, though, so do watch me closely."

Revka and Iyarra watched. At first, it didn't seem that anything was happening. Sister Muri stood perfectly still, not budging from beneath the large tree in whose shade they were standing. Her face seemed to take on a slightly glazed expression. There was a slight shifting of weight, and then...

And then...she didn't disappear, not really. She was there if you looked right at her, but somehow she became, well, easier to miss. Without any apparent outward change, she had faded into the background. Revka kept having to remind herself the girl was there. Iyarra, for her part, felt like she was trying to catch something out of the corner of her eye while it was right in front of her. She tilted her head back and forth a few times, trying to find a better angle. Her eyes were starting to water. "Okay," she said. "I give up. How are you doing that?"

Sister Muri shifted, and once again she was before them, plain as day. "It's good, isn't it? Basically, you, like, allow yourself to slip out of people's notice? Brother Sudgen calls it weaponized modesty, but really there's, uh, a bit more to it than that. It's, uh, kinda tricky, so don't feel bad if you don't get it right away. Uhm, shall we begin?"

In fact, it took several hours for either of them to make any headway. Revka, who tended to stand out in any case, found it particularly hard going. Iyarra, on the other hand, turned out to be rather good at it once she got the initial hang of the thing. By sunset, she was able to fade almost entirely from view.

Revka scratched her head. "I got to admit, Iyarra really has it down," she said.

Sister Muri nodded. "I'm not surprised, actually. She's, ah, like me, kind of. Very, uhm, not fond of being noticed and, er..." She waved a hand vaguely, blushing.

"Shy?" supplied Revka.

Sister Muri nodded. "Shy. Yes. Thank you."

Iyarra grinned at Revka. "See?" she teased. "There is an advantage to me being the shy one, after all."

"I suppose," chuckled Revka. "But you gotta admit I was pretty light on my feet this morning."

"Well, uhm, now you have a chance to prove it." Sister Muri pointed back toward the camp. "It's time we head back for dinner, you know? There should be two sentries between here and the fire pit. So, ah, why don't you see if you can make it past both of them?"

Revka grinned. "You're on!" She nodded at the others and plunged into the woods.

* * * *

About an hour later, Iyarra and Sister Muri reunited at the communal fire. "And how did you do?" asked the librarian.

Iyarra grinned. "Pretty good, actually. There were a couple of times I almost got caught. I had to hold still and wait for them to lose interest, but I never would have been able to do it before."

"Well, you did very well!" Sister Muri smiled. "And your friend?"

"Revka? Hasn't she shown up yet? She's usually much better at sneaky stuff than I am. She should be back by now."

"Hmm." Sister Muri scanned the camp. A few more of the Withdrawn were present, mostly wrapping up their tasks or talking in quiet groups. In a corner, a few were preparing the evening meal. There seemed to be no trace of Revka.

Sister Muri turned back to Iyarra. "I don't see her," she said. "It's possible she...er..."

Iyarra regarded the younger librarian. "Is something wrong?"

"Was...was that pine cone on your head there a moment ago?"

Iyarra reached up. Yup, there it was. Dead center on her head and standing upright too, by the feel of it. She sighed theatrically. "All right," she said. "Very funny. Where are you?"

Revka appeared by Iyarra's side. She cackled, flomping down in front of the fire. "Pretty good, huh?"

Iyarra rolled her eyes. She reached up and took off the pine cone, tossing it into the fire. "Showoff."

Revka grinned. "Sorry. Couldn't help it." She stretched out and looked over at Sister Muri. "Got here a little while ago and saw you weren't here yet. Decided to hide until you showed up."

"Very good." Sister Agata emerged from the main tent, Brother Sudgen in tow. "It seems we have a couple of fast learners."

"Yes, ma'am," said Sister Muri. "I think they're, uhm, ready for the next phase? Possibly?"

"Excellent." Sister Agata turned to the two women. "We shall start you tomorrow on observation. Our Sister Dowell will be instructing you. I hope you're good at picking up information quickly."

Revka grabbed an apple from the communal basket and began to cook it over the fire. "Oh, don't worry about that. 'Yarra and me, we're pretty hot stuff in the observation department. Heck, I'm a regular eagle eye, myself. Ask anyone."

Sister Agata raised an eyebrow. "Indeed? So if someone were to, for example, slip something onto *your* head while you were talking to me, you would notice?"

Revka blinked. "What? I mean, sure, obviously I would..." She trailed off. There were grins on the faces around the campfire. Now that she thought of it, she did feel a *little* pressure...

She reached up. Her hand closed on something smooth and flat. She tugged, and five books tumbled into her lap.

Behind her, Sister Muri smiled and said nothing.

* * * *

The next morning, the two were taken to a tent near the outskirts of the camp. Sister Dowell turned out to be a short, elderly woman with shock-white hair tied neatly into a bun. The tent held very little: a few mats, a bedroll, and a low table on which several books were stacked. As Revka looked around, she noticed that there was sort of a running theme present. Everything was meticulously organized. The cushions were perfectly squared and equidistant, and all arranged with geometric precision. Even the books were stacked in order of decreasing size and exactly centered on each other.

The old woman wore a set of small, horn-rimmed spectacles hanging on a chain around her neck. Such people are not to be trifled with.

"Sister Dowell," said Sister Agata. "These are Revka and Iyarra. Ladies, Sister Dowell here will be handling your observation training. Sister Dowell used to be the chief reference librarian in the Royal Library before she retired. During her years there, she learned how to retain large amounts of information very quickly. So, for example, if someone needed the population of East Blagistano—"

"One hundred twenty-nine thousand, four hundred and six," said Sister Dowell.

"...yes. Or the principal export of Mercia—"

"Rubber novelty items."

"Thank you. The point being, she can call it to mind instantaneously. Under her training, you will...well, just do the best you can."

In the interest of not bringing the narrative to a complete halt, we shall skip over the majority of the training. Those curious about such things will be interested to know that Sister Dowell employed a kind of mnemonic/mind palace hybrid in which she'd create imaginary spaces filled with icons, each of which stood for something else. It was, in the tradition of such homemade systems, entirely transparent to the creator and utterly incomprehensible to anyone else.

"For example," she said. "Suppose I wanted to memorize the contents of this tent. At a glance, I see the tables, the cushions, and so on. I merely create a mental image of this tent, and then around it, I put the things that go into it. The bedroll in the corner, for instance. It is a bed *roll* in a *corn*-er. So I just imagine a *roll* made of *corn*meal, and that immediately reminds me of what it is and where it is. You see? Simple."

"Uhm." Iyarra raised a tentative hand. "Pardon me, but why don't you just picture the bedroll?"

This did not seem to go over well. "I beg your pardon?"

"I mean, why not just do a mental picture of a bedroll, and not the bun—"

"Roll."

"Roll. Sorry. I'm not sure I understand the point."

Revka nodded. "It does kind of seem like going the long way around."

Sister Dowell smiled indulgently. "Oh, it may seem so," she said. "But that's because you are just getting started. I find it's quite easy once you learn how to do it."

"And how long does that take?"

"Seven months, two weeks, three days, eight hours, and twenty-seven minutes," replied Sister Dowell at once.

In the end, it was agreed that she would teach them a rather condensed version for fieldwork, and that they could come back later when they wanted to learn it properly. This shorter version proved actually rather useful. By the time the two exited the tent for supper, Revka felt that she could actually make use of the techniques, even if they made her head feel all woozy.

They were brought before the senior librarians again that evening. "Now, we would like to test what you've learned." Sister Agata gestured to a cloth draped over the floor. "Brother Sudgen will uncover the contents only for a count of five, then you will tell us as many items as you can recall. Ready?"

The two girls looked at each other and nodded. "Ready."

"Yeah."

Sister Agata nodded to Brother Sudgen. He whipped the cloth away.

A variety of items were laid out in an orderly manner. The two girls went silent, their eyes darting madly back and forth over the collection before the cloth was yanked back into place.

"All right," said Sister Agata. "Go ahead. What did you see?"

Revka looked up at Iyarra, who took a breath. "Two apples, dixie red delights, I think. A tobacco pipe."

Revka joined in. "Three quills, two black, one brown. Inkpot, two-thirds full."

"Three calamantrum leaves, a radish, and a Spotted Henry mushroom."

"Coins, two silver, and twenty-one copper. A chicken bone. A piece of string rolled up in a coil, and one of those strips of red silk I've seen you guys use as bookmarks."

"A light-brown book; I couldn't read the title. A small knife with a yellow handle and a chip near the base of the blade."

"A sandal, someone's spectacles, and a hunk of cheese."

"And two hard-boiled eggs."

"And one duck egg."

"Oh, yeah. One duck egg."

Revka looked up at the elders. "How was that?"

The three looked at the girls, dumbfounded. Sister Agata lifted a corner of the cloth and had a peek. "Yes. Er, yes indeed. Very good."

"Not bad," said Brother Sudgen.

"Better than you," said Sudgen Two.

"Oh, *shut up*."

Sister Agata coughed. "That was quite the performance, there. May I ask how you managed that?"

Revka grinned. "Simple," she said. "We just divided it up. She memorizes the left half, I memorize the right. Goes a lot faster that way. We figured it out while we were practicing."

Iyarra nodded. "Sister Dowell noticed we sort of naturally divvied the environment up anyway, so we sort of built our strategy around it."

"I see." Sister Agata regarded them. "I suppose it's a viable strategy, at least so long as you two are in the same place together, but do practice doing it entirely by yourself. You never know what circumstances may bring."

"Yes, ma'am."

"I must admit you two do work together awfully well."

"Bet that's not all they do," muttered Sudgen Two.

"That's *quite* enough!" snapped Sister Agata. She turned back to the two girls, who were carefully avoiding each other's eyes. "In any case, I think we will start you on our most important technique tomorrow. So, eat up and get plenty of rest tonight."

"Yeah," said Sudgen Two. "You'll need it."

Chapter Thirteen

THE NEXT MORNING FOUND them back in the same clearing as before. This time, there were two instructors waiting for them. The first was an elf, a bit short and stocky as elves went, with her hair tied back in pigtails. She wore a modified version of the gray librarian's robe and held a quarterstaff upright in one hand. Next to her was the hulking figure of Brother Conan. He had slipped out of the top half of his robes and tied the sleeves 'round his waist. The body thereby revealed was, put it like this, one you wouldn't generally expect on a librarian.

Actually, that's not necessarily fair. Some librarians are in excellent physical condition. Indeed, some have to be as a matter of necessity. Take the keepers of the Dark Library in the realm of Far Langor, where the magic-impregnated tomes therein must often be wrestled down and held forcibly in place before anyone can actually read them. Then there are the librarians of Lazak, where books are engraved in steel plates and can weigh several hundred pounds each, more if they have pictures. In the entire kingdom, there is only one dictionary, which takes up its own building in the capital. Looking up a word generally takes around three days, not counting time off for hernias. In any case, Brother Conan looked like he could take them all on with ease.

"Good morning," said the elven woman. "My name is Sister Tali. This is Brother Conan. Today, we are to begin training you in the most secret art of our order. It is the means by which we have managed to survive in the wild for so many years. Be warned, however, when you take on this knowledge, you also take the responsibility of handling it wisely. May we have your assurance that you will do so?"

The two women looked at each other, then nodded. "Uh, sure. Yeah. No problem," said Revka.

"Of course," added Iyarra.

"Very good," said Sister Tali. "Have a seat, and we shall teach you the founding principles of Bookshido."

The Librarians took hours to tell the story of Bookshido, including footnotes, so we've summarised it here for you. Bookshido is from the Lemurian words buke for book and shideo meaning to fight or struggle, the whole meaning to fight like they do in books. It is a technique for making use of narrative structure to gain an advantage in hand-to-hand combat. While impractical in what may be called real-world conditions, in sufficiently unreal environments it can make all the difference between victory and defeat. In a place like the Enchanted Forest, where the force of narrative impetus hangs heavy in the very air, a good knowledge of Bookshido can offer a huge advantage.

Bookshido traces its origins to the early days of the First Empire, when books were sparse and literacy rare, even among the ruling classes. In those days, the wandering librarians who moved from place to place with their precious cargo of books did not lend them out, but rather read them out loud, often in the public square or before a royal court. Those who followed this calling often found themselves trekking alone across wild, untamed wildernesses with nothing but their wits and a few survival guides, most published posthumously.

Among these was the great librarian-monk Turo, who it is said founded the art of Bookshido and laid down its founding principles. Turo set out from his village at the tender age of fourteen with a handful of scrolls and a desire to go out into the world and do some good. As is traditionally the case in these situations, he almost immediately landed in a world of trouble. Unfortunately, his only experience with combat had been the stories he had heard as a child. It didn't take long for him to discover that acting like a hero in a fairy tale was a good way to get your face pummeled.

Over time, he learned how to defend himself more competently and was eventually able to explore the farther reaches of the kingdom. It was during these wanderings that he made his first great discovery. It was in a small village—more of a glorified crossroads, really—when he was reading out some stories for the scant few that lived there in exchange for dinner and a bed for the night. As it happened, on that night, they were attacked by a group of bandits who had been stirring up trouble in the area. Turo, who had just been reading a particularly exciting bit, found himself slipping into his old habits, taking his moves right out of the very story he had been reading.

And this time—what the hell—they worked.

Later experimentation proved that, when in an environment sufficiently saturated by narrative causality (such as somewhere where stories were actively being told), a bleed-through effect allowed the rules of storybook fighting to retain their efficacy in actual combat. Over the years, it was found that this also applied to libraries, bookstores, and other environments naturally steeped in the power of stories. This is why the Withdrawn and other groups of warrior librarians had been able to defend themselves for hundreds of years against all manner of threats, and also why, to this day, nobody ever dares mess with librarians. Seriously. Just don't even try.

Revka and Iyarra listened in awe as the history of Bookshido was related to them. "You mean," said Revka after the others had finished. "That actually works?"

"I have to admit, it all sounds a bit unlikely," said Iyarra.

"Unlikely, yes," said Sister Tali. "But nevertheless so. Fortunately, here in the Enchanted Forest, the environment is particularly suited to the technique. I think, perhaps, a demonstration is in order." She pointed at Revka. "You. Attack Brother Conan."

Revka quirked an eyebrow. "I beg your pardon?" She tried to look Brother Conan up and down, but there was just too much of him. You had to look at him in shifts.

Sister Tali threw her an object. It was a toy sword, carefully wrapped in cloth scraps until the wooden "blade" was completely obscured. It was basically a sword-shaped pillow. "It's all right," she said. "We just want to see what you can do right now. When you're ready."

Brother Conan grunted and gave her a nod. Revka shrugged and readied the sword. She crouched a little, trying to find a good spot to strike, but there really weren't any. It was like looking for a weak point on a mountain.

To hell with it. She lunged forward, kicking her legs under her as she leapt. She slid across the soft grass, bringing the sword broadside across his shins. She tumbled, rolling upright behind him and delivering another blow at the back of the knees before he could turn to face her.

By the time he got around to where she had been, she was poking his ribs with the sword on her way back around. Okay. This seemed to be working. If she could keep it up, harry him and stay out of punching range, she—

A hand the size of a soup plate slapped across the back of her head and she went flying. There was a moment of vertigo as the world flew beneath her, the gut punch of a hard landing, and a mouthful of dirt. Ow.

"I think that's enough," said Sister Tali. "Not too bad. You can move quickly and have the ability to think ahead. That's good. We can build on that. Now, watch carefully." She picked up the sword, brushed it off until it was more or less clean, then nodded to Brother Conan. "Ready?"

Suddenly, she was in the air, handspringing backward toward him with the sword clenched in her teeth. He turned toward her, crouching, arms out, ready to defend himself.

She twirled, and suddenly the sword was in her hand, darting and swinging at him like lightning. He had pulled out a short sword of his own and was fighting her in apparent earnest. Sparks flew as their swords clashed. She leapt, laughed, and shouted insults. He spun frantically, lunging, trying to break through but somehow not able to do so.

As Revka watched, a little voice in the back of her head whispered that this was all wrong. Sister Tali's technique was all over the place. She kept whacking his sword. What's the point of that? It was more of a dance than a fight. And where were those sparks coming from? Swords don't spark, even the ones that aren't wrapped in several layers of cloth.

It was, in short, the biggest load of dragon splat she'd ever seen.

And then it was over. Sister Tali turned to the girls. "There, now. What did you think?"

Iyarra bit her lip, trying to find something polite to say. "Uhm...that was...different?"

Revka didn't bother with polite. "That was playacting," she said flatly. "That wasn't real fighting at all."

Sister Tali just smiled. "Indeed? Then perhaps you can show me how it is done." She nodded to Brother Conan, who tossed his sword to Revka. She caught it, swung it around a couple times, and nodded to Sister Tali. "Let's go."

Thirty seconds later, Revka was flat on her back, watching the forest spin lazily around her. She tried to shake off the brain fog and replay the last minute or so in her mind. She'd been sure she was going to mop the floor—okay, the ground—with Sister Tali, but somehow, it just hadn't happened. Revka had years of fighting and adventuring under her belt, and yet this skinny lady, with the most ridiculous technique Revka had ever seen, had utterly trounced her. She hadn't even gotten past her guard once. It had to be magic. *Had* to be.

Eventually, she managed to pull herself together enough to prop up on her elbows. "Okay," she groaned. "What just happened?"

Sister Tali was seated on the grass, quite unconcerned. "That," she said, "was Bookshido. What may have looked to you like the random flailings of a rank amateur were, in fact, the result of many years' study and technique. Sadly, we do not have years to teach you the finer points, but I think we can at least give you the basic techniques. That is, if I have your attention."

* * * *

The rest of the day was taken up in training. The two librarians taught Revka and Iyarra such time-honored techniques as improvising banter, catching thrown weapons and sending them back in one movement, and excessive but visually impressive acrobatics. Through it all, the two fought back and forth, trying and retrying the techniques until their instructors were satisfied.

"Technique nine, improvised weapons," Brother Conan announced. "You're cornered. You're unarmed. You reach behind you for something to defend yourself and pull back...?" He looked at the girls. "Anyone remember?"

Iyarra raised her hand. "Uhm, something useless but funny?"

"Such as...?"

Iyarra thought about it. "Like, a fork or a spoon?"

"Good, good. What else?"

Revka piped up. "Sporting equipment?"

"Good. Go on."

"A stick?"

"Not funny enough."

"A vegetable?"

"Better. Best, of course, if it's a humorously shaped one. One more."

The girls thought.

"Uhm," said Iyarra. "A fish?"

"Really any kind of animal," said Sister Tali. "Preferably living. Chickens are best, but really anything you can reliably throw at your opponent that will go berserk."

Iyarra nodded, and nudged Revka. "Remember Port South? And the octopus?"

Revka rolled her eyes. "Don't remind me," she said.

A little while later, Iyarra watched as her sword pinwheeled through the air, landing blade downward with a *thunk*. Brother Conan held her at bay, his sword pointed right at her chest. Sister Tali stepped forward.

"A male opponent has you pinned down," she said. "Now, if you were a male yourself, you would have the options of bluffing or trickery. As a female, your best bets are...what?"

Iyarra shifted a hoof, staring back at the sword. "Uhm...no, don't tell me..."

Revka opened her mouth to speak, but Sister Tali waved her off. "Take your time," she said to Iyarra.

"Oh!" Iyarra snapped her fingers. "Uhm, we either pretend to flirt with them or burst out crying."

"And why do we do that?"

"To take them off their guard."

"At which point...?"

"We knee them in the, uh...the...you know..."

Revka rolled her eyes. "Oh, for Krep's sake, Iyarra. Use your words."

"Okay, okay. The 'bits.'"

Sister Tali nodded. "Technique twenty-one. Crude, and frankly a bit embarrassing, but nonetheless, quite effective."

Iyarra raised a hand. "Is it any good against a female opponent?"

Sister Tali shook her head. "Not really," she said. "Apart from anything else, women aren't likely to fall for it. You *might* be able to buy some time by asking about some particularly striking bit of armor or weaponry. Try asking where she got it from. If you can get her to tell you how little she paid for it, you might be able to get out of fighting altogether."

"Hmm, not really my cup of grog." Revka frowned. "What if we just attack the broad hand to hand?"

Sister Tali coughed. "That comes under catfighting, and that...well, that's an entirely different set of techniques in itself. We haven't got time for that today."

"Pity," said Brother Conan.

Sister Tali shot him a look.

"In any case," she said, "you've both made excellent progress, and I think we have time for one more lesson. Based on what I've seen, I think we should finish off with Elementary Showboating."

"Oh, here we go. Over to you, right?" Iyarra grinned. She gave Revka a nudge.

Revka cracked her knuckles. "Oh, *hell* yes," she said. "Let's go."

* * * *

Dusk had fallen by the time the group found its way back to the camp. The two instructors agreed that, while more practice would undoubtedly do no end of good, Iyarra and Revka had a sufficient handle on the basics to serve them in fieldwork. Sister Agata seemed pleased.

"Very good. We shall discuss next steps soon, but first, why not show me something you learned today? Nothing too elaborate."

Iyarra looked down at Revka. "Candle trick?" she suggested.

"Candle trick." Revka nodded.

A few minutes later, a candelabrum was in place, with two thin candles lit and ready. The girls stationed themselves at either side.

Revka gave Iyarra a nod. "Okay," she said. "Go ahead."

Iyarra drew a sword. "Beware," she declaimed. "For I am quite deadly with a sword. Observe!" She bit her lip, narrowed her eyes at the nearest candle, and let fly.

The candle remained in place, apparently untouched. Revka sneered. "Ha! It seems you missed."

Iyarra just smiled. "Did I?" Right on cue, the top half of the candle fell away and onto the ground.

Revka gave her a tiny nod. "Not bad, not bad. Now, it's my turn." She brought her sword up and across, slashing downward in a smooth diagonal stroke. Before her, the other candle remained unaffected.

There was silence for a moment. Revka cleared her throat, giving Iyarra a meaningful glance.

Iyarra peered at the woman in confusion. *What?* She mouthed.

Revka's mouth formed the words, *Your line.*

"Oh!" Iyarra blushed. "Right. Sorry. Er, *Ah-ha-ha-haaaa!* You missed!"

Revka smiled. "Wait."

There was a moment of perfect stillness. Then the top half of the candle flame, neatly bisected, slid off and tumbled like a will-o'-the-wisp toward the ground.

Sister Agata nodded. "Very good. Timing could have been better, of course, but you will learn as you go along." She turned to the others. "What do you think?"

"Uhm, oh, I-I'm happy if you're happy," Sister Peasley spluttered. "I mean, the important thing is they did their best, right? Er, isn't it?"

Brother Sudgen just shrugged. "It'll do."

"Don't worry about us," Revka preened. "We're all over this. We've got the moves that, uh..." She trailed off. A look of concern pushed its way past her usual bravado. Something unpleasant was happening down in the region of her...

A moment later, she was flailing around, frantically trying to stomp out the fire in her boot with her other boot. When this inevitably resulted in two fires, she dropped to the ground, smothering the toes of her boots in the dark, loamy earth of the forest. For a moment, she lay there moaning and gazing despondently at her smoking footwear.

Sister Agata turned to Tali and Conan. "By the way, did you instruct them on the principles of slapstick and how they apply to a narrative environment?" she asked.

"Sorry, Miss. Didn't have time."

"I shouldn't worry," said the elder placidly. "I expect they'll pick it up as they go along."

"Yeah," said Sudgen Two. "They're clearly naturals."

"In any case," said Sister Agata. "I think they are ready for the final test. Kindly put the word out that we are pulling up stakes tomorrow. I'd like us well away by noon, if possible."

Brother Sudgen pursed his lips. "You really think these two are ready?"

Sister Agata watched as Iyarra fussed over Revka, trying to help her get her boots off. Mostly she was succeeding in dragging the woman along the ground. Sister Agata sighed.

"As ready as they'll ever be," she said.

Chapter Fourteen

THE MORNING WAS COOL, full of the crispness of waning summer. It only took a little while to gather up the camp and load it into the bow-top wagons that served for transport and mobile library. Soon, a convoy was working its way along an old forest road.

The day passed quietly, the group keeping on the move. The road was narrow, forcing them to travel single file the whole way. As such, there was not a lot of conversation. Occasionally, someone would start singing some favorite old librarian shanty, such as *Carry Me Back To The Stacks*, *The Girl From Circulation*, or the haunting *Dewey's Lament*. For a while, the forest would ring with voices in chorus, but for the most part, there was only the singing of the birds and the soporific rumble of wagon wheels.

At night, they made camp by a stream. The territory was rockier than their last camp, with a few small caves punctuating the landscape. As they sat around the communal dinner fire, the elders explained their plan.

"Now then," said Sister Agata. "Tomorrow, we should come to a place known as Rutger's Dip. It's a small valley, only accessible from the south. We shall set up camp at the entrance, and you shall proceed by yourselves along the trail to the goal."

Revka poked a baked apple out of the coals. "And that is?"

"At the far side of the valley, you will find a giant cavern. This is the home of a creature known as the Oraugh. The Oraugh lurks in the darkness, far beyond the light of the sun. It is said that he ventures forth from his stygian abyss no more than once a year. Into this place you must go and find him in his deepest sanctum."

Iyarra gulped. "A-and then what?"

Sister Agata gave them their instructions. There was a long silent moment.

Then, Iyarra spoke up. "Uhm...really?"

Sister Agata nodded. "That is your task. Do this, and we shall consider you one of us. With our talents combined, I feel quite sure that we can track down whatever is causing this debacle and restore the balance."

Revka piped up. "And if we fail?"

Sister Agata patted her on the shoulder. "Don't worry," she said. "We'll take care of it."

"Oh. Good."

"Yes," said Sudgen Two. "We'll give you a proper burial and everything."

* * * *

The next morning, the two women found themselves at the mouth of the valley. Final preparations were taking place.

Sister Agata handed Revka a slip of paper. "I've written everything down, just in case. Go in, do the job, and come back. Avoid any unnecessary unpleasantness. We will camp out here for five days, but you should be back in plenty of time. Now. You have torches?"

Iyarra pulled a couple out of her saddlebags. She gave one a little twirl.

"Good. Provisions?"

Revka nodded. "Got 'em."

"Any questions?"

Revka looked back to Iyarra, who shook her head. "I think we've got it."

"Very well." Sister Agata bowed her head, the others following suit. "We wish you luck. Remember your training. And come right back when you're done."

Revka swung herself onto Iyarra's back. "Don't you worry about that, ma'am," she drawled, tipping an imaginary hat. "We know how you hate late returns."

Iyarra rolled her eyes and set off.

* * * *

The valley consisted of two rows of hills slowly tapering toward each other like a giant Vee, with a large cavern mouth at the end. There was no marked trail going in, but then, one wasn't needed. It was pretty much your choice of two directions, in or out. The valley itself was sparsely populated with vegetation. Shrubs and smaller trees replaced the sylvan giants the pair had gotten used to seeing since their arrival in the Enchanted Forest.

"Revka?"

Revka shook herself. She had been zoning out for the last little while. "Mm? What?"

"Have you noticed what's odd about this place?"

Revka looked around. "Well, did you have something specific in mind? This whole place is pretty odd, when you get down to it. Kinda eerie."

"I'm talking about the birds."

Revka looked around. For a moment, she tilted an ear, listening, then shook her head. "What birds?" she said. "I'm not hearing any."

"Exactly."

"So?"

"So, when's the last time you remember not being surrounded by birds out here?" asked Iyarra.

"Well, uhm..." Revka thought about it. "To tell the truth, I'm not sure I recall one way or another. Can't really say I've noticed."

"Well, I have. And this is the first time. There were even some at the mouth of the valley."

"Weird. What do you think it means?"

"Well, I've heard that sometimes animals have mysterious senses. Like they can sense danger and stuff. It could be that."

"Hmm. Possibly. Or maybe there's just nothing much to eat around here."

"Could be."

They rode on.

It was early evening by the time they got to the end of the valley. The large cave mouth was hard to miss, opening as it did directly into the side of the hill. Vines and moss adorned the area around the entrance, adding a deep, lush green to the stony outcrop.

Skulls on poles flanked the entrance. That was a pretty good hint as well.

The two examined the grisly sight, neither wanting to be the first to speak. Finally, Revka hopped down off Iyarra's back and approached them. She peered closer, narrowing her eyes. Was it her imagination, or...?

"Animal skulls."

Iyarra tilted her head. "What?"

"Animal skulls." Revka pointed. "Just animals."

"Well, I didn't think they were plants."

"No, but I mean, no people skulls. Look, here's a rabbit, that's a deer, this is...huh."

"Huh?"

"Chipmunk."

"Oh. Huh."

"Right." Revka moved to the other pole. "Same deal here." She turned to Iyarra. "You know what I'm thinking?"

"What?"

"I think these were put here to scare us."

"Well, they're doing a good job, if you ask me."

"Anyway, this is it." Revka looked up at the sky. "Sun'll be going down soon. I suggest we make camp and head in first thing in the morning."

Iyarra nodded. "All right, but, er..."

"Yes?"

"Can we maybe camp somewhere out of sight of the cave? I have difficulty sleeping next to skulls."

"Really? You never said."

* * * *

A while later, a campfire crackled in a clear space just out of sight of the cave mouth. Some potatoes were cooking on a spit over the flames. Revka leaned back against Iyarra, watching the fire.

"Not a lot of game around here by the looks of it. Pretty desolate all around. No birds, hardly any animals. It's like everything just stays away."

Iyarra nodded. "I haven't smelled much of anything since we got here. I won't be sorry to leave this place behind, I can tell you."

Revka gave the spit a turn. "I'm with you there. Let's just get this thing over with and be done with it."

"Still," said Iyarra. "It's nice that we won't be fighting alone."

"True."

Iyarra smiled a little. "Although, I do miss having privacy. This is the first night we've had to ourselves in a while."

Revka nodded. "You know, you're right!" She poked at the fire, stirring it up. "We've been so busy, I hadn't thought about it."

Iyarra nodded. She smiled back at her partner, reaching over to tease her hair. "So," she said, "perhaps after dinner, we could, mm, have a little quality time?"

Revka laughed. "A little eat-drink-and-be-merry, huh?" She grinned over her shoulder at the centauress. "Why not?" She scooted closer, leaning against Iyarra's back. Her arms slipped around the horsewoman's top half. For a long moment they lay together, quiet and close.

"Revka?"

"Mmm?"

"I think the potatoes are burning."

"Krep!" Revka yanked the spit away and inspected the spuds.

Iyarra peered over. "They okay?"

"Just saved 'em." She passed one over gingerly. "Give it a minute. Still hot."

"Right." They ate in silence, each lost in her own thoughts.

After a while, Revka found herself staring into the fire. So, assuming they passed this little test, they and the librarians would...what? She still had no idea what to do. Maybe they had some kind of plan. She certainly didn't.

Behind her, Iyarra stirred. Revka felt the centauress's hand drifting up her arm to her shoulder. She smiled and turned to kiss the oncoming fingertips.

Iyarra grabbed her and tugged her over. Revka laughed and fell back on the soft grass.

Well, she could worry about it tomorrow.

* * * *

The next morning, the girls broke camp and headed down into the cave. It was a long, winding tunnel, with smaller tunnels branching off from time to time. Sister Agata had said that the Oraugh was about two men high, and there was only one path that allowed something of that size. In fact, as Revka examined the walls, it seemed they had been partially tunneled out, expanding the areas where nature had fallen short.

"Well," she said. "At least it's a fairly straightforward route." She frowned, lifting her torch for a better view. It wasn't that she minded being underground, not exactly. It was just that usually they were somewhere where other people were, or at least there had been people at some point. This place felt empty. What's more, it felt like it had been empty for a long time. Water dripped from the ceiling, the soft pat as it hit the ground echoing along the tunnel and providing the only real sound.

Behind her, Iyarra followed as close as she could. Unlike Revka, she *did* mind being underground. Centaurs were built for wide-open spaces. In the dark depths of the cave, there was nowhere to run, no horizon to fix one's eye on. What's more, it smelled wrong. She'd found herself in a surprising number of caves and dungeons and so on since taking up with Revka, and had come to know their scents well. Dungeons and old rotting temples fairly reeked with decay. In natural caverns, you got the scent of water, and a few living creatures here and there. There was a strong scent in this cave, a foul one she hadn't encountered before. That would be the Oraugh, no doubt, but other than that...

"Nothing," she said.

Revka looked over her shoulder. "Beg pardon?"

"There's nothing else down here. No bats, no lizards. Nothing. I think this is a dead cave."

"Can a cave be dead?"

Iyarra shivered. "It can," she said. "Trust me."

Revka didn't argue. "Well," she said. "At least that means there's nothing down here to attack us."

"Except the Oraugh."

"Right. The Oraugh." Revka wrinkled her nose. Somewhere, at the end of this winding tunnel, in a cave that even bats wouldn't haunt, the Oraugh was waiting. If they survived *that*, they would travel with a bunch of crazed, fanatical librarians to fight a supernatural wind and rescue a bunch of, let's face it, bad guys.

She wondered if other heroes went through stuff like this.

Heroes. That was the word. All her life she'd believed heroes were noble, morally unimpeachable paragons who went around righting wrongs and never, ever compromising their principles. Then she'd gone out into the world. She had been cold and hungry and forlorn, and sometimes survival was the thumb on the scale between right and wrong. It was better these days, goodness knows, but she still felt pangs of guilt remembering some of the things she'd done to survive. They would probably never go away completely.

Nothing for it, then.

Down and down went the would-be hero and her partner into the darkness, and behind them the light got further and further away.

Chapter Fifteen

IT WAS ABOUT AN hour later when Iyarra suddenly put a restraining hand on Revka's shoulder. She tapped the side of her nose and pointed down the tunnel.

Revka looked up at her. *You sure?* she mouthed.

Iyarra nodded and made a face.

Revka glanced up at her torch. If they were this close, how soon until he smelled them? She'd heard that cave creatures developed extremely acute senses to make up for the lack of light. Speaking of which, the torch would probably shine out like a beacon to anyone down there. Probably best to douse it if they didn't want the Oraugh getting the drop on them.

She stood on tiptoe, gesturing Iyarra to tilt her head down. "Can you follow just from smell if I put out the torch?" she whispered.

Iyarra hesitated, then nodded.

Revka gave her a light pat. She found a muddy puddle under a stalactite and used it to put the torch out. The darkness wrapped around them completely. She fumbled her way back to Iyarra and put the torch away. The woman lay a hand on Iyarra's withers and gave them a pat. Ready.

Woman and centauress began to ease their way down the tunnel, taking their time and going slow. Actually, the tunnel had been cleared out rather well as a path, with very little in the way of stray pebbles, or sudden yawning pits, or suchlike. In other circumstances, it would have been almost pleasant. Still, they kept the pace slow and deliberate, their movements stealthy and silent.

It had been maybe ten minutes, give or take, when they heard shuffling up ahead. The two moved to the side of the tunnel and held still. Something down there was working its way toward them. It moved with a heavy tread, punctuated with a wet *squish* as it came nearer. There was a snuffling sound as it approached.

Revka took a deep breath and tried to remember her training. Make yourself inconspicuous. Fade into the background. Easier said than done. She just wished her heart wasn't thumping so damned loudly. It was a miracle the thing couldn't hear it all the way down the tunnel.

Presently, the footsteps stopped. There was more snuffling about, and a low, guttural death rattle of a voice echoed through the dark caverns.

"Mreh. New smell. Unfamiliar, yes. Unwelcome." There were a few more steps forward. "Something lost? Something scrumptious?" It lumbered even closer. Revka was sure her heart would beat right out of her chest.

A minute passed. Then two. There was a grunting noise down the tunnel and the sound of retreating feet.

Revka silently counted to fifty. Then she gave Iyarra's hand a gentle squeeze. Time to move on.

Iyarra led the way, the scent now quite pungent in the still cavern air. They followed the tunnel down, the darkness only slightly impeding their progress. Neither needed to be told to be quiet. Even Iyarra's large hooves barely made a sound as she eased down into the depths.

After a while, Revka realized she was beginning to see light. Not enough to really see anything, just enough to give form to the darkness up ahead. The two slowed down, moving with extra caution. As they got closer, it became clear that the light was coming from a spot up ahead, in all likelihood the lair of the Oraugh.

They turned a corner, and now the light was coming out of a side passage. It flickered orange, and the telltale scent of ozone told of fire. Creeping forward, Revka risked a peek.

The chamber was vast and roughly ovoid, and absolutely filled with junk. Dead branches and brush, bones, scraps of rotting cloth, the remains of an old mattress, seemingly everything one might be able to scavenge from infrequent trips to the surface. The debris lay in various heaps around the room, in no particular arrangement that she could see. The small fire at the center was barely enough to melt a candle, but down in the bowels of the earth, it gave shape to the room and its contents. Most particularly to their owner.

The Oraugh slept on a pile of skins by the fire. The gangly thing was fish-belly white, with long, thin arms that ended in gnarled hands. A few gray wisps, dangling in scattered patches, hinted it had once been covered with hair. The Oraugh lay sprawled by the fire, limbs splayed in all directions. Here and there, bits of rag had been tied around it, serving as pockets or covering whatever it was the creature felt worth covering.

Revka tiptoed back to Iyarra and signaled her to wait, then dropped down into a crouch and stole around the corner and into the Oraugh's den. She remembered her instructions. Well, it was going to take a while, that was for sure. She just hoped he was a heavy sleeper.

Now that she was in, it seemed there was a bit of method to the place. At least, there were paths going between the various heaps of debris. Maybe she'd get lucky. She crawled forward, keeping her eyes peeled. Observation, that was the key. She remembered what Sister Dowell had taught them; take a picture with your mind. Remember shapes, remember colors. Fill in the details you need as and when you need them.

She worked her way around the den, checking heap after heap of junk. Nothing. She started to follow paths in closer, very close to the beast now. The stench was overwhelming. No wonder Iyarra had been able to follow it so easily. Once, passing close by his feet, she made the mistake of inhaling. She had to scuttle behind a pile of broken timber and cover her nose and mouth to keep from gagging.

She circled back around, keeping her eyes moving. So much stuff here. How long had this guy—this creature—been dragging trash down to this hole in the ground? At this rate, she'd be lucky if—

Wait.

She mentally rewound to the contents of the last heap of junk. There had been a crate, empty but serving as a crude table. There had been some random items, what might once have been fruit, and...she closed her eyes and recalled the scene.

Yup. There it was.

Holding her breath, she slowly backtracked and had a look. There, not two paces from the creature's hand and resting on top of the crate, was The Book.

Bingo.

She inched forward, moving on all fours. This close to him, she didn't dare breathe. Crouching behind the crate, she fumbled in her pouch for the slip of paper Sister Agata had given her. She held it up, just enough to catch the flickering light. That was it, all right. All ready to go.

Right.

One hand crawled up the side of the crate, around and over the top. Slowly now, working her way to the book. She felt the edge, slid a couple of fingers up over it, and lifted one corner.

Nothing.

Revka swallowed her breath. She eased it up the rest of the way and began to work it back. Steady movements, that was the key. Slow and easy, don't attract attention. For a moment, it sounded like the breathing changed on the other side of the box. She froze in place for what seemed like an hour, but nothing happened. Okay. Okay.

One smooth, easy movement and the book was in her hands. She allowed herself a silent sigh of relief. Now for stage two.

She picked up the little yellow slip and eased it slowly up along the side of the crate. Up and over now and inching toward the spot where the book had been. Just drop it and—

A giant, claw-like hand grabbed at her wrist. Revka was yanked over the box and brought face to face with the Oraugh. It was not a pretty face. It looked like someone had shaved a horse and given it a very bad nose job. Yellow eyes with pupils that almost swallowed up the fringe of red iris around them glared angrily at her. Mucousy-yellow spit strings hung in his open mouth, which revealed fungous riddled stumps that made Revka want to run right home and spend the rest of her life brushing her teeth. He snuffled at her, turning her this way and that.

"So," he growled, in a sickly gurgling voice. "Sneaking around Oraugh cave, yes? Stealing Oraugh treasures! Smelled you, Oraugh did! Make a fine snack of you, yes! What you think of that, hah? It make you sad? It make you cry?"

Revka steeled herself. So much for the subtle approach. Fixing her face with what she hoped was a fearless expression, she brandished the yellow slip in front of him. "Mister Oraugh, as a duly appointed representative of the Wandering Library, and on behalf of same, I am informing you that I am here to recover one copy of—" She took a quick glance at the slip. "—yes, one copy of *Bath Time for Mister Puppy*, currently standing at one year, three months, and five days—"

"Six days," Iyarra corrected. She came 'round the doorway, daggers in hand and looking as mean as Revka had ever seen her.

"Six days. Right. Six days overdue. Now, put me down nice and easy, and we'll waive the fine. Got it?"

The Oraugh's face cracked. He didn't put her down, but suddenly his expression was one of pure panic. "B-but...you can't! Not yet. Musn't! Oraugh not finish it yet!"

"Not finished it yet!?" Revka glanced down at the book in her hands. "It's, like, ten pages!"

"Oraugh slow reader."

"Oh, for the love of—" She stopped herself. "Look, you could have renewed it if you were having trouble, but we've been sent to retrieve the book, and that's what we're going to do. Now put me down."

For a moment, it seemed as if he was going to, but then a strange light entered his eyes. "If library people go, Oraugh no have puppy book." His eyes gleamed with malice. "But if Oraugh break library people, they no come back, and Oraugh have puppy book forever."

To understand what happened next, it is necessary to take a moment to set the scene. Revka was being held by one arm, dangling in front of the Oraugh, her feet just about half a meter off the ground. The Oraugh stooped, holding her up so they were face to face, his legs splayed out in a kind of half crouch. The upshot was, if Revka were to swing back a leg and kick, it would land squarely in the place most likely to make a male captor drop whatever he was doing.

She did. It did. And he did.

Revka was already rolling as she hit the ground. She tumbled to her feet and began to scamper away. "I'm sorry sir," she called over her shoulder. "But I'm afraid you're going to be subject to late penalties." It wasn't the best battle cry, she had to admit, but it wasn't like she had time to sit down and think of something really snappy. Besides, she'd just realized she'd wound up with the Oraugh between her and the exit. Damn.

Iyarra came vaulting over a heap of garbage, twin daggers at the ready. "YOU GET AWAY FROM HER!" she shouted. The Oraugh, whose mind was still on other things, tried a clumsy swipe to knock her away. She ducked, cannoned into him shoulder first, and sent him sprawling.

"Don't stab him!" Revka ran and leaped onto Iyarra's back. "I've got the book, let's just go!"

Iyarra nodded. She turned and bounded back toward the opening through which they'd come, vaulting over a few trash heaps in the way. A moment later, they were in the dark and trotting up the tunnel.

"Revka? Can we get some light? I don't like running in the dark."

"Hang on, let me get the torch lit." Revka began to scrabble through the saddlebags. "Can you smell the path?"

"Oh, yes. It's clear as a bell."

"Good. Just go as fast as you can. It won't be long before—"

Pure rage bellowed behind them, accompanied by the sound of lurching footsteps.

Revka groaned. "Yup. That's it."

Behind them, the light momentarily silhouetted the Oraugh as he came charging out of the cave toward them. Revka nudged Iyarra, who whinnied and took off into the darkness.

"How's that light coming?" Iyarra called out as she ran. The scent trail was pretty clear, but that really didn't make much of a difference. Running headlong through a pitch-black cave, in terms of enjoyable activities, ranked right down there with trying to do your taxes while being swarmed by mosquitos. And that's before you factor in an enraged creature chasing after you with a tree branch in one hand and a look of pure murder in his eyes.

Revka fussed through the bag until her hand closed on the other torch. "Just a second," she hollered. Flint and tinder, flint and tinder...second belt pouch, right? She tucked the torch under one arm and yanked them out. Behind her, she could hear the Oraugh gaining on them. She struck the flint against the tinder once, twice, finally a quick bit of light flared, which immediately went out.

Damn.

She shifted the torch into place and tried again. This time, it caught. She waved the torch into life and held it up so the way before them was illuminated. Of course, that also made them that much easier for the Oraugh to follow, but you can't have everything.

Iyarra bounded up the winding passage, pumping her arms in a desperate bid for speed. Revka tried to remember how far down they were and how much they had to go. It had taken a few hours to get down there, but that had been at a walking pace or slower. Iyarra wasn't built for speed, but she could keep going for ages, assuming nothing caught her first.

Just down the tunnel, maybe fifty lengths, the Oraugh was closing in on them. It had dropped the branch and was swinging its long arms in an attempt to build up some sort of momentum. He moved quickly, too quickly. Revka groaned. It was going to be a fight.

They rounded a corner, hitting a stretch where the path sloped steeply upward. Iyarra whimpered, the dancing light of the flame providing only sporadic guidance. Revka held the torch over Iyarra's shoulder, trying to provide what help she could.

The Oraugh lumbered after them, closing the gap quickly. "YOU GIVE BACK MISTER PUPPY BOOK!" he bellowed, waving a claw at Revka. Too late for a weapon. She swung the torch back around, waving it in his direction.

The effect was immediate. The creature screamed, shielding his eyes. He stumbled back and cowered until they got around another corner. Revka thought she heard the words 'light' and 'hurt' echo their way up the tunnel.

Well, that made sense, didn't it? He probably spent his whole life in the dark. Revka bet he didn't even come out, except at night. Of course he'd be sensitive to light. They could use that, if only they could...

A light went off in Revka's brain. She held the torch high as she could, and with her free hand began to rummage frantically in their medicine bag. Where was it, now? She knew there was some left. Comeoncomeon*comeon*...

"Not much longer now," Iyarra called back. "I think we're almost out."

"Great." Revka shuffled through the bottles. Painkiller, wound cleaner, bandage strips...aha! She picked up the blue bottle and held it to the torchlight. *Lydia Pinkblossom's Guaranteed Laxative Salts.* Perfect.

The Oraugh was closing on them again. It must have realized they were about to escape the cave. One clawed hand shielded its eyes from the worst of the torch's flame. No shouting now, no cowering from the flame that still dazzled eyes too used to darkness. Now there was just a determination to stop them no matter what.

Revka brought the torch back around so that it was facing their pursuer. She waited, letting him get closer and closer. She held the bottle ready, cork held carefully in her teeth. Had to time it just right...

The Oraugh reared back a claw, ready to swipe. Another pace or two, and he would be able to strike. Now or never.

Revka closed her eyes, pulled the cork out with her teeth, and shook the bottle at the torch's flame. The contents went flying out and into the fire, where they immediately burned with a brilliant white light that dazzled even through her tightly shut eyelids. The Oraugh screamed the feral howl of a maddened beast.

Revka risked a peek. The Oraugh had turned tail and was legging it down the tunnel as fast as it could, hands covering its eyes.

"What happened?" Iyarra called back. "It got all bright."

"Agnesiuh salsh."

"What?"

Revka rolled her eyes. She pushed the cork back into the bottle and tried again. "Magnesium salts," she said. "Trick my dad showed me once. They burn real bright. Think I scared him off."

"So we're safe?"

"Yeah. Well, as long as neither of us gets constipated."

"What?"

"Tell you later."

It was a short trot up the tunnel to the entrance. It was early afternoon, with not a cloud in the sky. Revka put out the torch and hopped down off Iyarra's back.

"Well, that's it," she said. She glanced back at the cave. "Don't reckon he's gonna be coming after us."

"I certainly hope not," said Iyarra. "Not after that."

"Right."

"That being said, if we could, maybe, camp nice and far away from the cave mouth, I think that would be good."

Revka glanced at the cave. If she strained her ears, she could almost imagine she heard the faintest echoes of a distant voice wailing, "Miiiiisterrrr Puppppeeee!"

"Yeah," she said. "I think that might be a good idea."

* * * *

It was a little after dark. The two sat before an extra-big campfire, roasting some yams that Iyarra had managed to bring along. Revka rested against Iyarra's back, occasionally leaning forward to turn the spuds with a stick.

"Well," she said. "That was certainly something."

Iyarra nodded. "I still can't believe we went through all that for a children's book."

Revka shrugged. "Well, I can't say he struck me as the high literature type. I mean, what would you expect a cave monster to read?"

Iyarra thought about it. "I suppose some kind of horror story, with all monsters and things? Maybe?"

"You think so?" Revka poked the fire. "I dunno, maybe they would. But I kind of see monsters as being more into cheerful stuff. Joke books and so on. Take 'em out of themselves, you know what I mean?"

"How about decor?" Iyarra grinned. "Like, *How to Decorate Your Dungeon*, that sort of thing."

Revka snickered. "Yeah! Or like, *1001 Ways to Cook Rat*. That'd be a bestseller."

"Gross. How about *The Swamp Creature Meets The Two-Headed Thing*? But it's a romance."

"Oh, man!" Revka cackled. "You can just see it, can't you? Blargo slithered a tentacle around Gunzark. Oh, you're the only creature for meeee! He gazed into her one eye as she stroked his manly thorax."

Iyarra snorted. "Okay, now I'm picturing a big old monster with her tentacles in curlers, eating chocolates and reading that."

Revka laughed. "Perfect!"

They watched the fire for a while.

"Revka?"

"Mm?"

"When dinner is over, you think you could read me the Mr. Puppy book?"

"Okay."

Chapter Sixteen

IT WAS, GIVE OR take, about midday as Revka and Iyarra found their way back to the librarians' camp. Revka slid down off Iyarra's back, brandishing the errant book. "One copy of *Bath Time for Mister Puppy*, slightly foxed, considerably dogeared, spine bent right back, and a stain on the back cover that I don't care to speculate about."

Sister Agata took the book gingerly and gave it a quick but expert inspection. "Rather unfortunate," she said. "But I've seen worse."

"Seriously?"

The elder woman chuckled. "My dear, when you've been a librarian for as long as I have, you cease to be amazed at the things people will do to books."

"Quite so." Brother Sudgen joined the group. "Bloodstains, scribbling over the pictures, pages ripped out and used as emergency handkerchiefs—"

"Or worse."

"Indeed. Food used as bookmarks."

"And books with bites taken out of them."

Iyarra did a double take. "Really!?"

"Well," said Sister Agata. "That only happened once. Never did get to the bottom of it." She shrugged. "In any case, we shall see to it that it's cleaned up and restored. It will be back on the shelves in no time." She handed the book to another robed figure, who scurried off.

"In any case. It would appear you have succeeded. Our congratulations. I'm afraid, however, that this brings us to the question of what to do next."

"Yeah, about that." Revka looked around at the group. "Do we have some kind of plan, or what?"

"Not yet," said Sister Agata. "But we shall discuss the matter tonight and see what we can come up with. In the meantime, I suggest you get some rest."

"And a bath," added Sudgen Two.

"Er, yes," said Sister Agata. "That as well."

* * * *

Villains

That night, the elder librarians brought Revka and Iyarra in for a council of war.

"While you were gone, we had some discussion as to how to proceed. Here is where things stand as of now, in our opinion. This thing is going to continue to abduct villains unless we can stop it. If we have any hope of doing so, we must be able to discover where it is taking them. Assuming the wind is some sort of magical entity—which I think is a safe enough assumption—it may be impossible to locate where they are being taken by conventional means."

Revka nodded. "That makes sense, sure. And we've seen the thing at work. I'd say it's pretty definitely magic of some sort."

Brother Sudgen leaned forward. "You two are the only ones to have been attacked and still be around to tell the tale. What can you tell us about what happened?"

Iyarra and Revka exchanged glances. "Well," began Revka. "First of all, Jack started chanting, and his eyes went all glowy."

"Kind of green."

"Right. Green. Then the wind picked up. Next thing we knew, he was floating off the ground, still chanting, but it wasn't like his voice anymore. It was creepy."

"I'd say eldritch."

"That too."

"About the wind?" Sister Peasley interjected.

"Oh. Right. Well, it just kind of came out of nowhere, if you see what I mean. One minute fine, next minute, typhoon."

"Tornado," interjected a robed figure.

"What?"

"Tornado. It wouldn't be a typhoon because those are only near the ocean."

"I thought those were hurricanes?" asked another librarian.

"OK, yes, hurricanes as well, but they wouldn't be there either. Same thing."

"Wait, so are hurricanes and cyclones the same?"

"Excuse me—"

"I *think* so? It may be according to how strong it is."

"Ex*cuse* me—"

"No, no. I read this once. See, there's this imaginary line—"

"*Ahem!*" Sister Agata cleared her throat. "If we could *please* restrict ourselves to the topic at hand?"

"Oh. Right. Sorry." Revka took a moment to find her way back on track. "Okay. So yes, the wind just popped up out of nowhere. I thought it was going to blow us away."

Iyarra piped up. "Did it go all dark for you too? Because once I felt myself going off the ground, everything kinda went black."

Revka nodded. "I saw that too, yeah. Or rather, didn't see it. Anyway, I could feel myself kind of…" She waved a hand, trying to find the word. "I was kind of drifting away. Like going to sleep, but all at once, if that makes any sense."

"And then?"

She shrugged. "And then there was this pain on my ankle, and the next thing I knew, I had a mouthful of dirt."

Iyarra nodded. "Pretty much the same here."

Sister Agata nodded. "I see. And have you felt any sort of lasting effects? Anything missing, or not working properly?"

"Same amount of toes?" asked Brother Sudgen.

The girls exchanged glances. "Yeah, as far as we can tell, everything's normal," said Revka.

"Glad to hear it," said Sister Agata. "Then I think we may have a suggestion. It is…well, far from ideal, but in lieu of any better ideas, I suppose I might as well put it forward."

Revka looked up at Iyarra, who shrugged. "Well," the woman said. "We might as well hear it. Heavens know we've got nothing. What's the idea?"

The older woman smiled and leaned forward. "Tell me," she said. "How do you look in black?"

* * * *

The strangest thing about the village of Killing Logan, deep in the heart of the Enchanted Forest, was of course, its name. It was inevitably the first thing people asked about when they encountered the town. Unsurprisingly, the residents had long since grown tired of explaining it over and over. Eventually, a sign had been put up, giving the history of the whole thing in detail. Annoyingly, for each visitor who read the story, there were at least five who preferred to collar some innocent passerby, generally while standing right next to the sign.

Therefore, it's just as well that we get it out of the way. So. A few hundred years ago, there was a giant named Logan, a fearsome beast of a man who routinely terrorized the inhabitants of the forest. He'd developed a habit of kicking over people's houses, helping himself to any local livestock, and squishing anyone who looked even vaguely heroic just out of general principle. After several weeks of putting up with this, the residents complained to the capitol, and the royal army was sent in to deal with him.

Using some clever trickery, they were able to lure him into a trap baited with a singing harp and a family sized keg of Nassatucket Fried Goose. Working quickly, they knocked him out with boulders from concealed catapults long enough to chain him up and render him quite immobile. Once that was complete, it became necessary to cut the giant's head off, this being the only surefire way to kill him for good.

This is easier said than done. The problems with cutting off a giant's head while it's still alive are that it's bigger than the average house, and the neck muscles tend to be very tough. Also, the giant is actively trying to bite anyone who comes near. It's a dangerous business, and one that takes a hell of a long time to get done. And so, a sort of camp grew up around the operation. Teams worked around the clock with twenty-man crosscut saws that had been made specially for the purpose. It wasn't long before farmers and traders began to show up, selling goods to the workers. A saloon opened, followed by an inn. Temporary buildings gave way to permanent ones. Families started moving in. Roads were laid down, which led to more commerce and more people. By the time the giant finally died, the town already had nine pubs, two ice cream parlors, and a stickball team.

These days, Killing Logan has little to do with the tourist trade. Actually, the main industry is logging. Of course, being in the Enchanted Forest, things are a little different. In addition to the usual skills required in the trade, local woodcutters receive special training in being humble, finding lost children, and how to extract old ladies from wolves.

On this particular day, Edwin, the tanner, was riding a donkey through a road in the woods. It had been a long day, and he was looking forward to getting home and having a nice dinner. The road was one he'd traveled nearly every day in his adult life, so he'd gotten into the habit of letting the donkey do the navigating while he lightly dozed in the saddle. As such, it's no surprise that the bandits were on top of him before he noticed they were there.

"Halt! Stand where you are!" The figure was dressed all in black, with a matching hood and mask. The horse—actually, a centauress, now he came to look—was likewise attired. Both were pointing crossbows at him. More or less.

"*And deliver!*" hissed the centauress. The human bandit tilted their head. "Eh?"

"Stand and deliver! It's what you're supposed to say! Remember?"

"Oh! Right. Right." The bandit regained their composure and raised the crossbow into a better position. "Okay, Mister! We've got you cornered! Now, hand over your garbage!"

* * * *

This demand might strike the reader as bizarre, and you wouldn't be wrong. There is an explanation, but to hear it we must turn back the clock to when the librarians held their council of war...

"Garbage!?" the girls exclaimed in unison.

Revka and Iyarra boggled at the senior librarians, who sat across the fire from them, and waited for an explanation.

Sister Peasley clasped her hands together. "Well," she said. "Er, the way we sort of see it, we ah, we need a villain, right? But we can't, uhm, ask you to go around really robbing and hurting people, can we?"

Sister Agata nodded. "Essentially, we wish for you to take on the trappings of evildoers without, er, doing evil. Not doing any actual harm. Well, as little as possible, at any rate."

Iyarra raised a hand. "Scuse me," she said. "But what happens if they ask us why we want to steal their garbage?"

Brother Sudgen shrugged. "Just tell them that you've got the crossbow, so you'll be the one asking the questions, thank you so very much."

"Hmm." Revka leaned back, glaring at the fire. She didn't say anything for a moment, then looked up at the librarians. "And this is the plan. Really?"

"I'm afraid it's the best one we've got, yes."

Iyarra pawed the ground. "I'm not entirely sure this is a good idea," she said.

"Of course not," said Sudgen Two. "It's a bloody awful idea."

"Unfortunately, it's the only reasonable one we've got," said Sister Agata. "We need a reliable villain, one we can trust, inasmuch as that is not a contradiction in terms. Someone who is trained in the story arts. Someone who can be relied upon."

"And is probably experienced in a little light larceny, unless I miss my guess," added Sudgen Two.

"Brother, that was entirely unnecessary."

"I know. Don't care."

Iyarra blew a raspberry at him.

"At any rate, this seems to be our best bet for establishing you as, excuse the expression, 'bad guys.' Our main objective here is to build up your reputation as quickly as possible. Let's just do that, then we can move on to the next phase. Now, any questions?"

Revka raised a hand. "So, just what are we meant to do with all this garbage we're going to be getting, anyhow?"

The librarian made a face. "Good grief, throw it away. What else?"

* * * *

Back in the forest, the tanner's mouth hung open, waiting for something coherent to come out. When it became clear that wasn't going to happen without help, he shook his head and tried again. "Uhm, I'm sorry?" he said. "You want my garbage?"

"That's right," said the human bandit. "All of it. Also any junk, trash, leavings, or, uhm...crud." She looked down at the centauress. "What was the other thing?"

"Residue."

"Right. Residue. Fork 'em over."

The man patted his purse in confusion. "I mean, I don't have much money..."

"Nobody said anything about money, pal. Keep your money. We just want your trash."

Edwin stared at the two outlaws for a moment, then decided it wasn't worth trying to understand. A quick search turned up a few loose bits of string, some leather scraps, and the paper he'd wrapped his lunch in that day. These were duly handed over and inspected by the masked pair.

"That's all you got?" the human one asked. "You're not holding out on us, are you?"

Edwin raised his hands in a conciliatory manner. "No ma'am," he said. "That's all I got, honest."

They studied him for a long moment. "All right," the human said. "Off you go, then."

Edwin clucked his tongue at his donkey and got out of there as quickly as he could. Criminals were bad enough, but crazy ones? Best to clear off before they got really nuts.

He didn't think any more about it until a couple of days later at the village inn, while having a bit of after-work ale and gossip. Some of the lads were sitting around a table, watching a glass. There seemed to be a bit of a discussion going on.

Dorrf, the thatcher, scratched his nose reflectively. "I think it's supposed to float, but it's been a while since I've done it. I could be wrong."

Someone else shook their head. "It's sink, you know. I'm sure of it."

Dorrf looked over at them. "Really? I dunno."

Edwin strolled over. "What's going on?"

Art, the miller's apprentice, looked up. "Oh, Ed. You know eggs?"

"I know of them."

"You know the thing where you test to see if an egg is good by dropping it in water?"

"Oh that, yeah. Uhm, what about it?"

"Do you remember if it's supposed to float or sink? If it's good, I mean."

Edwin scratched his chin. "I think sink is good, unless I'm remembering it wrong."

Dorrf looked up at him. "You sure about that?"

"Pretty sure. Pretty sure."

"So, er, what about when an egg bobs up and down and beats itself against the side of the glass?"

They watched it for a minute.

"Where did you even get that thing, anyhow?"

"Found it in the back of the pantry."

"Oh."

They watched it some more. It seemed to be going faster now.

"I think," said Edwin, "that's probably not a good sign, right there. I don't know about you fellas, but I try not to eat things that are moving around."

Dorrf nodded. "One for the garbage, I'm thinkin', yup."

Art chortled. "Yeah? Better be careful, they might pinch it."

Edwin looked up. "How's that, now?"

"Oh, didn't you hear?" Art sat up. "Old Zeb was throwing out some scraps the other night after dinner, couple o' masked hoodlums held 'em up and took the scraps. Also the broken leg off his stool. Wouldn't take anything else."

"Good grief," said Edwin. "That sounds like what happened to me."

He told them the story. Dorrf sat back and let out a low whistle. "Come to think of it," he said. "I had some scrap leather heaped up outside I've been meaning to get rid of. Was gone the other day. I just thought the missus had given it away or something."

Behind the bar, Dak Haliday smeared a mug with an old rag, thereby rendering it somewhat dirtier. "I heard that over in Argot, they'd had some folks waylayin' people and taking their junk. I mean, I thought they were joking, but if it's really happening, that's...well, I don't know what to make of that."

"You better be careful," Art joked. "They take your garbage, you got nothing left to serve!"

Dak rolled his eyes at the laughter. "Yeah, yeah. Very funny. But what I want to know is, who are these people, and what do they want our garbage for?"

Art shrugged. "Who cares?" he said. "It's garbage."

"Garbage it may be," said Edwin. "But I didn't much care for being held up for it, I can tell you."

"Maybe it's secretly valuable? Like, they've found a way to turn junk into gold or something."

"Art, if they've found a way to turn table scraps into gold, I don't think they need to go around stealing my scrap paper at bowpoint."

"Well, I'll tell you one thing," said Dorrf. "I'm gonna hang on to my garbage. Lock it away where no one can get to it."

"That's gonna go over well with the wife."

"I don't care. It's my garbage and by Yog, I'm keeping it. Who's with me?"

There followed the kind of silence that only comes from a room full of people waiting for someone else to speak. Nobody quite caught anyone else's eye. Finally, Edwin coughed.

"Well, you go ahead and do that, but I think I'm just going to avoid the whole thing and get rid of my trash as fast as possible."

It was at this point that a loud, wet crashing noise interrupted the conversation. The glass with the egg had tipped over, spilling water all over the tabletop. The egg itself rolled to the edge, down onto a bench, off the bench to the floor, and out the door before anyone thought to stop it. From outside, there was a faint "wheeee" noise as it rolled away.

At that, as they say, the evening broke up.

* * * *

That night, Edwin lay in bed, trying to figure it all out. Who would go around stealing garbage? What on earth did they get out of it? Should he hang on to his junk, or just let 'em have it?

Well, it was all too much for him. He shrugged it off and went to sleep, and didn't think about it again until the next day, when the fertilizer *really* hit the windmill.

Chapter Seventeen

THE WORD SPREAD FROM one end of town to another, traveling at the speed of gossip. What had once been dismissed as a prank or the work of eccentrics took on a new and horrible cast. They weren't joking around anymore. Someone had broken into the town hall and emptied *all* of the wastebaskets.

To understand what happened next, it is important to understand a little about the land in which our tale is told. This was a world of magic, where dragons filled the skies and centaurs roamed in great herds among the sweeping plains. It was a world of wizards and sorceresses, of creatures dark and evil lurking in deserted caverns. It was, in fact, a world of action and adventure, where men were men, women were women, and liability insurance was not even remotely a thing. In short, it was the kind of place where everyone was too busy to have any sort of regular garbage collection.

Consequently, your options were either burn it, bury it, or for preference, leave it in a pile out back. Ask the average resident of a fantasy kingdom what they did with their leavings, and nine times out of ten, they'd be too busy running from a dragon to give you any kind of coherent answer. About the only people who did anything approaching recycling were the really poor, who never threw anything away simply because they couldn't afford to.

The point is, nobody really gave garbage that much thought. That is, until somebody started stealing it.

That night, the people of Killing Logan had a town meeting. The town hall was packed with angry villagers, all shouting and arguing at cross purposes.

"What I want to know is," bellowed Dorrf, "just what is the board of eldermen doing to protect our gods-given garbage?"

This roused a cheer from the back. Several people took up the call, firing it across the room to the mayor and the board. Mayor Den, who more or less mayored when he wasn't busy at the sawmill, fingered his chain of office nervously. It was a well-known fact that the IQ of a crowd is roughly that of its loudest member. Just at the moment, there seemed to be several contenders. He sighed and raised his hands for calm.

"Ladies, gentlemen, please." He raised his voice as best he could above the hubbub. "Calm down, I beg you, please! We don't know what's happening any more than you do, but I beg you to bear in mind that, after all, it is only worthless junk we're talking about."

"*Worthless junk!?*" Dorrf shook his fist. "You're talking about our birthright! Stolen out from under us! I tell you, no garbage is safe!"

"Well, yes," said Mayor Den. "But I ask you, who on earth would go around stealing trash?"

"Foreigners!"

"*Foreigners!?*"

"I *seen* 'em! Coming over here, taking our junk!"

"Elves!" shouted an old woman at the back, waving her cane. "They come in the night! Steal my garbage and ravish me five ways from Friday!"

That shut the room up. There was a moment of horrible silence as everyone tried and failed to avoid the mental picture.

The mayor coughed. "Er, yes," he said. "Well, be that as it may, I really don't see what we are meant to do about it. I've got the sheriff's men and the guards stepping up their night patrols, but we can't have people standing around guarding people's trash heaps."

"Then we'll do it ourselves!" Dorrf leapt onto a chair, swinging his hat. "So help me, we'll start a citizen's trash committee! We'll patrol night and day if we have to, and hunt down every last garbage thief!"

"And foreigners!"

"And elves!"

"And left-handed—"

"*QUIET!*" The Mayor bellowed, fists clenched with the effort of making himself heard. "All right! Nobody's starting any mobs and that's final! Now look." He took a deep breath. "There's the old granary outside town we don't use anymore. I propose we use it as a municipal rubbish repository. We'll put some good locks on the door, and have guards stationed. All right? That will do until this whole thing blows over. That work for everyone?" He sighed as a hand went up. "Yes?"

The widow Morgan put her hand down. "Does that mean that everyone's trash will be mixing?" she asked. "Only I was rather hoping to keep mine, well, separate."

"Separate?" snarled an old man in the back. "What's the matter, lady? My trash not good enough to mix with yours?"

"Oh, it's not that. Dear me, no. It's just that I feel your, er, leavings would be better suited among their own kind. Besides," she added. "I don't have trash. I have *refuse*."

"Refuse!?" hooted the old man. "What the hell is the difference?"

"About two tax brackets," came a voice from the back.

"All right, all right." Mayor Den rubbed his temples. "That's enough. I say we're going with a municipal trash repository, and that's it. If you don't want to have your junk there, that's fine, but you're on your own. Don't come crying to us when you haven't got a banana peel left to call your own, that's all."

* * * *

Meanwhile, in another part of the woods, the Enchanted Forest's newest criminal masterminds were having a spot of difficulty.

"Okay, look." Revka rubbed her temples. "Finish your apple, and we'll take the core, all right?"

"Well, I'm not going to wolf it down all at once. Not right here." The old man sat on his donkey, arms folded. "I've got a good half an hour's ride ahead of me. I'm pacing myself. Besides," he added. "It's bad for your digestion, eating too fast. Disrupts the humors."

"Fine. Fine." Revka sighed. "And you're sure that's the only garbage you have?"

"Quite sure, yes."

"Fine. OK, how about this. You come by this way every day?"

"Most every day, yes."

"Great. You hang on to the apple core, and we'll just catch you next time. That sound reasonable?"

"Well, I don't want to be any trouble," muttered the alleged victim.

"Oh, no trouble at all. As I said, we'd have to come out anyway. Isn't that right?" She nudged Iyarra, who nodded. "Oh, yes. Totally true."

The man turned the half-eaten apple over in his hand, studying it. "Well...oh, all right."

Revka breathed a sigh of relief. "Thank goodness," she said.

From around a bend in the road there came the sound of hoofbeats. A horse came into view, its rider covered head to toe in black. He lifted a crossbow, aiming it at the group. "Stand and deli—Oh, what the bloody hell is this?"

Revka glared. "Hey, back off," she said. "This is our patch!"

"*Your* patch!?" The highwayman spat. "I don't see your name on it!"

"Well, we were here first!" Revka waved a dagger at him. "Now, go on. Clear out. We're busy here."

"Well, maybe I will, or maybe I won't," he leered. "Maybe this fellow doesn't *want* to get robbed by you, ever think of that? You there!" The masked man nodded to the prospective victim. "Who would you prefer to be robbed by? These two clods or a seasoned professional like me? I've got nine years behind the mask, I do."

The older man fumbled his hat in his hands, looking down. "I don't want to be any trouble," he mumbled. "Don't bring me into the middle of this, please."

"Oh, come on. Look." The highwayman jabbed a thumb at Iyarra and Revka. "I bet these two haven't even threatened you properly. Hm? Did they?"

"Well, they did a *bit*." The old man shrugged. "Though to tell the truth I didn't really feel all that threatened, actually."

"Ha!" The bandit leered at the girls. "You see? Rank amateurs! Now me—" He brought the tip of his crossbow to the old man's neck. "—I'll put the fear of the gods right into you."

Iyarra nudged back at Revka. "Oo. He's good."

"Well, I try." He nodded curtly to the two women, then turned his attention back to the victim. "Now then, sir. Any gold or jewels on your person? Or whatever few little coppers you might have about you? I'm not particular."

"Coppers? Well, I have a few." The old man shrugged. "But they were just going to take my apple core."

"When you were finished with it."

"Right. When I was finished with it."

"Apple core?" The highwayman looked askance at the two. "What do you want that for?"

Revka had had enough. "Look, Mister," she growled. "Do we go around telling you how to do *your* job? No? All right, then. Besides, we were here first. We called dibs."

"Dibs? *Dibs!?* We are highwaymen. Well, *I* am a highwayman, don't know what you two are. And we do not call dibs!"

Revka waved a placating hand. "All right. All right. No need to get all worked up. Obviously, the fairest thing is to let him decide." She turned to the old man. "Now sir, which would you prefer; to have your invaluables taken by a pioneering duo of criminal masterminds, or to have this Johnny-come-lately show up and take your money like any other run-of-the-mill criminal?"

"Well, I'd kind of like to just go home."

"Sir, that's really not helpful. I don't think you're entering into the spirit of the thing."

"And who are you calling Johnny-come-lately, anyway? How long have you two clowns been at this?"

"Okay, granted, not long, but we like to think we're bringing much-needed fresh ideas and innovation into the world of crime."

Iyarra nodded. "We're disrupting the dominant paradigm."

There was a moment of silence as everyone turned to stare at her.

"What?" she said. "We are."

"Okay," said the other bandit. "Like how?"

Revka looked blank. "Like how what?"

"How are you disrupting the...the whatever-you-said? Go on." He turned to the old man. "You watch," he said. "I bet they've got nothing."

"Okay, no, uhm, give me a second." Revka thought fast. "Well, for one thing, we have..." She scrambled frantically in Iyarra's saddlebags. "Ah! Yes. This lovely souvenir mug, our gift to new customers with a robbery of equal or greater value."

The old man brightened. "Oh, that's nice. Er, I don't suppose an apple core would count?"

"Just one? Oh, no sir. We'd need to get at least a medium bag of table scraps. Or some broken crockery. That would work."

"Oh." He looked crestfallen. "I'm afraid all of my dishes and things are in good repair." He looked up. "Maybe I could smash a few?"

"Hmm, I dunno," said Revka. "That's not really bona fide junk, is it? Not if we know you smashed it on purpose."

"You wouldn't have to tell anyone," he said. "I'd keep my lips sealed!"

"Well, we really shouldn't," said Revka. "But in your case, sure. I think we could let it slide."

"Oh, thanks very much!" The old man's brow furrowed. "Er, you wouldn't tell anyone, would you?"

"Sir, you have my word as a crook."

"Oh, good."

"I don't believe this!" The other bandit's fist hit his saddle with a thump. "Why are you even talking about this? We are *bandits*. We *take*! I've never heard anything so ridiculous in all my life. Why—"

The old man held up his hands. "All right, all right. That's enough. Now, you're both very good robbers, and I will say that I am legitimately terrified by both of you...and also more than a little confused. But I think that, since the young ladies were here first, it's only fair to let them go ahead."

"Thank you."

"Don't mention it."

The bandit sneered. "I think you're forgetting something," he said. Once again the crossbow was planted against the old man's head. "Now, I think that you two had better run along and leave me to my business. Off you go."

"No." Suddenly Iyarra's hands were holding daggers. She twirled one, giving the other bandit as mean a look she could manage through her mask. "We were here first. He chose us. He's our victim. Go away."

"Right." Revka pulled out a dagger as well. "And if you have any tricksy ideas, just remember, you've got a crossbow with one bolt. There's two of us, and we've both got knives. Wanna do the math?"

The bandit looked at the two women, made a swift mental calculation, and sighed. He slung his crossbow over his shoulder. "Fine." He glared at the old man. "But don't come crying to me later, right?" He turned his horse around and rode off. "Don't know what this business is coming to," he grumbled as he disappeared around the bend.

"Well," said Revka. "That was awkward." She turned back to the old man and gave him a bright smile. "Sorry about all that. So, tomorrow?"

* * * *

"Man, what a pain." Revka dumped the day's haul on the outskirts of the camp. There was already quite the heap there, moldering in the afternoon sun.

"Anything good?" Brother Sudgen was leaning against a tree, nose buried in a book. Behind him, another book was wedged in the crook of a branch, hanging open.

"If it were any good, we wouldn't be taking it," said Revka.

"Fair point." Sudgen glanced over the day's takings. Well, day's leavings, more like. Heavy on the food scraps, but a little scrap paper here and there. Also what appeared to be a broken wheel spoke. "How are things going out there?"

Villains

Revka shrugged. "Could be better. We had a little competition out on the road, but we chased him off. So far it's just small potatoes, though." She kicked lightly at an errant rock, sending it into the woods.

"I see," said Sister Agata, joining them. "Well, I think we're doing well by laying down the general groundwork, but you're quite right that you won't achieve notoriety carrying on like this."

"*Page!*" called out Sudgen Two. Brother Sudgen sighed. He turned around to the other book and flipped to the next page.

"Well, we need to think of a way to pick things up," said Revka. "I'm not sure I'm keen to keep at this forever."

"Revka's right," said Iyarra. "I mean, I know we're not stealing anything of value, but I still don't like it. We need to speed things up if we possibly can."

Sudgen nodded. "Quite. Some of us have been discussing that very problem. I think that tonight—"

"*Page!*"

"I just turned it!"

"It's mostly picture!"

Brother Sudgen sighed. He flipped to the next page in Sudgen Two's book and turned back to the conversation. "As I was saying, tonight we need to discuss this matter further. Bad you may be, but notorious is what we are looking for."

Iyarra took off her black cloak, folding it neatly. "Well, how do we do that?"

"I don't know," Sister Agata said. "I only hope that, between us, we can figure something out."

* * * *

That night, Revka and Iyarra were summoned to the senior librarians' camp after dinner. Several robed figures were sitting around the central fire, talking quietly. Sister Agata gave the two women a nod and beckoned them to have a seat.

"Now then. It seems you've been doing well getting out there and, well, vaguely inconveniencing innocent civilians left and right. The bit at the town hall was effective, but we really aren't crossing over into what I would call actual villainy. Something's missing, and I've called this meeting to see if we can work out what it is."

"Well," said Brother Sudgen, who was leaning against a nearby wagon. "I hate to be the one to throw this idea out there, but perhaps it's time we discussed actually being villainous. I don't think we're going to get anywhere with this song and dance. I mean, nobody tells stories about a big bad wolf who goes to little pigs' houses and, say, tries to sell them things."

"Your point is made, Brother, but as I have said before, we will not harm people if we can possibly avoid it. We're skating quite close to actual harm as it is, I'd say. Now, there's got to be something we're missing. Let's talk it over."

"Well, okay." Revka sat down, plucking a blade of grass and toying with it. "Way I figure it, you don't get into the fairy-tale books from just doing typical petty criminal type stuff. On the other hand, I don't think it's really down to the scale. You know?"

Iyarra nodded. "That makes sense," she said. "A fairy-tale villain doesn't have to be super vicious, they just have to be memorable."

"All right, let's talk about that," said Sister Agata. "Are we talking about exploring some sort of gimmick?"

Sister Peasley raised a tentative hand. "I, uhm, thought stealing garbage *was* the gimmick?"

"Fair point." Sister Agata got up and began to count off points on her fingers. "So, we have a unique modus operandi, one that certainly gets the public's attention and more or less guarantees we've got a niche all to ourselves. All very useful, yet we haven't sufficiently captured the public's imagination to achieve the kind of infamy we require. So. What makes the difference between a run-of-the-mill bad guy and a villain?"

Iyarra traced a hoof in the ground. "Like, other than a hero?"

The camp went quiet. There was one of those moments that was filled with the silence of pennies dropping in several minds at once.

One of the librarians looked up at Sister Agata. "She's right, you know. Any good villain has a foil. Everybody knows that."

"Yes, yes..." And now Sister Agata was pacing back and forth, gesturing as she spoke. "Of course. We need someone specific. We've been going at this all scattershot. Different victims every day. We need to focus on a specific target. Or rather, bring a specific target against us."

"Okay," said Revka. "But if that's the case, where do we find ourselves a hero? I mean, you can't just go down to the store and pick one up, last I checked."

Sudgen drummed his fingers against the wagon. "I think, perhaps, it is probably in our best interest to provide one of our own. Shouldn't be too difficult. We'll just have one of our people ride out and foil them a few times. No problem there."

"Uhm." It was Sister Peasley again. She half raised a tentative hand. "I think maybe it will take a little more than that?" she said.

Sister Agata turned to her. "What do you mean, Sister?" she said kindly. "Go on, tell us."

"Well..." The young librarian cleared her throat. "I read a lot of those stories, when I was a children's librarian. Story corner and so on, you know? And, uhm, as I recall, it was more like the hero had to *match* the villain, you see? So a predator against prey, or a little animal against a big one. That sort of thing. I mean, not all of the time." She waved a flustered arm. "There are plenty of examples of others, but I do remember that the really good ones—the memorable ones, you might say—well, they, uhm, worked that way."

After a moment, Sister Agata nodded. "Yes," she said. "Yes I believe you're right." She turned to the others. "Well, you heard her. What's the opposite of someone who goes around stealing trash? Thinking caps on, everyone."

The meeting went quiet. Revka scratched the side of her head thoughtfully. "A litterbug?"

"Not heroic enough."

"Someone who gives out free trash?"

"Can't see anyone getting behind that, really."

More silence.

Iyarra coughed. "I, ah, I don't think there actually is one," she ventured.

"Actually," said a voice from the back. A younger librarian pushed his way forward, holding a scrap of paper. "I was in town today and they had these posted everywhere." He showed it to Sister Agata. She read it over, then handed it to Sudgen, who read it out to the others.

Revka and Iyarra listened along with the rest of the group, then looked at each other and nodded. "Well, all right," Revka said. "That sounds about right, but where do we find a suitable candidate?"

Suddenly, from the forest outside the camp, there came a terrifying noise. It was like a screech and a roar mixed together by someone who did special effects for sci-fi movies and who was getting double overtime. As suddenly as it had begun, the sound was truncated by a loud *thump*, followed by silence.

The group looked at each other, then ran as one to the source of the noise.

On the edge of the camp, standing next to a torch on a long pole, was Brother Conan. He loomed over the inert form of the morga, which lay crumpled in a large, furry lump at his feet.

"Came out of the woods," Brother Conan explained, massaging some feeling back into his fist. "Guess he must have smelled our cooking or something." Even sprawled out on the ground, the creature was an imposing sight. Seven feet tall if an inch, with long arms that ended in claws that could rip through a tree. One leg kicked a little, but otherwise it stayed still.

Revka boggled. "Good grief," she said. "What did you do?"

He shrugged. "I hit it," he said.

The committee looked at each other. And back at Brother Conan. And back to each other. And nodded.

Brother Conan, still flexing his fingers, looked around at the others with mild confusion. "Uhm," he said. "What's going on?"

Sister Agata stepped forward. Her smile could have melted iron. "Brother Conan." She slipped an arm into his. "Let Brother Sebastian take your watch for a while. We have something we'd like to discuss with you."

Chapter Eighteen

SEE THE VILLAGE SQUARE, all cobbles and stone. The sun is up, and so is the town. People don't waste perfectly good daylight around here. A few market stalls are already open. From a small building wafts of baking bread, and the distant hammering of the blacksmith echoes over the town.

See the town hall, with the bulletin board out front. See the old timber, gray with age, that in other places is called barn wood but here is just wood, because sooner or later it all looks like that. See the handbill, tacked to the board, rustling softly in the early autumn breeze.

Now. See the shape move across the field of vision, outlined black against the morning sun. It strides with purpose, making no noise, as it heads toward a building in the center of the town.

And now the shadow is a silhouette, framed in a doorway and taking up most of it. The morning sunbeams push through and around where they can, giving the stranger a haloed appearance.

Givney, the town clerk, blinks in surprise at the sudden eclipse. He looks up, and further up. There's a *lot* of up. He stares for a moment, then remembers himself. "Come in," he manages. "Er, may I help you?"

The shape steps into the town hall and slowly resolves as the eyes get used to the light. The man is large, solidly built. It must be a man, Givney thinks to himself, because oak trees don't grow like that. He wears a hat with a wide brim, just the thing for hiding his eyes. Draped over his shapeless, gray robe is a simple garment, not much more than a woven blanket with a hole in the middle for the neck. An old leather belt hangs underneath, just visible.

Givney clears his throat. "Can—can I help you?"

The stranger approaches the desk. His voice, when it comes, is like the purr of a sleeping dragon. "I hear tell," he says, "that you people have a bit of a problem."

Givney straightens up, remembering himself. "Er, well, yes," he says. "I take it you're here about the position?"

The stranger doesn't answer right away. With rattlesnake speed, he rakes a match across Givney's desk. He lights a pencil-thin cigarillo, taking his time. A lazy cloud of blue smoke drifts across the desk. "Yeah," he says. "That's about the size of it."

Givney looks him over. Big. Scary. Quiet. Could mean anything. Still, they do need help. And this guy looks like he could hold off an army. "All right," he says. "Pay is ten crowns a week. We start first thing tomorrow morning. Be here at sunrise. Will that work for you?" And then, because it pays to be polite to someone twice your size, he adds, "Sir?"

The stranger nods. "Tomorrow." He turns to go.

"Wait!" Givney holds out a hand. "Before you go, I need your name."

The giant man pauses on the threshold, half turning. For a moment he doesn't say anything.

"I, er, I need it for the payroll," Givney holds up a sheet of paper. "You know. So you can get paid."

"They call me..." The man pauses. He steps out into the morning sun. He turns once more and looks Givney directly in the eye.

"They call me Larry."

* * * *

Brother Sudgen looked up from his book. "Larry?"

Brother Conan pulled off the hat and poncho, setting them aside. "It was all I could think of, okay?" he said. "Anyway, it's done. I start work first thing tomorrow morning."

"Good." Revka was off to one side, preparing some rabbits she had caught earlier. She nodded at Iyarra, who had gathered a small mound of nuts and was carefully sorting through them. "When do you want us to show up?"

"Not right away." Sister Agata moved to collect Brother Conan's disguise, handing them off to a junior librarian. "I think perhaps it would arouse their suspicion if you showed up immediately. Besides, we don't quite know what we're dealing with. I propose that Brother Conan goes and does the rounds tomorrow, so he can make himself familiar with the setting. What to expect, how many other people, and so on. Once he has done that, he can inform us, and we can proceed with rather more foreknowledge than if we just go charging in. Are we in agreement?"

"Works for me." Revka said.

"Sure." Iyarra nodded.

Brother Conan shrugged. "Up to you," he said.

"Very well." Sister Agata nodded to the group. "You will report back tomorrow evening. In the meantime, we will wait. And plan."

* * * *

Villains

The next day passed without incident. 'Larry' arrived at the town hall just before dawn to discover he was one of only three men on the job. One was a boy—couldn't have been more than fourteen—who moved like a sack full of elbows with bad acne. The other was somewhat sturdier, but had a half-glazed look on his face, which put Brother Conan in mind of a wax doll that had been left in the sun too long. They were called Ponach and Jeb, and Brother Conan quickly realized that he was going to do most of the heavy lifting, and *all* of the heavy thinking.

Still, the work wasn't too bad. The group went from house to house, collecting up the garbage and hauling it to the old granary. The main area of the village was finished by lunchtime, but there were several homes out along the roads or in the woods, which took up most of the afternoon.

As they trudged through the woods on their way to pick up from the local charcoal burner, the trio fell to chatting.

"And he said I had a natural talent for accumulating junk," Ponach was saying. His Adam's apple was bigger than his chin, and as he talked, it bobbed up and down alarmingly. "I just got fired from the wheelwright's, so I figured why not?"

"Why'd you get fired from the wheelwright's?" Larry strolled along, a half-empty sack over his shoulder.

"There was kind of an accident," the boy said. "Some of the wheels got loose."

"Sorry? Got loose?"

"Well, I was putting some up in the storage racks, and I kind of hit the wrong thing and sent about forty cartwheels flying out the door."

"Good grief."

"Oh, yeah. We were running around all day chasing them down."

"One of 'em wound up on our roof," said Jeb. "Never did work out how it got there."

Brother Conan let out a low whistle. "Well, I can see how there'd be trouble over that," he said.

"Oh, sure," said Ponach. "Wasn't as bad as when I was apprenticed to the blacksmith, though."

"Yeah?" Brother Co—sorry, Larry tilted his head in the boy's direction. "Do I want to know what happened there?"

"Welded the hammer to the anvil."

"Eh? How in the world did you manage to do that?"

"You know, that's exactly what the blacksmith said."

"Huh." Brother Conan turned to Jeb. "So, how about you? You have a job before this?"

Jeb straightened up. "Indeed I did," he said. "I were a dragon spotter."

"A what?"

"Dragon spotter. Very important job, too."

"No kidding? How many did you spot?"

"Never seen one in my life."

"You don't say."

"Oh, it weren't for lack of tryin'." Jeb nodded his head vigorously up and down, only occasionally getting lost on the way. "Every day, I would go out into the woods. There's this big old cave, and I would sit by the entrance and wait to see if a dragon showed up. If it did, I was to come right back and tell the mayor."

"I see." They walked on for a while. "And you did this how long?"

"Oh, *years*. Got five crowns every week, too."

"Huh."

Jeb gave the others what he apparently considered a sly grin. "Actually," he confided. "The cave weren't big enough for a man to lie down in. No way a dragon'd fit in it. I didn't say nothin', though. I just think maybe they weren't very smart."

"You don't say."

Larry mulled this over as they trudged along the forest path.

* * * *

They got back into town just as the sun was beginning to sink below the tree line. The town clerk unlocked the granary, and they dumped the day's takings into a corner. The trio was paid and dismissed with instructions to return in a week.

Brother Conan headed back through the woods to the librarians' camp. That night, around the council fire, he gave his report.

"A week?" Brother Sudgen groaned. "We don't have that kind of time to hang around."

"Agreed." Sister Agata looked up at Brother Conan. "You say it was you and two others?"

"That's right. Some kid and a guy they pay to stay out of town. Not exactly intellectual heavyweights."

"Nevertheless. We don't want anyone unduly injured." She sat back a moment, her eyes closed. Around the fire, the rest of the council fell silent. When she spoke, her voice came from a faraway place.

"Am I right in remembering tomorrow is market day?"

Some of the others nodded. "That's right, ma'am," said a younger librarian.

"Good, good." She paced around the council fire. "If my surmise is correct, a nice big crowd will be just what we need. Of course, we'll have to make sure they are kept out of harm's way, but we should be able to arrange that easily enough." She looked around. "Iyarra and Revka, where are they?"

"Off by the main fire pit," said someone. "Off telling some of those stories of theirs again."

"Run and fetch them, please," said Sister Agata. "I think it's time we brought this little drama to a head."

* * * *

The next morning was cloudy and cool, the last vestiges of summer trickling away. The trees were just beginning to take on the faintest tints of orange and red, and a crispness in the air hinted that autumn was about to ignite its full burn.

Market day meant everyone showed up early and stalls lined the entire village square. Goods from all over Killing Logan and beyond were on display, and the square filled with the smells of roast meat, spiced apples, and livestock. It was a good crowd this week. People tended to stock up during the autumn months so winter wouldn't leave them wanting.

Things had been going for a good several hours when there was a sudden commotion. Off by the town hall, a centauress reared up on her hind legs. The woman riding astride her was dressed all in black, holding a bag slung over one shoulder. She threw back her head and laughed. *"NYA, HAHAHA-HAAA! COWER, YOU HAPLESS FOOLS! FOR WE, THE GARBAGE GANG, HAVE COME FOR YOUR TRASH! HAHAHAHA-HAAAA!"*

"Ha, ha, ha, ha," added the centauress.

The rider waved a crossbow in the air. "Now, then. Here's how this is going to go down. You're all gonna come up here, one at a time, and empty all your useless items into this here sack. No welshing, no hiding. And I don't think I need to tell you what will happen if you try to put something of actual value in here. Do I?"

A long look at the faces in the crowd made it clear that she would, in fact, need to tell them. "We'll shoot you," she sighed. "Everybody got that? Yes? What?"

A villager in the back put his hand down. "Why?"

"Why? Why what?"

"Why do you want our garbage?"

Revka groaned. She had occasionally bent the law a little, here and there, in a strictly informal sort of way, survival and so on, but this was just ridiculous. It was some comfort to know she wasn't cut out for out-and-out banditry. She was going to be glad when this charade was all over, and that was the truth.

"Look," she said. "All you need to know is I'm the one with the crossbow, all right? This is not a good time to be asking questions. Just do as I say, and everything will be just fine. Now, let's get started, shall we?" Out of the corner of her eye, she scanned the crowd. Dammit, where was he?

She cleared her throat and tried again. "So, if everyone will just line up here, we will *get started*." Pause. "I *said*, we can ge—"

"Not a chance, Garbage Gang!"

The crowd parted. Larry stood in the middle of the square in his slouch hat and poncho. He took a long draw on his cigarillo and flexed his arms out, ready for action.

Finally.

"Well, well, we meet again, our dread nemesis...Larry." There was only the slightest hesitation. "But I'm afraid you're too late. We're going to clean this town out and there's nothing you can do to stop it."

Brother Conan flipped his poncho aside, revealing as impressive an array of weapons as a group of itinerant librarians could scrounge up on short notice. He shook his head slowly. "No way," he said. "This ends now." He waved off the sheriff, who had moved up beside him. "No. I've got this. You keep the townsfolk out of the way. You leave these two to me."

The sheriff nodded, all too happy to leave the dangerous stuff to the big guy. He turned to the townsfolk. "You heard 'em, people. Let's everybody cleared out of here. Come on, now." The crowd grumbled at the prospect of missing the show. Nonetheless, they retreated to the various side streets and buildings, where they jostled for a good view.

Iyarra began to gallop toward the center of the empty square. Brother Conan waited, biding his time until she was about to gallop right over him. At the last second, he tumbled to one side, regaining his feet and watching as centauress and rider tried to swing around for the return trip.

"A fine feint," Revka cried. "But not quite good enough!" She drew a dagger and spurred Iyarra into another charge. This time he stayed put, using his own knife to carefully parry the blade.

Revka leaped from Iyarra's back and charged. She cannoned into their ersatz nemesis, rebounding slightly off his gigantic frame but managing to make it look good anyway. For a moment, the two grappled. Grunts and imprecations were interspersed with sotto voce comments along the lines of "Watch your leg," and "Take it easy, man. Just make it *look* good."

The wind stirred.

The three combatants crossed and recrossed, taking wild but (if one was paying attention) not especially fast or accurate swings at one another. There had been hardly any time to rehearse, so the trio just kept the momentum going as best they could and tried to make it look as real as possible. All around them, the villagers watched. And believed.

Revka watched as Iyarra reared up on her hind legs, neatly avoiding Brother Conan's dagger. A sheet of paper swirled past her field of vision, then tumbled away. The wind was definitely picking up. She dropped, feinted, and caught Iyarra's eye. The horsewoman nodded; she'd seen it too.

Their opponent sniffed the air. He nodded briefly to the girls and lunged at them with a fairly convincing "*Hiyahhh!*" They ducked, countered, and sent him sprawling onto the ground.

Revka quickly cleared the space between them. She put her hands on her hips, standing over him with her best bad-guy scowl. "So! We've got you at last! Any last words?"

The wind *roared*.

There it was again, that gut-plunging sensation of falling in several directions at once. Revka felt her consciousness drifting away, fading into nothingness. Behind her, Iyarra whinnied in fear.

Suddenly, there was silence.

* * * *

Nobody ever quite pieced together what happened that day. The mysterious stranger had been fighting those two bandits, right in the middle of the square. He'd been doing well, too. Then suddenly, he was flat on his back. It looked like they were about to strike him down for good, but…somehow, it didn't happen. The stranger stood alone in the square. The bandits were gone, the threat lifted for good.

And as for the stranger? Well, those who were there say he disappeared himself, vanishing right in the midst of the crowd that rushed to congratulate him. Some say he disappeared in a puff of smoke. Others swear he turned into a bird and flew away. There was even one guy who swore he saw a big man in gray robes toss a hat away and leg it down an alley, but nobody's going to believe a story like that. It was probably aliens.

From that day forward, garbage men were the most loved and respected members of the community. Women idolized them, men envied them, children wanted to grow up to be them. Wherever garbage men went, people stepped aside and gave them room, although admittedly, this might have had something to do with the smell. Junior Garbage Collector sets shot to the top of the annual Winterturning wish lists, where they remain to this day.

And everyone lived happily and hygienically ever after.

THE END...right?

Chapter Nineteen

IT WAS A BEAUTIFUL day.

Revka leaned back, feeling the gentle rocking movement of Iyarra's muscles beneath her. She closed her eyes and took a deep breath of the good, fresh air. Birds were singing, and a soft breeze was just enough to temper the warm autumn sun. Life was good.

"I think we should head on down to the coast," she said. "Nice and warm, and we could laze around on the beach for a while. What do you think?"

Iyarra's head bobbed up and down in agreement. Revka fished an apple out of a bag and began to munch on it, thoughtfully. "Maybe we can get on a boat, eh? Take a voyage, see the Green Lands or the City of Mirrors. Of course," she added, "I know you're not a big fan of boats, so maybe we'll skip that. Still, I wouldn't mind seeing those places someday."

Iyarra didn't deign to comment. Before them, the road stretched on, leading to who knew how many different adventures and a thousand amazing places. Someday, Revka would see them all.

She took another bite of the apple. Where had she got this one, anyhow? She hoped that she'd picked up some extra, wherever it was. Well, it didn't matter too much, did it? There were always other apples. She took another bite, eyes closed, as a stray rivulet of juice ran down one side of her mouth. Delicious. When they passed the eyes that watched them from the forest, she missed them completely.

* * * *

It was a beautiful day.

Iyarra cantered across the endless plains, laughing and basking in the warm summer sun. Her family was there, and with them the rest of the herd. Revka perched quietly on her back, her weight familiar and reassuring. All around Iyarra, her family laughed and sang and swapped stories as they followed the soft grass. Ahead was the scent of water and the promise of a good night's rest beneath the stars.

That evening, they camped out by a small pond. There was fresh bread and hot stew, and the younger members of the herd sang for them. Iyarra ate and sang and felt herself absorbed into the comforting embrace of her people. And no one noticed the thing on the hill overlooking the camp.

* * * *

In a candy-colored shack in an all-but-empty part of the Enchanted Forest, Mother Vieille was sunk into her favorite overstuffed chair, idly scratching a doll with a fork. The figure was odd-looking, lashed together from the scraps at the bottom of any sewing kit, but nonetheless bearing an uncanny resemblance to the old woman herself. She raked the fork up and down, right at the spot on her back where she couldn't reach. The day was done, there was stew on the fire, and later she would—

There was a pricking of her thumbs.

Mother Vieille didn't panic. She put the doll away, nice and gentle, because you couldn't be too careful. She stood in the middle of the room, her hands held apart as if she was holding an invisible ball. She closed her eyes and bobbed a little on the balls of her feet, as if testing the ground. She let her mind *Wander*. Her consciousness uncurled, winding out in an ever-expanding spiral into the woods.

Out into the world, now. A note, familiar...but off somehow. A single wrong note in a symphony...if you've got the knowing of it, that one note can stand out all the more. Closer, now. Letting her senses do the work, drilling down.

Ah. There it was.

She opened her eyes. For a moment she did nothing, just stood staring into space. She shook her head sadly. "I warned 'em," she said. "I warned 'em. Knew it was gonna happen, but what can a body do?"

Outside, the evening cool had set in. She stepped down the crazy paving, shawl wrapped tight around her, until she found what she was looking for. She knocked a couple of times, and without waiting for an answer said, "All right, you. Those poor girls have gone and got themselves in trouble. You run along and fetch 'em out, you hear? I'll be here."

There was silence, but Mother Vieille seemed satisfied. She grunted and hobbled back into the cottage.

A few seconds later, there was a rattling, clanking sound from the front yard.

Then silence.

* * * *

It was a beautiful day.

Day passed into night. Sometimes it was one, sometimes the other. Sometimes it would move between the two without the intermediaries of dawn and dusk, but you never noticed that. It was always now, and it was always fine.

One day, Revka and Iyarra were fighting their way through a pack of vargs, nasty creatures with the body of a man, the head of a warthog, and the attitude of a junior high vice principal. The girls slashed and whirled against the foes, striking them down one after another. Revka was in particularly fine form, receiving not so much as a scratch as one varg after another fell to her fighting prowess.

When the fight was over, the girls began to gather up the loot. Lots of gold and some nice weapons. Revka loaded as much as she could into Iyarra's saddlebags and took one last look around to see if there were any treasures left behind. She was just nosing around the edges of the scene when an odd shape caught her eye.

Out a ways from the battle, an old box stood in a little clearing, about the size of a couple of men standing side by side. The box had once been gaily painted, but time had worn most of it away. There was writing, or at least the remains of writing. And a…face? There couldn't be someone in there, surely?

She felt herself moving toward the thing. It felt familiar somehow, like a word you're looking for but can't quite recall. Something tickled at the back of her brain. She patted at her belt pouches and found a dagger suddenly in her hand. Odd.

Behind her, she heard Iyarra stamping impatiently. Revka shook her head and turned back. Whatever was in that box, it wasn't important.

She mounted up on Iyarra's back and gave her a pat. Horsewoman and rider made their way out of the camp toward the main road. Behind them, painted eyes watched them go.

* * * *

On the Red Plains, the Greatfoot clan made camp by a cool, clear stream. The night was warm and fragrant, and Iyarra felt like stretching her legs a little. With Revka on her back, she trotted out a ways, past the firelights of the camp and up to the top of a hill. The moon was in crescent and the sky was absolutely filled with stars. They lay out on the soft grass, just gazing up at the night sky.

"They say," Iyarra said, "that some of those are worlds with people on them. One of Father's friends told me, when we visited. Of course, the elves say they're beacons placed in the sky to help you find your way. I suppose that makes sense too, but there are an awful lot of them just for navigating, don't you think?"

There was no answer. Iyarra leaned over and gave Revka a nudge. "Hey," she said. "You fall asleep on me?"

Iyarra would be the first to admit that she's not the smartest thing on four legs. The Greatfoot clan had a rich oral tradition and centuries of accumulated wisdom in what might be called "steppe smarts," but it was hard to acquire much in the way of book learning when you didn't even have a written language. Still, she had a natural feeling for her surroundings. In the same way that an experienced engineer detects the tiniest change in the hum of a machine, she began to feel something tickle at her senses. Something was *off*.

She rolled over and nudged Revka again, a little more urgently this time. "Uhm, Revka? Hon?"

Again, there was no answer.

Something gripped Iyarra's heart. It wasn't quite fear, not exactly, but perhaps the feeling of a space being made for fear to arrive. She hauled herself right way up and shook at Revka's shoulder. "Revka?" she said, a little louder than she meant to. "Revka? Can you hear me?"

Revka rolled over. She rubbed her eyes and looked up at the centauress, her face catching the light of the moon.

To understand what happened next, try the following: go to a costume store and buy a rubber mask that almost, but not quite, looks like you. One night, when your significant other is fast asleep, put the mask on.

Now, wait for them to wake up.

See that face they just made?

Well, that's exactly the face Iyarra made when she saw Revka.

(Incidentally, this would probably be a good time to apologize to your significant other, maybe take them to dinner or something. Just don't tell them where you got the idea.)

It was...it was Revka, but it wasn't. All the elements were there, to be sure, but the thing missing was the whole. Like a very good doll, or a bad special effect. Iyarra had never heard of the uncanny valley, but Revka's face landed right, smack dab in the middle of it.

People talk about nightmares. They invoke images of bug-eyed monsters, shadowy things standing around you, silent and still. Those aren't the real nightmares. Nightmares begin when something familiar twists into something alien. Suddenly, the world you're accustomed to becomes different, becomes *wrong*. It doesn't even have to be a big thing; movement where there should be stillness, silence when there should be sound. That's when the little alarm goes off in the back of the brain, and the oldest program of all hotwires itself into the mind. Fight or flight.

Iyarra screamed.

She was on her hooves before she knew it and galloping off in a random direction. The moon bathed the landscape in a silvery light. The plains stretched out in all directions. She ran and ran, putting as much distance between her and...*that*...as possible.

After a couple of minutes, she realized she probably ought to head back toward the camp and her herd. Unfortunately, the direction she chose in her flight had led her away from the campfires. To get back to them, she'd have to find her way past that...that *thing*. Besides—and the thought made her shudder—what if the herd were like Revka as well? She tried to remember faces so familiar she barely looked at them.

She risked a glance over her shoulder. Whatever it was, it wasn't following her. There was that, at least. She allowed herself to stop, and she tried to think. What would Revka do in a situation like this? Honestly, Iyarra had no idea.

Now that she'd stopped and looked around, there *was* something. The landscape was pretty empty, barring the occasional tree, but a little ways off stood what appeared to be a large box. Not something you generally saw in the plains, actually. She peered at the oddity, tilting her head in mild bemusement. There was something about it, something familiar...

Well, she wasn't going back to the camp, not with that fake Revka around. She might as well investigate the box. Besides, it didn't feel dangerous. She trotted gingerly forward. It was fairly large, about the size of two men. There was glass in the front, and inside—

Iyarra stood still for a moment, waiting for her heart to calm down. It was just a dummy, nothing more. The eyes were painted on, the clothes hung loosely over a carved wooden form. It wasn't like the creepy thing she'd run from. In fact, now that she was closer, that nagging familiarity was really hitting her hard.

She licked her suddenly dry lips and forced herself to go forward. Revka would, wouldn't she? Of course she would.

Well, there you are, then.

As she moved in closer, she began to pick out more details. There was a ball in the glassed-in area in front of the dummy, and writing above and below. Revka's patient tutoring had given her a passing familiarity with the printed word, provided she went easy and didn't try all the words at once. She got close enough to read the wavy banner at the top. *Find Fame—Fortune—Romance.*

She heard a clink and saw a glint of metal. One copper coin dropped into the change slot.

Iyarra took the coin and turned it over a couple of times. Well, it was a penny. And there was a slot for it, right there. Sometimes, you just follow the road that's in front of you.

She inserted the penny.

The machine came to life...well, almost life. A dim, hesitant light flickered on behind the painted glass eyes of the fortune teller, and its hands began to move in jerky motions around the crystal ball. From somewhere in the depths of the machine came a tune which would have been mysterious and evocative were it not being plunked out on an old music cylinder desperately in need of oiling. After a few seconds, the extravaganza shuddered to a halt, and a card dropped into a waiting hopper.

BEWARE OF HAPPY ENDINGS.

Iyarra blinked at the card. Where had she heard that? Sometime recently. Something familiar. The machine...it was part of the same memory, and there had been...what?

She turned the card over and over in her hand. She knew it was important. She'd seen it before, but she couldn't quite remember where.

Come to think of it, there was a lot she couldn't remember. Like how had she and Revka gotten back to her herd? It had been months since they'd last seen them. The air smelled of spring, but she couldn't remember winter. They had...they were going to go somewhere, weren't they? It had been autumn, and they were headed south ahead of the cold, but something happened, right? And there had been the woods, and she and Revka...

Revka. The thought struck her like lightning. Something had happened to Revka. Something had hurt her. They had taken her Revka away and replaced her with that *thing* back there. And now they were in her head, trying to make her forget.

Iyarra, like much of her kind, was gentle by nature and nonviolent whenever possible, but the thought of Revka off somewhere in trouble, while she was stuffed into this—this *lie*—was enough to make her blood boil. She screamed and wheeled around, looking for someone or something to kick. She wanted to gallop back to the puppet that had been left for her and tear it to pieces. She made to move, but suddenly found herself trapped. The wide-open spaces still stretched out before her, but now she was constricted, barely able to even move her arms away from her body. She bucked and writhed, fighting the invisible force that held her in place.

A wet tearing sound preceded a sudden jolt, and Iyarra found herself landing on a cold, stone floor, shaking with fear.

Iyarra staggered up to her hooves and waited for the world to stop spinning. She felt weak and hungry, and the world smelled wrong. She managed to stand and take a look around.

It seemed she was in some sort of cave, dimly lit and surrounded on all sides by gray stone. Odd. It didn't smell like a cave at all. There was light, of a sort, but it seemed to come from nowhere and cast no shadows. She turned around and saw a strange thing hanging down from the ceiling. It looked like someone had dipped a lily in tar. It caught the light in a way she didn't like at all. The stalk wound its way up to the ceiling, where it snaked off into the distance.

Now that she looked around properly, she could see others. They were figures, each wearing one of the black flower things on its head like a cap. The nearest appeared to be some kind of fishman, tall and lean with scales trailing down his back. He was hunched up, doing something which she couldn't quite see. She cowered for a moment, waiting to see if he was going to attack, but the creature paid her no mind at all.

Cautiously, she stepped forward. His skin was smooth and dark green, and made Iyarra think of swamps. His underjaw was large, and his eyes were uniform yellow with just the tiniest pupils, right in the center. A stalk coming out of his forehead arched upward and out. The luminescent bulb on the end cast a sickly, yellow-green light over the scene.

As she got closer, the creature continued to ignore her. It held its webbed hands close to its mouth, which it was opening and shutting rhythmically as if—yes, as if it was eating something. From time to time, it would take big bites out of whatever it was, tearing bits away with its fang-like teeth.

Gingerly, she reached out and touched one shoulder. No reaction. She tried shaking the fishman a little. Still nothing. "Hey!" she shouted. Her voice echoing too loud through the stone corridor. If the creature heard her, it gave no sign.

She looked at the black flower cap on its head. The petals lay flat against the creature's head, apparently holding the rest in place. Perhaps if she—

The fishman screeched as she tugged at one of the petals. He fell to the ground, curling up in a tight ball of agony. Iyarra pulled her hand away quickly. Well, better not do that again.

Revka. Revka would be in one of these things. Iyarra looked around for the next one and trotted over. Some man with a mustache. He seemed to be laughing about something. She moved on.

There were more down the long passage of the cave. She checked each as she came to them. Monsters, beasts, men, and women. Maybe these were the villains she and Revka had been sent to find? Iyarra wished she could find Revka. She was better at this sort of thing.

After a while, she heard a noise. This was a surprise, because up until that point, the place had been almost completely silent. Even her footsteps, which should have echoed across the cavern walls, were strangely muffled. There was no mistaking it, though. Somebody was singing.

She turned a corner, moving faster now. A ragged figure slumped against a wall, little more than skin and bones, knees hugged to its chest. As Iyarra approached, it sang a tuneless little thing to itself. The figure didn't pay Iyarra any mind, and in fact, didn't appear to see her.

Iyarra coughed. "Uhm, hello?" she whispered, not wanting to be rude. "Excuse me?"

The singing stopped. The figure lifted its head, held it more or less steady for a few moments, then dropped it again.

Iyarra came closer. "Excuse me," she said. "Do you know if—"

The head bobbed down and to the side, turning itself more toward the centauress.

Iyarra gasped.

"Hello," said Jack.

Chapter Twenty

ONCE UPON A TIME, there was a boy named Jack.

Jack was the third son of a humble woodcutter. His eldest brother was brave and strong, and could run a hundred leagues at a stretch. His next-eldest brother was wise, could speak any language, and could answer any riddle posed to him, no matter how tricky. And Jack...well, Jack could do none of these things. Indeed, he was rather slow and simple, and frankly a bit silly, but above all, Jack was a dreamer.

Jack would dream of great adventures, of slaying giants and sailing distant seas. Of outwitting witches and finding treasure. And marrying princesses. He dreamed about that one a lot. As his brothers grew up and flourished, he stayed home and read the old stories, again and again.

Finally, the day came that his eldest brother left the family home to seek his fortune. Not too long afterward, his next-eldest did likewise. Jack realized that it was his turn. He would go forth into the world and have adventures just like he'd always dreamed of. One day, soon after his eighteenth birthday, he set off with a bindle over his shoulder and headed out into the wide world.

After three days of traveling, he found himself in a deep, dark forest. He made his way along, following the track that snaked its way through. He came upon an old woman, bent double with age and care, struggling to haul a load of firewood back to her cottage. Jack immediately offered to carry the wood for her, and spent the rest of the day hauling what felt like the better part of a tree on his back. He staggered after the old woman, who hobbled slowly along until they got to a ramshackle hut in a clearing by a stream.

And then, to Jack's great surprise, the old woman did not turn out to be a good fairy and was not just pretending to be a helpless old woman to test his kindness. She then proceeded not to tell him the answer to a riddle posed by an ogre, who was conveniently holding a princess hostage nearby. Nor did she give him a golden key to unlock a secret chest in a long-forgotten dungeon. She did give him some liniment for his back, though. So there was that, even if it was a bit whiffy.

Clearly, this was going to be harder than he thought.

Some days later, Jack came across a pool fed by a small waterfall, which hid a cave just big enough to crawl inside. Sensing this was the perfect hiding spot for a treasure, or possibly a long-forgotten magical item, he resolved to explore the cave. He worked his way in, lit a torch, and followed the curve of the tunnel until it came to a dead end about ten paces in. There, before his astonished gaze, was absolutely nothing. No treasure, no swords, not even an abandoned food wrapper, and those things get everywhere.

Dejected, he made his way back to the entrance, only to find it had begun to rain. Between that and the fact that it was almost evening, he wound up spending the night deep in the shelter of the cave. As he slept, he dreamed of seven maidens clothed in white, each on a golden horse. They sang to him in a tongue he did not understand and rode into the sky. Then he was one of them, and the others were all his relatives, and they were on their way to a family gathering that he really didn't want to attend. When they got there, he was made to recite his school lessons, but he couldn't remember them. He could only bleat like a sheep. Everybody laughed and said he would have to go and live as a fish. They threw him into a pond and went away.

The next morning, he woke up to discover that the cave was home to something in the way of ten thousand fleas, ticks, and other crawling things, all of whom had made themselves at home on his person.

This was really not going according to plan.

A few days later, the still-scratching boy came upon a hermit by the side of the road. The hermit explained that he had sworn a vow of poverty. His only sustenance came from selling the various holy relics he had acquired on his travels. Touched, Jack purchased from him a holy ring, cast in purest gold, which protected the wearer against ague, splots, and the galloping lurgi.

The next day, he came to a village where he heard tell of a woman who was ill. He brought the ring to her house, only to be told by her family that the so-called hermit was a known swindler and that his "holy" rings were generally poor imitations bought by the sack. Not only that, but Jack noticed the damned thing was turning his finger green.

He went away into the woods, lamenting his lot. "Oh, why?" he cried. "Why can't I find fame and fortune, and have a life of glorious adventure? Where are the princesses to save? Where are the treasures to find? Where, for that matter, is my money belt, which I swear I had on me when I met that damnable hermit? How can I be a hero in a world which seeks no heroics?"

"Thou wouldst be a hero?"

Villains

Jack looked around, but there was no one there. The voice was not an unpleasant one. Actually, it had a smooth, enticing lilt. "I would...verily, but it seems the world will not have me so."

"Mayhap we are able to do something about that."

Jack looked around. "Who are you?" he asked.

"That is not important. If a hero thou wouldst be, we have it in our power to make you the greatest of them all...that is, if thou wilt do what we bid of thee."

Jack nodded. "I would do anything to be a hero," he said.

"That's the spirit. We think we shall be very useful to each other."

* * * *

In the cave, Iyarra knelt beside Jack, listening.

"So this thing," she said. "It said it would help you to be a hero, but you'd have to do as it said. Do I have that right?"

He nodded. "I thought I was going to fight the bad guys, you know? It said it would guide my hand, and that the evildoers of the world would fall to my sword. Then it said it knew where we could find some villains. It could kind of sense evil. There was this monster, you see, chasing after a girl. So I got my sword out, all ready to fight, and then..."

"And then?"

"And then everything went all funny, and..." He shrugged. "Later, when I woke up, it told me that I had vanquished them. Saved the day. I guess I wanted to believe it." He shook his head.

"Anyway, we went to the Enchanted Forest, because everybody knows there's all sorts of monsters and things there. It was so...*good* at finding them, you know? Like it knew right where they were." Jack stopped and looked down, drawing on the stone floor with a finger. "I never remembered what happened when we found them. Not ever."

Iyarra nodded. "I see," she said quietly. "And then you met up with us?"

"That's right. I was so excited to meet two real, honest-to-goodness heroes. I couldn't believe you two would let me tag along. You were both so helpful, giving me all that advice..." He trailed off, staring at his shoes.

"And then Miss Revka said all that about helping the villains. I felt betrayed, you know? Like you had tricked me. I just got so mad." He rubbed the back of his head, hesitant to go on. "Uhm. But something went wrong that time. There was this wind. And all those people in robes? They were hanging onto you with ropes. I saw the looks on your faces and—" He gulped. "—and I ran."

Iyarra nodded. "The Librarians. When they rescued us, it must have broken whatever was keeping you from seeing what was happening."

"Librarians?"

"I'll explain later." She gave a little smile. "Or maybe Revka will. She's better at explaining things than I am. Anyway," she added, "what happened after that?"

"Well, I tried to talk to...you know, *it*. I told it I didn't think that what we were doing was right, you know? I said that I didn't want to do it anymore. And that for the next one we should just take them to the nearest town, hand them over to the sheriff or something. And then it said..."

"...Yes?"

Jack closed his eyes. "It said...it said that if I was going to stand in its way, then I was no better than the rest of them. There was this wind, and I felt like I was falling. Everything went black and...well, here I am."

Iyarra nodded. "I see." She looked around the cavern. In the distance, more bodies could be seen, each with the sickly black thing attached to its head and snaking up into the darkness. "The black things on everyone's heads, do you know what they're all about?"

He shrugged. "As far as I can tell, it seems to be the bad guys we captured," he said. "I thought it was like a jail at first, but now I'm not so sure." He rubbed his head. "Actually, I think it may be feeding on them."

"Feeding on them?"

He nodded. "I think so. Maybe it eats their dreams or something. Have you noticed they're all moving? I saw a witch acting like she was stirring up some kind of potion. And there was a troll earlier. I guess he was dreaming of fighting, because he looked like he was swinging a club around. I think they're dreaming, and somehow it gets something from that. Don't ask me what."

"You know," said Iyarra, "when I was...well, when I had the thing on, it was like I was having a wonderful dream. Everything was nice and perfect, but it wasn't right, somehow. I remember running and singing and spending time with my family, but there weren't any of the ordinary times, you know? Like, when you're just sitting around, or waiting for something, or whatever. It's like it skipped over the boring bits."

Jack thought for a minute. "I suppose that makes sense, actually," he said. "I think this thing, whatever it is, works in stories. When it feeds on your dreams, it follows the same rules. It's like how stories often have people eating and drinking, but they never go to the water closet." He thought some more. "Not most stories, anyway."

Iyarra stood up and walked over to the nearest body. This one was a witch—or at least, a woman dressed as one. Black dress, broomstick, the whole bit. There was even a pointy hat on the ground next to her. She was waving her free hand, her mouth forming inaudible syllables. Probably cursing someone. Iyarra poked gingerly at the woman, who wobbled a little bit, but utterly ignored the centauress.

"I think," Iyarra said, "that this is when we go and find Revka."

* * * *

It was difficult for Iyarra to say how much time passed. It seemed like a long time, could have even been days. With no sun or moon, it wasn't easy to get any sort of real bearing on things. Oddly, Iyarra never found herself feeling hungry or thirsty, no matter how long they walked.

"Story rules again," said Jack. "I think, wherever we are, the same rules apply. I mean, I can't remember the last time I ate or drank something. By rights, I should be dead by now. They don't eat ordinary meals in stories, because no one wants to read about that, you know? It's like it happens outside the story. All the ordinary stuff. I think that's what's going on."

There were more of the black tentacle things hanging down from the ceiling as they traveled along. Iyarra tried counting them, but gave up once they got past twelve or so. Most of them were attached to people, provided you were really flexible with your definition of people. There were monsters, and creatures who were like animals but stood upright and wore clothes. There was even another centaur, though not from any clan Iyarra knew. Some of the creatures reminded her of the basement lab they had explored, and the strange things floating in the jars. She shivered.

Eventually, they found Revka standing alone in a sparse side passage. She didn't seem hurt in any way that Iyarra could see. In fact, as they watched, Revka's arms twitched back and forth a little, as if fighting unseen enemies.

Jack peered at her. "Is she all right?"

"Oh yes. She does that in her sleep sometimes." Iyarra frowned at the black cap, giving it a little poke. "Well," she said. "You don't have any idea how we get this thing off, do you?"

Jack shrugged. "Search me. I didn't even know about them until I came here. I suppose there's some sort of trick to it."

Iyarra stepped back and thought. Revka would come up with some super clever plan, and it would probably work. Or sort of work. Or it wouldn't work, but it would cause something else to happen, and they'd get what they wanted anyway. If only she could think like Revka...

No. Only Revka could solve this Revka's way. Iyarra would have to find her own way to solve the problem. She knew she wasn't clever, but she wasn't helpless, right?

So what could she do?

"There was another one," she said. "Back where I got out. I tried to pull his off, but it wouldn't come. When I tried, he just sort of screamed and doubled up."

"Maybe it burrows into them," Jack suggested. "There's these bugs I've heard of, when they sting you, they have these barbs. If you try to pull them out, they're even worse. Could be something like that. Do you think?"

Iyarra shook her head. "I don't think so," she said. "I remember it hurt when I got out, but not that much. Still..." She bundled up her hair and held it up out of the way. "Here, have a look. Any marks or anything?"

Jack peered around the centauress's head. "None that I can see," he admitted. "Bend your head down. Let me see the top. Hmm, nope. Everything seems fine. Not even a scar or anything."

"Well, then it can't be attached too hard. I know when I got out, I didn't feel any pain or anything. Not in the head, I mean. I guess it just makes you think you're in pain if someone tries to take it off you."

"Good grief," said Jack. "Actually," he added, "come to think of it, how *did* you get out?"

"Well, in my dreams, I was just there with Revka. Then somehow, nothing was right, you know? I remember getting scared and running, then there was—oh, my gosh!" She slapped her forehead. "The box!"

"The box? What box?"

"The fortune-teller box! We met this lady earlier, see, and she had this box with a fortune teller in it. But not a real one, I mean a wooden one. She told us our future and said to beware of happy endings. The box said the same thing, and I was like, oh no! And I realized I was trapped, but then I got out."

Jack blinked, his head tilted in the classic, confused-puppy position. "I'm sorry," he said. "But could you maybe run that by me again?"

* * * *

The full explanation took some time, but Jack managed to get there in the end. "So what you're saying is that this box from the lady showed up and made you realize that none of your dream was real," he said.

Iyarra nodded. "Well, there was a little more to it, but yes."

Jack looked over at Revka. She was standing with her feet wide apart, bouncing up and down a little. She swiveled her head from side to side, taking in the nonexistent scenery with evident enjoyment. "So maybe there's a way to get her to know that she's stuck in a dream, but how do we tell her?"

Iyarra pursed her lips. "Good question." She leaned down to Revka and gave her a poke. "Hello?" She tried again. "Revka? Revka, if you can hear me, wave."

Revka didn't respond. She just stood staring into the middle distance.

Jack moved over and took a breath. "Hey!" he shouted. "Hello in there! Can you hear us?"

Iyarra flinched. "I don't think that's going to work," she said.

"Nuts." Jack sat back down again. After a moment or two, his eyes found their way to the stalk growing out of Revka's cap. "You know, we could try to cut through it."

Iyarra poked the strand snaking up into the darkness. "You think that would work?"

"Might."

"You have a knife?"

He fished one out of his belt. "Right here," he said.

Iyarra hesitated, remembering the fishman. "All right," she said. "But at the first sign she's in pain, you're to stop."

Jack nodded and moved into position. He laid his free hand on top of Revka's head, holding it steady, then began, very gently, to slide the knife back and forth against the cord. For a moment, nothing happened.

Revka let out a scream that made Iyarra's heart jump into her mouth, and Jack yanked the blade away with a yelp.

"OK, I don't think that was a good idea," said Iyarra. Revka had stopped screaming the instant the blade was taken away and gone back to staring off into empty space. Jack put his knife away and examined the cord. "Funny," he said. "The black stuff? It's just a skin. Underneath it's all pink. Come look."

Iyarra worked her way around to the other side. Sure enough, the knife had cut away the thin black skin and revealed a shiny pink underneath. "Good grief," she said.

Jack nodded. "Must just be there to protect this," he said, giving the tube an experimental poke. "I wonder if—*ow!*"

"What? What's wrong?"

Jack yanked his finger back. "That thing. I touched it, and it zapped me."

"Zapped you?"

"Yeah. Like, not real painful, but it felt like I was somewhere else. I think I saw her, too. Here, you try it."

Iyarra hesitated a moment, then laid a single cautious digit against the exposed tube.

The smell of the woods. The dappled sunlight of a small clearing. Birdsong. And Revka, stalking a small animal through the ground cover.

She yanked her hand back. Jack was still there, watching her. "Well?" he said. "Did you see her?"

She nodded.

"You think it's her dream?"

"Probably."

"You think we can talk to her?

"I'm going to try," she said. "I think one of us should stay behind and keep watch. You keep an eye on us, all right? If anything happens, pull my hand away from her."

"Will it work?"

"Don't know, but it's worth a shot."

"Uhm sure, all right, but do you think—"

"Thinking is not my job." A small, private smile curved Iyarra's lips.

* * * *

There was the scent of pine, the soft rustle of dead brown needles on the ground. Off in the distance, a stream burbled, and from every surface hung heavy, green moss. The place felt warm and humid...and old.

There was a small camp set off a little from the stream, the remains of a campfire. A few bits of familiar laundry that had been hung up to dry.

And a knife at her throat.

Revka stepped into view, keeping the knife steady. "All right, you," she growled. "Who the hell are you, and *what have you done with Iyarra?*

Chapter Twenty-One

IYARRA GULPED. SHE held very still, afraid to even breathe hard lest the knife pierce her skin. She put her hands up in the air very slowly. Revka stood where she was, glaring at her as if she was a total stranger.

"Revka?" Iyarra whispered. "It's me. Don't you recognize me?"

Revka scowled. "Cut the bull. I saw Iyarra disappear with my own eyes, just before *you* showed up." She narrowed her eyes. "You've got the voice right, I'll grant you that, but come on, you couldn't even get the right shape. Where'd you send her, huh? You might as well tell me now, save yourself some trouble."

"But I—" Iyarra stopped, running the last few lines back again in her head. "Wait. What do you mean I'm not the right shape?"

Revka smirked. "Missed one little detail, didn't ya?" She chuckled. "Thought you could fool me. Well, forget it."

Iyarra looked down at her hands. Same old hands. Down below, big old hooves, two more legs in the back. Everything seemed to be in order. "Sorry," she said. "I don't know what you're talking about. Everything looks all right to me."

"Oh, does it?" Revka smirked. "Well, why don't we have a proper look? There's the stream over there. Go on." She moved the knife down, giving Iyarra a little nudge in the ribs. "Have a look for yourself."

Iyarra obediently moved toward the stream, dreading what she would see. The trees covered the stream, right where it settled into a smallish pool, forming an almost perfect mirror. She collected herself, then bent down to have a look.

It was a nightmare. Some hellish thing looked back at her, all teeth and bones and flesh wrapped and tied over something that could only be called a face on technicalities. She screamed, throwing her hands up reflexively and turning away.

Behind her, Revka snorted. "Yeah, not exactly an oil painting, are ya? Now, start talking."

Iyarra recovered enough to try to put together some sort of answer, but nothing was coming. She fumbled and waved her arms around as if she could pull a coherent answer from the air. Where could she begin? How could she explain what was happening when she looked like...looked like...

Hang *on*.

Iyarra knelt and held an arm over the pool. She studied the scene before her. The image in the pool was every bit as horrible as what she had seen before. Above, her actual arm seemed normal. She waved it back and forth experimentally, waggled her fingers a bit. No, it wasn't her imagination, was it?

"Oh my," she whispered.

Revka leaned over her shoulder. "What are you doing?" she demanded. "You're not doing some kind of weird magic, are you?"

Iyarra shook her head. "Watch," she said. She moved her forearm to the right, as fast as she could. "Did you see?"

Revka craned. "See what?"

"Watch the arm. Watch it move. Here." She brought it to the left, sharp. "There! It did it again!"

Revka tilted her head. "Did what again?" Her eyes narrowed. "If this is some kind of trick…"

"It didn't move! It just jumped from one place to the other! It can't keep up! Something's making me look like this, but it can't keep up if I go fast enough. Here. I'll do it again." She waved her arm back and forth as fast as she could. In the water, the reflection jumped and flickered madly as it tried to keep up.

Revka took a step back. "Good grief," she whispered. "You mean, it's some kind of spell or something?"

"Yes!"

Revka tilted her head, eyeing Iyarra cautiously. "…okay. That's odd. Maybe you do have some sort of spell or something on you, but that doesn't mean you're Iyarra. Gonna need to see some more proof than that."

Iyarra sighed. "All right, all right…uhm, how about something only I would know? Like the time we were in Crowhaven and you hired yourself out as a dance instructor? Or your nickname when you were a kid? Oh, I know! Sometimes when you drink a lot you ask me to—"

"Okay! Okay!" Revka waved her hands. "That's enough." She stepped back and rubbed her chin the way she did when she was thinking. After a moment, she held up a finger. "Wait right here." She trotted back to the camp and returned almost immediately with a blanket. She shook it out, threw it out behind Iyarra, and stepped back.

"Well," she said. "There's a thing. You are now an ugly monster with a large blanket hanging in midair right behind you." She patted Iyarra's hide through the blanket and brushed lightly over the surface, noting the undercurrent of equine muscles. "I see," Revka said quietly.

Villains

Iyarra looked anxiously behind her. "Now do you believe me?"

Revka pursed her lips. "Almost," she said. "There's one way to make sure." She patted again. "Your haunches should be about here...yup, there they are. So, if I move down a little and along here..."

A loud yelp echoed through the woods, sending birds and beasts scattering in all directions.

Revka moved her hand away and grinned. "Yup," she said. "It's you, all right." She patted Iyarra's flank. "Come on," she said. "I think you'd better tell me what's going on."

* * * *

"...and then I touched the little pink tube thing again, and...well, here we are."

The two sat on opposite ends of the campfire. Iyarra was her old self again. Once Revka could see through the disguise, it had melted away. Revka, who had been unusually quiet, finally broke the silence. "I see. Wow. And you say this thing is just attached to my head?"

Iyarra nodded. "That's right, yes. We tried cutting it, but you screamed and thrashed around a lot, so we stopped."

"You know," said Revka. "A while ago...was it yesterday? Could have been days...anyway, I remember having this *wave* of pain come over me. Like something was attacking me, but there wasn't anything at all. It was pretty scary, I recall. I bet that was it."

Iyarra nodded. "I think time doesn't really flow right in this place." She shrugged a little. "Anyway, we've got to get you out of here."

"Right. So, how did you say you got out again?"

"Well, once I realized it wasn't real, I started fighting. It's like I could feel myself being trapped. I kicked and fought, and suddenly, there I was."

Revka thought about it. "Hm, okay. I wonder if, now that I know it's there..." She reached up to her head, patting around the top. "Actually, there *is* something there." She gave a little tug and winced. "Okay, that smarts. Did it hurt for you?"

Iyarra shook her head. "Honestly, I was too busy panicking. I must have yanked it out while I was thrashing around."

"I see." Revka sighed and took a deep breath. "Well, looks like there's only one thing for it." She began to tug on the invisible cord, gritting her teeth. "Come...on...dammit, will you...ghhh!" She stopped, panting. "I can't do it," she said. "I just don't have the leverage. You'll have to do it."

Iyarra bit her lip. "Are you sure? I don't want to hurt you."

"I know, hon, but it looks like it's the only way. Come on around."

Iyarra obediently circled around to Revka's back. She reached down, moving her hand into the space just over Revka's head. Sure enough, she could feel the cord in place. She got a good, hard grip on it. "Ready?"

Revka nodded. "Ready," she said. "And just keep going unless I tell you to stop. Hard as you can, now, okay? Promise?"

"Right." Iyarra braced herself and tugged.

There was a moment's resistance, an ugly tearing sound, the distant echo of a scream, and blackness.

* * * *

Revka dragged her head off the floor, letting out a loud groan. "Okay, that...I did not enjoy that." She looked around groggily. "Uhm, everyone okay?"

Iyarra sat up. "I think so," she said. "Jack, you okay?"

No reply. She looked over to where Jack was sea—to where Jack had been seated. "Oh, nuts," she muttered. "Now *he's* gone."

The two got to their feet. "All right," said Revka. "Where'd the little twerp run off to?"

"Search me," said Iyarra. "But I was only in there a little while. He couldn't have gone far." She tilted her head and started to sniff at the air.

"Any hint?" said Revka.

Iyarra nodded. "Oh, yeah. In a place like this? They might as well paint a trail on the floor, but..."

"But what?"

"But there's something else. It's like..." She waved a hand. "Well, you know I can smell fear, right?"

"Yeah, of course."

"Okay, well, this is like that, but it's kind of different. Animals all have their own smells, but you can tell it's the smell of some animal. Even if you don't know which one it is. This is...well, this is like that, but if fear were a creature? Then, uh, this is what it would smell like. Er, if that makes any sense."

"I think I see what you mean." Revka nodded slowly. "All right. We go slow." She pulled out her sword, testing the weight of it. "You got your daggers?"

Iyarra nodded. She fished them out and readied them. "Revka?"

"Mm?"

"What do we do if they've got him?"

Revka shrugged. "What do we always do? We improvise."

* * * *

It wasn't very long at all before they found Jack recumbent on the ground, unconscious and with a black cord affixed to the top of his head.

The two stood over him, taking in the sight. "Odd," said Iyarra. "When I first found him, he was free. I guess whatever it is decided to take care of that."

Revka looked around. "No signs of a struggle," she said. "You'd almost think he went willingly."

"Maybe they hypnotized him? It sounded like they already had a way into his head."

"Could be. Could be a trap. Wait here." She dropped to all fours and crawled along the edge of the wall toward the next bend in the tunnel. Iyarra waited obediently, watching her. Revka slowed to a snail's pace, checking each step before she took it. It seemed to take ages for her to fully disappear around the corner.

A moment later, she came trotting back into view. She shook her head.

"Nobody there," she said. "Not for a long way."

"All right," said Iyarra. "So, shall we go in and fetch him?"

"I expect so. How did you say you guys did it with me?"

"Well, we just shaved a little of the cover off the cord." Iyarra pointed. "See? Be careful not to cut the actual tube, though."

Revka nodded. She switched to her smaller knife and began to carefully work at the tube's outer coating. It took a little finesse, but before too long, she was able to expose a fair amount of the pink tubing. "Okay," she said. "Now what?"

Iyarra knelt down next to Jack. She gingerly clasped the tube and—*a country road, cresting a hill with a village down below.*

She yanked her hand back.

Revka looked up at her. "Worked, did it?"

"Yup."

Revka reached up and took hold of the pink tube. Almost immediately, she yelped and yanked her hand away. "Good grief!"

"You saw it?"

"Yeah. That's crazy. There was all trees and birds and everything. It was like we were back in the woods. I mean, that's what you saw too, right?"

"Yup."

"Funny thing, though," Revka frowned. "I didn't see Jack."

Iyarra tilted her head. "Now that you mention it, I didn't either," she said. "Funny. You would think he'd be there, it being his dream and all."

"Well, it's not like we got a good look. Anyway, it looks like it works. Shall we go in?"

"Do you think it will let us both in at once?"

Revka shrugged. "Don't see why not."

"All right, but..."

"What?"

"Would you hold my hand when we go in? I don't want to come out of this and have you be disappeared too."

"You bet." Revka smiled and reached over and took the centauress's hand. "You ready?"

Iyarra nodded. She gave Revka's hand an extra squeeze, then reached out and grasped the tube.

And off they went.

* * * *

The country road crested a gently sloping hill and wound down in a lazy sort of way 'til it got to the village. It was the usual sort of town you got in these places, just a strip of buildings on either side of the road. A bit of a creek off to one side served as the town's water supply. The land around had been cleared for farming, and sheep and goats could be seen grazing in the distance. Off the other side of the village, the road wound on in search of something more interesting.

Revka and Iyarra stood on the crest of the hill, gazing down at the view. For a long moment, Revka studied the town below, shading her eyes from the sun. "Well, I don't see him," she said at last. "Doesn't mean he's not down there. I guess we go down and start searching?"

"Uh, Revka..."

"Of course, the people might not take kindly to that. Though I guess being imaginary people they wouldn't mind too bad. Hey, you think this is his hometown?"

"Revka...?"

"Bet that's it. It looks like the kind of place a little—"

"*Revka.*"

Revka finally shut up. "What? You see him?"

"No. I was just wondering about the words."

"Oh, the words." Pause. "Wait. What words?"

Iyarra pointed. High in the air, words floated over the landscape in letters taller than any building Revka had ever seen. She read them, then read them again, because she couldn't quite believe it the first time.

"Oh," she said weakly. "*Those* words."

The two stood on the hill looking up. Four words and three dots. Just like that. Hanging out in the middle of the sky.

Iyarra rubbed her neck. "You think it's magic?"

Revka shrugged. "Hard to say. Not sure what would count as magic here. Remember, this is in Jack's head—and I still don't see him, by the way—so maybe this goes on in his head all the time."

"Well, maybe, but I didn't have big letters floating around when I was hooked up to that...thing."

"Oh, me neither, but it wasn't like real life, either. I mean, it was kind of real, but more like how you *want* reality to be, if you see what I mean."

"Oh, I know exactly what you mean." Iyarra nodded up at the words. "So that's what's in his head, then." She read it again.

Once upon a time...

There was a noise behind her. A figure came up the hill along the road, whistling tunelessly to himself, with a bindle slung over one shoulder. He looked more than a little familiar.

"Hello," he said. "My name is Jack."

CHAPTER TWENTY-TWO

IYARRA and Revka looked down into the open, honest, and almost completely vacant face of Jack. He smiled up at them, radiating unworldliness from every pore.

Revka cleared her throat. "Er, yes," she said in her talking-to-a-stunned-five-year-old voice. "We know. We've met. Revka and Iyarra, remember?" She waved her hand between them. "From the Enchanted Forest? And the cave?"

Jack's brow furrowed. "Cave? What cave?"

"The one we're all trapped in, remember? With all of the monsters and witches and things all hanging around with those weird hose things on their heads? Any of this ringing a bell?"

"Oh, no," said Jack. "I'm sure I would remember if something like that happened. I've just left home to seek my fortune and become a hero. I was going to head down into that village to see if I could be of any help there. Care to join me?"

"I really don't think so." Revka put her hands on Jack's shoulders and looked him in the eye. "Okay, Jack, I need you to listen carefully to what I'm about to tell you. This—" She waved a hand around. "—is not real. It's a dream. You're trapped in a cave with us, and there's this thing that's doing this to you. We don't know what it is, but it's plugged into your brain. We've got to stop it, and to do that, we've got to get you out of here. Got that?"

Jack's mouth dropped open. For a moment, he looked like he was about to speak, but a spasm rocked his body, sending his bindle flying into the bushes by the side of the road. Just for a fraction of a second, Revka could have sworn his body twisted in ways no human body should. She yanked her hands away, watching in horror.

Just as quickly as it had started, he was all right again. The bindle was back over his shoulder, the smile back on his face.

"Hello," he said. "My name is Jack. I've just left home to seek my fortune and become a hero. I was going to head down into that village to see if I could be of any help there. Care to join me?"

Revka exchanged glances with Iyarra. "Er, *maybe*." She held up a finger. "Excuse us just a moment. I need to confer with my partner here. Don't go away."

"Okay," Revka said when she and Iyarra had moved out of earshot. "Did you see what I think I saw? Because I'm not sure if I really saw that."

Iyarra nodded. "Oh, I saw it all right." She made a grim face, looking more than a little bit green. The average equine stomach comes in around six times that of your average human model, so when their stomachs turn, they *really* turn. That had not been a good moment for her.

"Any idea what that was about?"

"Not sure. Maybe the whatever-it-is is doing it to keep him from realizing what happened."

"Could be. Could be." Revka drummed her fingers on Iyarra's back. "May make things tricky, getting him out of here and all."

"So what do we do?"

Revka shrugged. "For now, I guess we humor him."

The pair went back to where a bemused Jack was waiting in the middle of the road. "Well," said Revka brightly. "Hello there, Jack. My name is Revka, and this here is Iyarra. We'd be tickled pink to go along with you. Wouldn't we, 'Yarra?"

"Oh yeah," said Iyarra. "Tickled pink."

Jack brightened. "Wonderful," he said. "I just know we'll find all sorts of adventures." He set off down the hill, whistling a chipper little tune as he went.

Revka turned to Iyarra. "Well, shall we?"

* * * *

The walk down to the village was short but pleasant. It was a nice enough looking place. Rather cleaner than such places tended to be in Revka's experience. Still, if this was going on in Jack's head, then this was probably just how he saw things.

Lucky bugger.

As they entered the town proper, Revka couldn't help but notice that there were far fewer people around than she would expect for that time of day. A couple of merchants in their stalls, a blacksmith, one old man who stood silently watching them and puffing his pipe. That was another odd thing; nobody was talking. The few people visible—and more than a few hidden behind shutters and cracked-open doors, if Revka was any judge—were silent as church mice, waiting to see what would happen next. Frankly, it gave her the willies.

The three stood in the middle of the town, such as it was, and looked around. Still quiet. More people appeared, all silent, all watching them. Without looking down, Revka let her hand drop down by her side, hoping the kid had imagined some weapons for her in this dream. She felt the comforting bulk of her sheathed knife and relaxed a little.

By now, more people were coming out. They were what Revka thought of as typical village folk: guys in smocks, fat, middle-aged women, and old fellows with whiskers. There were a few young people here and there. All of the villagers gazed at the trio in silence.

The three clustered together. "Okay people," Revka said out the side of her mouth. "Anyone have any ideas what's going on?"

"Not me," whispered Iyarra. "I just wish somebody would say something."

Jack looked around with apparent interest. "Perhaps they're waiting for us to start," he suggested.

"Hm." Revka cleared her throat. She stepped forward, holding up a hand. "Uhm, hi," she hazarded. "We come in peace. You know, peace? Anyone? Peace?"

That seemed to have some effect, even if it wasn't what Revka expected. An older gentleman, whose hair had migrated from the top of his head to just above his lip, stepped past her as if she was hardly there. "Thank goodness you've come," he said to Jack. "We've been waiting for you."

Iyarra did a double take. "Wait, Jack, you know these people?" she asked.

The old man smiled. "Know him? Why, he's the hero, come to save us all. Aren't you, young sir?" The old man put his hands out in welcome, smiling warmly at Jack. Jack opened his mouth to speak, but Revka got there first.

"Well, he's more of a trainee hero. An apprentice, you might say. Fortunately, as it happens, my colleague here and myself are fully capable of handling any standard, hero-type emergen—"

There was a lurching sensation, like someone had grabbed the world and yanked it back. If Revka had known what record players were, she would have likened the sensation to the world jumping back a groove, complete with the fingers-on-a-chalkboard screech as the dream unceremoniously rewound. Iyarra and Revka exchanged glances. If anyone else had experienced it, they gave no sign.

The old man stepped past Revka and put a hand on Jack's shoulder. "Thank goodness you've come," he said. "We've been waiting for you."

There was an expectant silence. Revka nudged Iyarra. "Go on."

Iyarra tilted her head. "What? Oh! Right. Sorry," she said. "Do you know him?"

The old man smiled. "Know him? Why, he's the hero, come to save us all! Aren't you, sir?"

Jack beamed. "Why yes," he said. "How may I assist you fine people?"

The old man pointed up the road. A castle sat alone, perched at the top of a hill that Revka was prepared to swear hadn't been there before. "An ogre has taken up residence in the old castle. He comes down at night and steals our food. He's even threatened to kidnap our children to slave for him!"

Revka looked the castle over. It was a bit of a wreck, frankly. Old stone walls, bits of masonry beginning to crumble. Even from a distance, she could tell the place was in a state of serious disrepair. Her brow furrowed. "There's somebody living in *that!?*"

Iyarra nodded. "Tell me about it. I mean, even an ogre."

"Never you mind." Jack puffed out his chest. "I will rid you of this dread menace! You just leave everything to me!"

"To us." Revka sidled up. "You weren't thinking of leaving your faithful sidekicks behind, were you?"

You could almost see the wheels turning in his head. "Why...yes. That's right. You are my sidekicks. Of course. How could I leave you two behind? Let's go!" He reached down, pulled a sword out of a scabbard that had *definitely* not been there before, and pointed up the road. "To the castle!"

The girls exchanged glances. Iyarra raised her eyebrows at Revka, who just shrugged. "To the castle," she said.

Iyarra nodded. "To the castle."

* * * *

The road had once been wide and clear cut, but years of neglect had clearly taken their toll. The three followed the course as it wound its way up the hill, switching back again and again as it worked its way up the slope.

"So," whispered Iyarra once Jack was sufficiently ahead of them. "What is going on here, anyway?"

"Well," said Revka, kicking a stray piece of gravel. "I think I may have an idea. Remember the words in the sky?"

"Mm-hm?"

"Look again."

Obediently, Iyarra looked. The sky was clear, with only the occasional wisp of a cloud drifting by. "Oh."

"Yup. And you heard the way those people talked back there? You ever people hear talk like that before?"

"Well, no." Iyarra shook her head. "It seemed kind of, I don't know, stilted? Like, it wasn't quite regular speech. I don't think I've heard anything like it before."

"Well I have, when I was a kid. We had these storybooks, y'see, full of fairy tales and whatnot. And they all talked like, 'Oh, goodness me. You must save us!' Like that, you know? And we know that our friend here wants to be a hero, right?"

"Yeah."

"Okay. So what I figure is, this is his dream world. We know this whatever-it-is gives you what you want to dream about, right? Well, I think this is a story, and he's a storybook hero. I reckon we aren't going to get him out of here without helping him get all the way through to the end."

Iyarra whistled low. "Wow," she said. "You really think so?"

"Seems like the most likely explanation to me."

"I suppose..." Iyarra made a face. "Thing is, though..."

"Mm?"

"The heroing. He's, uh...he's not very good at it, is he?"

Revka grinned. "Well," she said. "We'll just have to help him get good."

* * * *

The castle, such as it was, had clearly had time to settle in. The foundation stones looked as if they had more or less grown out of the ground. In fact, once you got up close, it was a bit difficult to tell where the landscape ended and the castle began. The trio inspected the structure with a fair measure of doubt.

"Picturesque old heap," said Revka. She kicked a stone, which went tumbling into what had once been a moat, but was now essentially a ditch with pretensions. She nudged the drawbridge with her toe. "Wood's in bad shape," she said. "Iyarra, I'm not sure if—"

The drawbridge whipped up with a crash, nearly taking Revka's leg with it. "Okay," she said as Iyarra pulled her back to her feet. "So much for plan A. Any ideas?" The two girls turned to Jack, who immediately assumed the deer-in-the-torchlight position.

"What, me? Oh, uhm, I dunno. I guess I sort of just assumed we would sneak in. Uhm, somehow?" He wilted a little.

Revka stepped over and clapped a hand on his shoulder. "First time?"

"What? No!" Bless him, you could actually see his eyes moving back and forth, as if hastily reading some long-remembered text. "I've done this, oh, hundreds of times. It's just that, usually, you sneak in dressed as a washerwoman. Or, uhm, a…secret passage? I think?"

"You sneak in dressed as a secret passage?"

"Hush, Iyarra." Revka faced Jack. "Oh, a secret passage. Well, why didn't you say so?" Revka swept her arm out before them. "Lead on, fella!"

Jack stood there for a moment, frozen with indecision.

Revka decided to be kind. "Okay, tell you what. How about me an' Iyarra go ahead and see if we can find a way in. If you see us making any mistakes, you just sing out, all right? How's that sound?"

Jack sagged with relief. He nodded vigorously. "Oh, yes! I mean, yes, that would be fine." He stepped back a little. "So, uhm, out of interest, where do you think you should start?"

"Well, that's very kind of you." Revka cracked her knuckles. "I suppose we might as well start by working our way around the perimeter of the castle." She grinned. "If that's all right with you."

"Uhm, yes. Yes, that sounds…good. Okay. Uhm, off you go, then."

"Thank you ever so very much."

* * * *

As it happened, the journey around the castle was a bit of a hike. Between the stones, the weeds, and the generally decrepit nature of the place, they actually had to go the long way around some of the larger obstacles and double back. Eventually, however, they found themselves at the back of the wall. Or rather, where the wall had been. A good chunk of it had caved in, providing a convenient gap once one had clambered through the moat and scraped the mud off.

"Okay." Revka looked around. "Thoughts?"

Jack stepped forward. "All right," he said. "If I were an ogre, where would I be?"

The girls exchanged glances. "The kitchen?" suggested Iyarra.

"The treasury?" offered Revka. "That's where I'd go."

Jack screwed his face up into a look of intense concentration, or possibly constipation. Really, it could have gone either way. Eventually, he said, "No, I think he'll be in the throne room. He's probably sitting on the throne, counting his ill-gotten gains and laughing an evil laugh."

This was a new one on Revka. "What, just laughing?"

"Oh, yeah. They do that, you know. Villains, I mean."

"Just sit around, laughing? Like, ha, ha, ha, it's hilarious how evil I am? That sort of thing?"

Jack made a face. "Well, maybe not *quite* like that, but sort of. I read it. All the big bad guys do it. So we just have to sneak in, listen for the laugh, and we'll find him. Easy."

Iyarra quirked an eyebrow at Revka, who shrugged. "What the hay?" she said. "It's not the worst idea I've ever heard. Okay, Jack, lead on."

They crept around the back of the main building until an open doorway took them to the back kitchens. The place had clearly been built to cater for some heavy-duty feasts, once upon a time. The pantry itself was bigger than any house Revka had ever been in, and the main kitchen had a whole wall of ovens, spits, cooking pots, and firepits to keep it all going. Jack might be a bit of a twerp, but he sure could conjure up a good castle. They moved through the big empty spaces, keeping as quiet as they could.

The way out led to a maze of passages that, to Revka's eye, looked more or less the same. Jack moved through them quickly though, as if he knew the way. Of course, he was making all this up, so he more or less did. A narrow passage opened into a wider one, with tapestries hanging along one wall. Up ahead, they heard the sound of distant snoring.

The three crept along the passage, Iyarra moving extra slowly to keep her hooves from echoing off the stone floor. The trip down the hall seemed to take ages. The silence spread until there was only the snoring and the thumping of their heartbeats.

Finally, they came to an open intersection. To the left, the hall opened into a large area filled with old tables and benches, most of which had been shoved haphazardly against the wall. There was a general sense of neglected grandeur, of bygone luxuries left to decay. The three slowly brought their heads around the corner and peeked.

The ogre was slumped in the throne at the far end of the room. There was a high table set before him, with plates covered in half-eaten grub. He was large and bald, his only hair covering his arms and belly. An old ermine cape hung over his shoulders as a sort of makeshift blanket, and his feet were propped upon an empty spot on the table.

In the middle of the room, someone had cleared a space and built a fire pit. Beside it, several chairs and other pieces of furniture had been dragged into place and smashed to bits. The ogre might not have had a lot of food, but he clearly wasn't going to be wanting for firewood any time soon.

Revka nodded to the others. She pointed down along the side wall, then along the back and right up behind the ogre's throne. The others nodded, and the group set out.

They crept around the corner, keeping close to the wall. If the progress in the hallway had been slow, this was practically a crawl. The ogre's snore filled the room, echoing off the walls and rebounding on itself. It occurred to Revka, rather belatedly, that there was no way he was going to hear anything short of a brass band with all that going on.

She turned round to Iyarra to tell her she could lay off the sneaking, and only then noticed that Jack had disappeared. Curse that boy, where the hell did he go?

"Quit this place at once, foul fiend!"

Jack was standing foursquare in the middle of the room. He held his sword aloft, legs spread, every inch the picture-book hero. In his makeshift throne, the ogre snorted, rumbled, and woke.

Revka put her hand over her eyes as the ogre threw the table aside with a mighty roar. "Jack," she muttered. "You almighty twit."

Chapter Twenty-Three

THE OGRE LEAPED DOWN to the floor, brandishing a table leg as a makeshift club. "WHO DARES DISTURB ME?" he bellowed.

Jack didn't even budge. "I do," he said. "The villagers have had enough of you, and they sent me to get rid of you. I advise you to quit this place at once and never come back."

The ogre's laugh echoed through the castle. "You!? They sent you? Do you actually think you have a chance against me, you little human?"

Jack stuck his chin out, inasmuch as he had one. "That's right," he said quietly.

"Okay, seriously?" The ogre was no longer shouting. It stood not ten paces away, looking the boy over. "Are you actually going to go through with this?"

Jack waved his sword in the ogre's direction. "It is my duty as a hero," he declared with the serene confidence of a complete idiot.

The ogre growled. He covered his face with a large, hairy hand for a moment, then tried again. "Look," he said. "You seem like a nice kid, but you know I'm going to cream you, right? I mean, look at you." He gestured toward Jack with his free hand. "You're a kid. Don't look like you've ever shaved in your life. You're holding the sword wrong too. Bet you've never been in a proper fight. And now you come in here, against me, who has wrestled animals three times your size to the ground. I mean, how was this supposed to play out, just out of interest? I just want to know what you thought was going to happen here."

Jack didn't even hesitate. "I will vanquish you, because I am good and you are evil, and good always triumphs in the end."

The ogre let out a low whistle. "Good grief," he said. "You really got it bad, don'tcha kid? Well, I'll tell you what." He sauntered toward Jack, swinging his club back and forth. "I'd feel kinda bad about bashing your head in, it being barely used and all, so I'll just break your arms and send you back to the village. Best offer you're gonna get today. And when you get back there, tell 'em to send up some greens next time, will ya? I'm not getting any roughage up here."

"You may joke—"

"I don't."

"You may joke, but I'm not leaving until you're gone. Your reign of terror ends this day!"

"Yeah, yeah. Sure, kid. Whatever you say." He stopped just within skull-crushing distance and looked Jack over. "Tell me something," he said. "Before we get started here, what possessed you to come up here all by yourself to tackle an ogre like me?"

"Oh, I'm not all by myself," said Jack quickly. "I've got my friends with me too." He pointed behind the ogre to where Revka and Iyarra were just sneaking up behind him.

Iyarra groaned. She cupped her hand over her face and muttered a quick stream of Low Equine. Revka threw her hands up. "Way to go, kid," she said. "Smooth job. Thanks a heap."

The ogre's face broke into an unexpected grin. "Well, well," he said. "Three against one, eh? Now, that's more like it." He cracked his huge knuckles. "This should be fun. Won't hurt the pantry, either. Save me a hunting trip. Well, now. Who wants to go first?"

"Now, wait." Revka held up her hands in a placating gesture. "Let's not be too hasty here. Before we start swinging swords and clubs and things, let's just talk about this, can we? Look, we just want to know if there's any way we can talk you into leaving. You know, pack up and move somewhere else. It can't be great, can it, big old stinky castle like this? I mean it's practically falling apart as it is. And you know this place is going to be an absolute bear to heat in the winter."

"True," added Iyarra. "And the maintenance? You know a place like this is just going to be one thing after another."

"Well, you have a fair point." The ogre scratched his chin. "But here's the thing; I'm basically evil. If I need something repaired, I go down to the village and smash stuff until they promise to come up and fix it. If I need food, I grab some. Basically, my whole thing is I get people to solve my problems for me. Simple but effective, you know? So I think I'm gonna stick to what works. Now, you three wanna beat it, or what?"

"Got any arguments for that?" Iyarra hissed out the side of her mouth as she nudged Revka in the ribs.

"Nothing comes to mind, no." Revka coughed. "Uhm, well. Under the circumstances, I think we can safely say negotiations have failed." She turned to Jack. "Over to you, kid. What's the plan?"

Jack did the bit with the sword again. "We fight him and slay him with righteous justice!"

"Yeah, I thought it was going to be something like that. All right, let's get on with it."

It is an acknowledged fact that odds of three to one are no picnic, even when the one is an ogre, and one of the three couldn't fight his way out of a paper bag. By mutual agreement, Revka and Iyarra spent most of their time trying to distract the ogre away from Jack, who seemed determined to charge in and whale on him without any sort of strategy or basic tactical sense.

It has to be said, though, the kid had guts. Not a lick of sense, but hey, guts. He kept charging at the ogre and swinging his sword like a man possessed. Once in a while, he'd nick the ogre somewhere in the area of the thighs, only to get backhanded or kicked across the room. He always sprang right back up, though, and came charging back in right up to the point where the whole thing went to hell.

Dodging around the ogre's left side, he moved in to strike a quick blow up at the monster's exposed ribcage. Unfortunately, it was exposed because the ogre had his arms raised, about to bring the club down on Jack in a very fatal way. Revka, seeing what was about to happen, cannoned into Jack from behind. She managed to get him out of the way, but caught the corner of the club across her back. This sent her flying into Iyarra, who had been setting up for a rear attack. The two spilled onto the floor just in time for Jack to stumble backward, trip over his own feet, and drop his sword.

The ogre regarded the two women impassively. "Well," he said. "I can't say it hasn't been fun, but I think it's time we wrap this up. It's going to take forever to get you guys properly butchered, and I don't want to be all night in the cold room. Any last requests?"

Iyarra put up a sheepish hand. "First offense?"

The ogre snorted. "Funny. Now, be good and hold still, and it'll be nice and quick. You wiggle around a lot, this is going to take longer, and believe me, you don't want that."

"Wait!" Revka held out a hand. "Look, you beat us. Fair's fair and all that, but before you finish us off, just tell me something. Who are you, anyway?"

The ogre chuckled. He put his hands akimbo, posing a little as he spoke. "You have the honor of being defeated by the great Bugar, scourge of the Wolfjaw Mountains! Slayer of sixteen separate knights, dasher of hopes, squasher of...I'm sorry is there something funny going on here?"

Revka and Iyarra looked at each other, both trying unsuccessfully to stifle a laugh. "I'm sorry, I'm sorry." Revka waved a hand as she tried to collect herself. "It's just, what did you say your name was again?"

The ogre peered at them quizzically for a moment, then grunted. "I said, I am the great Bugar, scourge of—" But they were off again.

Revka lost what composure she'd had. "Oh, my gosh!" She cackled. She looked up at the menacing figure. "Your name is actually Booger!?"

"What? No! It's Bugar! *Gar!* Don't call me that! I hate it when people call me that!"

Revka nudged Iyarra. "He's right," she said. "We shouldn't make fun. After all," she grinned, "growing up with a name like that? You know he was constantly being *picked* on!"

Iyarra snorted through her laughter. "Gross! Yeah, people would probably say, 'Is your name really Booger?' And then he'd say, 'No, *itsnot!*'"

"Ooo, good one!" Revka clapped her hands, laughing loudly. "Oh, wait! I got another—"

"Enough!" the ogre thundered, raising his club again. "I'm going to smash you both to pieces!" He hesitated a moment, as if something in the previous statement sounded wrong in some indefinable way, but shrugged it off and prepared to attack. He hefted his club over his head and prepared to deliver the death blow.

He stood there a brief second, club wavering in the air. His expression changed to a puzzled frown, then a look of genuine surprise. He dropped the club, wobbled a bit, and began to pitch forward. Revka barely rolled out of the way as the ogre hit the floor followed by Jack, who had forgotten to let go of the sword.

"Nice." Revka darted forward and gave the ogre one in the neck for good measure. "Was beginning to think you'd never make your move back there." She gave the body an experimental kick, but the life was definitely gone. "So. Job done, I guess."

Jack tugged the sword out of the ogre's back with some difficulty, then stood over the body, panting. "I did it," he murmured. "I actually did it."

Revka slapped him on the back. "Yeah, kid, not bad at all."

Jack caught himself and tried to recover. "I mean," he said. "I got another one. Ogres, you know. No big deal, really. When you're a big hero like me, you see dozens of..." He trailed off. "You...you aren't buying any of this, are you?"

The two women shook their heads. "Nope," said Revka. "But you did good. I bet if we leave now, we could get back to the village before nightfall. What do you say?"

The boy shook his head. "You don't understand," he said. "All my life I've dreamed of doing something like this. Rescuing princesses, slaying dragons, even fighting ogres just like...just like..." He looked around the room at the castle walls, and finally down at the inert form of the ogre.

"Just like this," he whispered. "It's all right out of my dream." He poked at the ogre's body with his sword. "He even looks exactly the same as I imagined. This is...this is another dream, isn't it?" He looked up at the two women, as if seeing them for the first time. "Revka? Iyarra? What are you doing here? Where *is* here?"

Revka patted him gently on the shoulder. "You may want to sit down," she said. "This is going to take some explaining."

* * * *

The three sat in the ruined castle. Jack stared at the floor, swinging his legs idly. "So that's it?"

"Afraid so," said Revka. "It basically looks in your head to see what it is you want, then gives it to you. And you stay asleep, or under its spell, or whatever it's doing. We haven't figured that out yet, unfortunately."

"Good grief," the boy whispered. "And it got you both too?"

"Oh, yeah," said Revka. "Fortunately, Iyarra was able to go in and lead me out, just like we're here to do for you."

"Really?" Jack turned to Iyarra. "And how did you manage to escape?"

The centauress scraped a hoof along the stone floor. "Long story," she said. "I think I had a little outside help."

"Anyway," said Revka. "It seems like once you know where you are, you can actually escape. The thing on top of your head? See if you can feel it."

Jack reached up. His eyes went wide. "Gosh."

"Right? Now hold still." Revka moved around behind him. "This is going to hurt a bit, but not for long."

Jack nodded and braced himself. "Okay."

Revka found the spot. She wrapped a hand around the invisible cord. "Ready?"

"Ready."

There was darkness, a burst of color, and a wrenching sensation as the world snapped back into place.

The trio lay on the cave floor, panting. Revka groaned and waited for the world to stop spinning. Apparently, this didn't get any easier with repetition. She managed to sit up and rub her temples until some of the pain faded away.

Villains

Iyarra clambered to her hooves. "Everyone okay?"

Revka cricked her neck and managed to nod. "Oh, more or less," she said. She gave Jack a tap. "Hey there," she said. "Still with us?"

Jack sat up slowly, kneading his temples. "Oh, ow," he muttered. "I feel terrible. Did that really happen?"

"Well, not *really*, really," said Revka. "It was, uh..." She waved a hand vaguely.

"A story being told inside your head," Iyarra supplied.

"Yeah. That. It was a real imaginary thing, so to speak."

Jack didn't answer. He sat up, rocking back and forth, staring off into the middle distance. After a long moment, he spoke. "You know what?" he said. "I don't think I'm really the hero type."

"Oh now, come on." Revka gave him a reassuring pat. "Nobody starts off as an expert. We all gotta learn our way along. Why, when I—"

Jack shook his head. "I don't mean that," he said. "I mean, I think I've been fooling myself all this time." He got up and waved an arm around the cave. "All my life, I've read these stories, and dreamed of being a hero just like the ones I'd read about, but I never had any idea what it was really all about. I mean, I thought it was all bravado and medals, and being noble while everyone swoons over you, but it's not like that at all, is it?"

The two women exchanged embarrassed looks. "Well, not as a general rule, no," admitted Revka. "Honestly, most of it is just finding your way to the next meal."

"Which is not to say," Iyarra cut in, "that we *don't* have real neat adventures. It's just that you don't usually notice it at the time."

"Right," said Revka. "Normally you're just thinking, 'Man, I hope I don't die in the next few minutes.' It's not until later that you look back and you're like, wow. That was really something."

"Exactly, yeah."

"So it's just basically survival?"

"Well, it's more than that." Revka rubbed the back of her neck, trying to find the words. "It's like, sometimes you're going along, minding your own business, then suddenly there's this thing that has to be done, you see? And if you don't do it, nobody will."

Iyarra nodded. "That's it," she said.

Jack looked up at the two. "Really? Just doing what has to be done?"

"Pretty much."

"Our elders have a saying," said Iyarra. "If not me, then no one. If not now, then never. It means it's up to us to fix what is broken, even when there's no reward or recognition or anything. It's just what you do."

"Yup."

Jack sighed. "See? I don't think I could do that. All I've got is a dream. And heroing is no job for dreamers." He picked up a pebble and threw it, sending it skidding across the cavern floor.

"I think I need to go away and think for a while," he said.

Iyarra looked around. "Go away where?" she asked. "We're all stuck in this cave."

"Just...alone. For a little while. I need to think about things." He smiled. "You go on without me. I wouldn't want to get in your way."

"Now, hold on," said Revka, but the boy was already walking down the tunnel, back the way they had come before.

The two women watched him go. "Should we go after him?" asked Iyarra.

Revka shook her head. "Let him go," she said. "I think he's got some thinking to do."

Iyarra nodded. "All right," she said. "So, what about us?"

Revka shrugged. "I guess we go on," she said. "Somewhere in this cave is whatever is doing this. I guess we'd better hunt it down."

"And then?"

"And then...well, hope like hell we think of something."

* * * *

They continued down the tunnel, following the tendrils that snaked along the ceiling. Every so often, they would come across another victim, silently acting out whatever deeds were taking place in their heads. It seemed to Revka, as they moved along, that the tunnel was getting larger. The tentacles that snaked along the ceiling were getting thicker and joining together as they went.

After what might have been an hour, inasmuch as she could judge, the end of the tunnel opened up ahead. There was a feeling of a large space beyond. Revka motioned to Iyarra, who nodded, and shuffled close to the wall.

The duo crept their way toward the opening. Revka moved close to the edge, then peeked around the corner.

A vast chamber stretched farther than the dim light would let them see. Tunnels came from several directions. Each had black tentacles coming from them and snaking up into the darkness. There were more creatures here, dozens of them, and each of them unlike anything either woman had ever seen. A creature apparently made of stone, with long diamond tusks, moved in a strange and unidentifiable pantomime. A rainbow-colored blob floated in midair, occasionally burbling to itself. A slime-covered creature crawled along the floor, its tentacles reaching out in front as it went. Every creature was tethered to a black tentacle, which snaked up into the darkness. The two women crept into the cave, passing creature after grotesque creature.

Iyarra tiptoed past a green-gray thing that looked like someone had sewn a dog's head to an ape's body and left it out in the rain for a few years. "What *are* these things?" she whispered.

"No idea." Revka shook her head. "But I don't think they're from our neck of the woods."

After a few minutes, they came to what must have been the center of the chamber. A bulbous, black, glistening thing sat in the middle, the dim light of the cavern catching it oil-slick in unwholesome ways. A tree-trunk-thick stalk stretched from its center up to the roof of the chamber, where all the tentacles came together. Every few seconds, the main part would grow a little, then shrink back.

Revka stepped forward, Iyarra trailing behind her. The two women gazed at the sight, trying to make sense of it. "You ever see anything like that?" Revka whispered.

Iyarra shook her head. "Not me," she said. "I don't even know what it is."

"Well, no, you wouldn't."

"I mean, I don't know if it's an animal, or plant, or what."

"Oh, I see." Revka tilted her head. "Looks kind of planty," she said after a moment. "But plants don't move, do they? This one almost looks like it's breathing. I wonder if—"

There was a voice, or rather, the sensation of a voice. It was like the words were just dropped straight into their brains. The utterance felt cool, almost reptilian, with an echoed hiss trailing behind.

I really think it's time we stopped playing games, don't you?

Chapter Twenty-Four

REVKA LOOKED UP AT Iyarra, who nodded. She'd heard it, too. Revka cleared her throat. "Excuse me," she said. "Um, who exactly are we talking to? Sorry."

To me.

"Yes, but who are you? I'm Rev—"

I know who you are. Have I not ridden your minds? But you seek a name. I fear I have no use for such a thing. I am merely myself.

"Huh. Okay, uhm…you," Revka stepped toward the ebony mass in the middle of the room. "You mind telling us what is going on?"

The voice laughed. *I have a better idea. Why don't you tell me? I should like to hear what you think.*

"Okay." Revka began to sidle around the room, picking her words with care. "I think that you're behind this whole thing with the disappearing villains."

Go on.

"I think…" Revka licked her lips. "I think that you're tapping into them, somehow. You feed them this kind of dream, and in return they give you…give you…"

Keep going, the voice said. *You're doing very well. What do they give me, pray?*

Revka racked her brains. "Is it…is it something only bad guys have? Because I noticed you took us, too."

There was laughter. *Oh, no. Everyone has it. They just have more. Go on.*

Revka looked at Iyarra, who shrugged. "Maybe using them as some sort of food?" She hazarded.

Close, but not the way you mean. Keep trying.

"Look." Revka had had enough. "We don't know, okay? And nobody's here to play a stupid guessing game."

Oh, but you're so close! I'll even give you a hint. You're using it now. And if you were using it more, you would know.

"What's that mean? You don't mean intelligence, do you? You're not sucking their smarts out or something?"

"Imagination," Iyarra said. "You're taking their imagination."

Well done! I knew you would guess it! The voice was positively giddy. *You are correct. I give them a place to dream and they feed me the fruits of their dreams.*

Revka shook her head. "Sorry. Wait. You mean you actually *eat* imagination?"

Oh, yes. Villains are such fertile sources of it, you know. Heads so full of ambition and dreams, so easy to harvest. They are innately tied to the narrative power. And, of course, there are so very many of them.

"But it's just imagination. Just...you know, making things up. I don't see how it could be food."

Just making things up? JUST making things up? Do you honestly not understand the power you have? I have traveled across eons, moving from star to star, and I tell you that not one world in a thousand is capable of supporting even the most primitive life. Of those, not even one in ten thousand ever gains a creature capable of imagination. Did you never think to ask yourself what makes you different from the beasts that roam this world? Why you have the power to speak, and build, and learn, and become?

There was a sound very like a sigh. *And yet, and yet...you have this exquisite power, to be able to look at the world and say, this could be otherwise. You use that power to entertain your children. To make each other laugh. You are beasts who have learned to dream, and thus you are capable of anything. And you treat it like the most natural thing in the world.*

"Now, look," said Revka. "We were told that if the villains were all taken away, all the life would drain out of the world. I'm not sure if I quite understood it, but—"

Oh, existence would continue, said the voice. *Don't you worry about that. You would still get up in the morning. People would be born and die. The world would carry on.*

Iyarra narrowed her eyes. "But existence isn't the same as life, is it? I mean, we'd be alive, but if you're saying what I think you're saying, we wouldn't be *people* anymore. We'd be like..." She waved an arm vaguely, then turned to Revka.

"Uhm, aardvarks?"

"Well yeah, but really any animal." She shook her head. "I don't think we'd like that at all."

And now the voice took on a note of sardonic glee. *Well, now. That's just the thing. You wouldn't mind it at all. You wouldn't be able to. Those who cannot dream cannot comprehend what it is to dream.*

Whole worlds spin on, emptied of their imagination, yet they live. And they do not suffer. For suffering needs the idea that things could be better, and that is beyond them now. Really, when you think about it, I'm doing them a favor.

Revka shook her head. "You're a monster," she whispered.

Monster!? The voice was sharp with rage. *How dare you? Look around. These are the monsters! From every world, I find them and take them and render them harmless. I am the very opposite of a monster! I am the ultimate benefactor. Entire worlds bathe in dreamless sleep because of me! My destiny, stolen from me by such as you, I claim anew!*

"Stolen?" said Revka. "What the hell are you talking about?"

You heroes, it sneered. *You ride the stories to your happy endings, never thinking about those who must fail that you may succeed. Shall I tell you what I am, little heroes?*

I am the Father, slain that his son may avenge him.

I am the Warrior, whose death tells the danger ahead.

I am the Second Son, destined to fail so the third may prevail.

I am every set of bones at the entrance to the dragon's cave.

I am every character who was smarter, stronger, wiser, more deserving...but not chosen.

In every story I am found. And in time I have grown in power. I have chosen myself. Now, I do what you never could. I take all of the evil from the world. I leave it in perfect peace. If that happens to also mean the end of heroes...well. I don't really see a problem, do you?

And now two tentacles snaked down from the ceiling, heading toward Iyarra and Revka. *But now, I think it's time we finished our little discussion. I'm afraid I can't force you to accept the conduits, seeing as you seem to have found your way out. Perhaps I can persuade you to go peaceably. I believe I can weave you into a shared dream together. You two are quite rich veins indeed, you know, and I should regret having to destroy you.*

Revka eyed the tentacles. "Yeah," she muttered. "We wouldn't be too thrilled about it ourselves." They were coming closer, weaving with a snakelike hypnotic rhythm. Her hand found her belt and closed around the hilt of her sword.

"Look," said Iyarra. "You don't need to drain them all, do you? I mean, surely, you could leave something?"

Laughter. *Have you been listening? It will be centuries before I find another source as rich as this. And you would have me starve in the meantime? How very heartless of you. No,* the voice sneered. *I believe I shall stick to the plan as it is, thank you anyway. Now, then. What is it to be? A beautiful dream or a painful death? Make your choice. I grow weary of this.*

Revka caught Iyarra's eye. The centauress nodded.

"Well," said Revka slowly. "Since you put it that way, I suppose we have no choice."

Very good. Now, if you'll just—

Revka raised a hand. "You don't understand. I said we have no choice, and we don't. You see, there's no way we could allow you to hook us up to those things while you drain our world."

"Yeah." Iyarra stepped forward, shaking her arms loose and drawing out her daggers. "Give up without a fight? You may have been in our heads, but you didn't learn anything about us."

So be it.

The tentacles lashed out at once, whipping toward the two women at speed. Revka tumbled to one side, just managing to avoid hers, while Iyarra caught a glancing blow on her flank. She stumbled, but recovered enough to slash at the tentacle before it could react.

Revka rolled, brandished her sword, and slashed at the tentacle hard. It whipped out of the way, the tip of the blade only knocking away a scrap of the black, oily skin. She growled and dove at the tentacle again, going for a direct jab. She missed completely and staggered forward.

Iyarra, meanwhile, had managed to get a grip on hers. She wasn't as fast as Revka, but when you're half a giant farm horse, you tend to stay where you damn well please. She wrestled the tentacle to the ground, then struck with one of her daggers. A yellow-green ichor sprayed out of the wound, and the tentacle thrashed wildly beneath her. Iyarra brought all her weight onto it and kept stabbing away until it stopped moving. All the while, the bulbous creature screamed in agony and rage.

"Good girl!" shouted Revka. She made a leap for the one attacking her and hung on for dear life. She tried to stab at it with her sword. "Help me with this one!"

Iyarra galloped across to Revka and brought the tentacle down with a flying tackle. "Got it!" she yelled. "Give it a good whack!"

Revka let go. She dropped to the ground and brought her sword down hard, right at the end where the lily cap was attached. The scream was even louder this time. Iyarra shifted her weight just enough to let the tentacle whip away and back into the darkness.

Revka got to her feet, panting. The two women looked around. Was that it? Surely it couldn't be as simple as...

Iyarra heard them first. Footsteps, yes, and the shuffling of things that couldn't be called feet. Strange shapes emerged from the darkness. Creatures of every color and size, empty-eyed beings closed in on them from every direction. Some were already fighting. They came grasping, pounding, and swinging fists. They had no weapons, but that was no real comfort. When you're a hulking creature twice the size of your opponent and made entirely of stone, a weapon is really rather optional.

Revka swore. She adjusted her grip on the sword and started toward the nearest target. A pinkish-gray thing that looked like a brain with teeth squished its way toward her, making disgusting slurping noises as it came. Revka wondered how much of a threat it could be, moving slowly as it did and with no visible arms or—

Without warning, the thing spit a glob of thick, green gunk right at her. Revka just managed to dodge the gunk, which hit the stone floor with a faint sizzling noise and etched a pit in the stone. Okay. That stuff was definitely bad news. She trotted around, sidestepping while drawing closer. The thing tried to follow her, but she easily outmaneuvered it until she was able to get behind it. She brought her sword down into the heart of the creature and it expired on the spot.

Iyarra, meanwhile, was finding herself more than occupied. Some spindly, insect-like things, almost as tall as she was, had come for her, but their fragile, outer shells had proven quite helpless against her powerful kicks. The results were not pretty to look at, but she got the job done. Now, one of the stone giants had closed with her and was swinging its giant hammer fists. She ducked and weaved out of their way but was unable to find an opening. Not that she would know what to do if she had. None of her weapons would penetrate stone, and as for her hooves? It would be like, well, like kicking a mountain. "Revka!" She called, ducking yet another swinging fist. "Little help here, please?"

Revka tackled the winged, remora-looking thing that had been menacing her, and wrestled it to the ground. She sliced off the head, or at least, what the thing had for a head. The corpse flailed around underneath her, spraying reddish-brown blood all over the cave before it finally subsided. She scrambled to her feet and ran toward the centauress.

Iyarra was backing away from the stone creature, leading it in a sort of slow circle. Revka crept around behind the creature and looked it over, hoping a weak spot might suggest itself. Nothing. Back, neck, legs...all stone. Damn. She hazarded a glance between the behemoth's legs. All stone down there, too? Well, that just wasn't fair. Hell, the only thing that wasn't made of rock on that thing was...

Bingo.

"Yarra!" Revka sheathed her sword and pulled out a couple of small daggers. "Keep him occupied!"

Iyarra rolled her eyes. "Not a problem." She ducked and stumbled back again.

Revka licked her lips, watching the creature's movement and choosing her moment. When the thing crouched, she made her move. One leap and she was on its back, two daggers wedged between plates of rock. She scrambled her way up, using the daggers to find purchase on the monster's back. The thing swayed, waving an arm vaguely behind it, but it wasn't nearly fast or agile enough. She reached the shoulder.

Revka plunged one dagger into a shoulder, then brought the other one up and straight into the black cord. The creature reared violently and brought its two titanic hands down over the top of its head, howling with pain. Revka worked as fast as she could, hacking away at the outer skin of the cord before slicing into the tender pink beneath. It was over in a second. The monster swayed, stumbled, and fell straight back with a thump that echoed across the cavern.

Revka, who had just managed to leap clear, landed badly a few steps away. She sat up and rubbed her head, groaning. Iyarra hurried over and helped her up. "Are you all right?"

"Rough landing," Revka said. "But I'm good." She looked around. There were others, too many others, and now they were keeping their distance. While the girls had been fighting, several of the creatures had formed a wall around the pair. They stood now, mute, empty-eyed, and swaying, hemming the two women in.

"Krep," muttered Revka. She sidled close to Iyarra. "Okay," she whispered. "I think we can take that slug-looking thing on the right. It and the blobby thing look like the weakest links. If we—"

A dozen of the long, black tentacles came from all directions, descending and lashing themselves around the two women before they could react. Iyarra found herself splayed out, one tentacle on each leg, holding her quite immobile. Revka was bound from shoulder to feet by three different cords. She struggled against the bonds, but was unable to even make them budge.

INSIGNIFICANT CREATURES! The voice boomed throughout the cavern. *You had your chance, but now I will destroy you! I will lock you away in never-ending nightmares. You will beg for death, but there will be no respite. I will make you watch as I drain your planet dry, then I will leave you to wander its soulless wastes, the only ones left to carry the knowledge of what has been lost.*

Of what you failed to stop.

"I suppose," said Revka weakly, "that it's too late to reconsider your previous offer?"

Shut up.

"Ah. Thought so."

Now, just hold still.

Two new tentacles snaked into the room, each with a bulb on the end. As the two women watched, the bulbs began to grow. Thin layers of black skin peeled away and dropped like petals from a dead rose. *This is going to hurt.*

The shedding outer layers left a smaller, inner set of petals. These opened out slowly, revealing a small, pink bud in the middle. It glistened unwholesomely in the cave light and was covered with what appeared to be fine, white hairs. Revka writhed hard against the tentacles that held her, but couldn't escape.

"Stop."

Revka blinked and looked around for the source of the voice. It wasn't her, and it wasn't Iyarra. She tried to turn her head, but could only manage it about halfway.

But halfway was enough.

"Well, I'll be," she murmured.

A shape stood silhouetted against one of the tunnel mouths. It was tall, a bit lanky. Not what you'd, necessarily call a hero's physique. There was something in the way it carried itself, though. It was the stance of someone who had had enough and who would quietly, calmly walk through goddamn walls if they had to.

The shape stepped forward, a young man with short, sandy hair, dressed in simple traveling clothes. The peaked, green cap on his head had a feather in it.

"Hello," he said quietly. "My name is Jack."

Chapter Twenty-Five

LAUGHTER SHOOK THE ROOM. *Ah, yes. And here we have our little hero, in at the end to save the day. I do have that right, yes? You with no sword, no plan, no anything. And yet you come. Why, it's almost charming.*

I think I'll kill you last.

Jack stepped forward. His voice trembled slightly and wasn't completely free of adolescent cracking, but there was a steadiness that hadn't been there before. "I'm here to stop you," he said simply. "This...all this...it has to stop."

Revka groaned. "Kid," she cried. "Get out of here. Find help. Tell people what's going on. There's some people in the forest! They—" A tentacle smacked the back of her head, momentarily stunning her into silence.

Do you actually imagine you have a chance against me, boy? I made you. I bound myself to you. When you wanted to play at being a hero, I gave you the power to actually do so. Oh yes, that's right! The voice took on a gleeful note. *Your friends don't know, do they? Why don't you tell them? Tell them what you did, and why you cannot touch me.*

Revka and Iyarra found themselves lifted up and turned around to face him. He stood alone, empty-handed, but with an expression of absolute calm. He looked at the two women, then spoke quietly. "When I first went off to become a hero, I didn't have much luck. Didn't really know much about the world. I guess I still don't. I thought if I just went out and did like they do in the stories, it would all work out, you know?"

"Well, it didn't take long for me to find out it doesn't work that way. I'll spare you the details, but anyway, this...*thing* found me." He gestured toward the glistening, black entity. "Said it could help me. Said I'd be the biggest hero of them all. That together we'd wipe out villainy forever. I mean, why wouldn't I want that, right? So it told me to...to..."

Revka groaned. "Oh, kid," she whispered. "What did you do?"

"It said it needed an avatar, a body to help it. I would let it bind itself to me, and it would share its powers. We would hunt down any villains and defeat them, but that's not what happened, is it?" And now his voice rang with anger. "You were just using me! You didn't care about good or evil, you just wanted to feed!" His voice dropped. "And I fell for it."

Yes, the voice said quietly. *Yes, you did.*

"Uhm, look," said Iyarra. "Any chance you could, maybe, let him go? You already beat us, and he knows you got him, so there's no point in keeping him, is there? I mean, you might as well."

Oh, but I can't do that. Tell them why, boy.

Jack looked down at his shoes. "When this thing bound itself to me," he said, "it was permanent. I can't break from it. If it dies, I die. If it severs the connection, I die. I'm stuck with it for life."

The creature laughed. *That's right! So if you want to go on living, you're just going to have to continue being a good boy and fetching me more vict—ah, I beg your pardon. I mean catching more ne'er-do-wells for me, but it's not all bad. You can still pretend you're one of the good guys, if you want. Tell yourself that enough times and who knows? You may actually come to believe it.*

Jack shook his head. "No," he said quietly. "It ends here. You see," he began to walk forward, a strange gleam in his eye. "I've figured it out. This, all this..." He waved his hand around the room. "This is all just another story. It's obvious. I mean, good grief, you even *sound* like a villain! Do you hear yourself? But you can't help it, can you? Because you are a creature of stories, and you can't be any other way."

"But it's okay." He stretched out a hand. "Because a story has to follow rules. And believe me, I know how stories work."

And then there was a sword. Nothing fancy, no ornate etchings on the blade or jewels in the pommel. Just a simple, clean, very sharp blade.

Foolish boy.

Even the girls could hear the not-quite-hidden tinge of fear.

This isn't one of your stories. This is real. And you're going to find out just how real it is. I own you. Your life is mine. If you want to continue breathing, you will do as I say. Now, take that sword of yours and kill these two. Do not hesitate. Remember, I can always find another to do my bidding. Now. Kill them.

Jack shook his head. "It's too late," he whispered. "I told you I figured out that this is a story, but that's not all. I've worked out which kind of story this is. You see, in this story, the hero is led astray, but in the end, he sacrifices himself so that evil may be defeated." He turned to the two women. "Revka? Iyarra? Thank you for everything you taught me." He turned back to the black creature and began to step toward it, sword in hand.

Revka groaned. "Oh, Krep. Look, kid, whatever you're thinking..." The tentacles slid off and away, and she slumped to the cave floor. They whipped at Jack, trying to catch him, to trip him up. He just parried them without even looking. The creature screeched and bellowed imprecations that echoed throughout the cave. Jack kept walking. He got close, unstoppable now, moving on sheer narrative momentum, and then...he leapt.

Rules.

Everything, no matter what it is, has rules it has to obey. There are rules of movement and nature, rules of work and play, and in a story, rules of narrative. The third son always succeeds. The true love's kiss breaks the spell. And when the hero makes a desperate, last-minute sacrifice, there is only one way that it can go.

It's possible that no force on earth could have stopped Jack in his leap. He held the sword, two-handed above his head, and brought it down, hilt deep, into the heart of the creature.

There was...not a sound. It was more of a feeling. A sensation of pain and rage and defeat that shot through the cave and everyone in it. Iyarra and Revka doubled over in pain. The world shook as if it was going to come crashing down on them. An eye-searing light preceded a chaotic confusion of shapes, then darkness and total silence.

After a moment, Revka cracked her eyes open. As they adjusted to the darkness, the familiar shapes of the old forest came into view. Dead leaves rustled under her. She shifted to a sitting position. Iyarra was next to her, rubbing her head and groaning.

Revka laid a hand on Iyarra's shoulder. "You all right, hon?"

"Just sore." Iyarra nodded. "Nothing that won't heal." She jerked a thumb to one side. "It's him I'm worried about."

Revka craned her neck to see. Several paces away, in a small clearing, lay Jack.

She hurried over. He was in a bad way. His body seemed gaunt, rail thin, his skin an unhealthy pale. He was breathing, but only just.

One eye managed to focus on Revka. "We...we made it out?" he whispered.

Revka nodded. "Yeah, looks like. At least, I think." She reached up and tapped the top of her head. Nothing there. "OK, yeah. I think we're good. You got it, kid. Good job."

Jack tried to smile. "Then I saved the...the day?" he managed.

"Yeah, kid. You totally did. Bona-fide-hero stuff. But listen, we need to get you out of here. Get you to a doctor, okay? I need you to stay with me."

Jack shook his head. "Too late," he whispered. "Remember what that thing said? Tied to me. Can feel my life going. Almost gone."

"Oh now, don't say that!" Revka's voice took on a desperate cheeriness. "A few weeks' rest and we'll have you up and around in no time! You'll see. You'll be fine, guy. We'll help you."

He just laughed. "Could almost...believe you, but...it's okay. I was the hero. All my life...wanted to be the hero. I did it. What...no one else can, right?"

"Yeah, but—"

He held up a hand. "Please. Revka, Iyarra...you taught me...how to be...real hero...thank you."

"Oh kid, don't talk like this. It's gonna be all right, I promise. We're just gonna...kid?" She peered closer. There was no mistaking the emptiness behind the eyes that she knew all too well. "Oh, *kid.*"

His jaw hung open and his eyes went half-lidded. She tried to close them, but they wouldn't stay shut. "Dammit," she whispered, and leaned back.

As she knelt beside his body, she felt a hand on her shoulder, and looked up.

Iyarra gave her shoulder a pat. "Er, I didn't want to interrupt, but there's like a hundred monsters and witches and things, all milling around. I think things are about to get kind of hairy."

Chapter Twenty-Six

REVKA STOOD UP. ALL around them, others were getting to their feet. Some were getting to their paws or their tentacles. One was just hovering in midair. They looked confused and out of sorts, milling around and trying to get their bearings. It wouldn't be long before they started asking questions.

Revka and Iyarra began to back away. "What do we do?" whispered Iyarra.

"Dunno," Revka side-mouthed. "Give me a second, maybe I can think of something." Some of the nearby creatures were beginning to eye them suspiciously. There had to be a way to get out of this...

Ah.

"Okay," Revka whispered, trying to keep still. "I think I have a plan. Just...follow my lead. Okay?"

Iyarra nodded. "Okay," she whispered. "Whatever it is, I hope it works."

A couple of witches were muttering to each other, casting glances at the two. An ogre pulled himself up and gave them a suspicious glare.

Well, now or never.

Revka threw her head back and laughed. "NYA-HA HA HA HA HAAAAAA!"

Iyarra blinked. What the hay?

Revka swept her arms out, holding one in the air like a bad actor. "The fools! The blind, blind fools! They thought they could defeat *me*, Revka the Terrible! But I showed them, oh yes. I showed them all. YA-HAHAHAHAHAAAA! Igor, laugh with me!"

"What?" Iyarra ducked her head and whispered.

"That's you. You're Igor," Revka murmured, hiding her mouth behind a theatrical gesture of her hand.

"Oh. Right," Iyarra whispered. She lifted her head and laughed aloud. "Ahahahahaha."

"Great job, hon."

"So perish all meddling do-gooders!" Revka called out. That got their attention. Several of the baddies cheered. A few waved their fists, or whatever else they had.

"And now!" Revka reached down. Thank goodness all her stuff was still there, right where it belonged. She pulled her sword out of its scabbard and held it aloft. "Come, Igor! Let us return to my lair, so that we may formulate a plan to destroy them, once and for all."

At this, all the villains and monsters and creatures gave a rousing cheer. Several brandished weapons. They turned as one and took off in all directions. Within a minute, the clearing was empty.

"Wow," said Iyarra. "I can't believe that worked."

Revka put her sword away. "To tell you the truth," she said, "neither can I." She shrugged and gave Iyarra a lopsided grin. "Still, what the hell?"

Iyarra folded her hands in front of her. "So," she said. "I guess we head back, now?"

"Not just yet," said Revka. "There's something we have to do."

* * * *

The sun was just beginning to duck behind the trees as the two women made their way out of the forest. Behind them, right where the sun lit a small clearing, a small mound of freshly turned earth rested. There was no greenery there, but a few flowers had been carefully moved into place. A stick had been driven into the ground. On it hung a battered, green-felt hat with a broken feather.

Time passed. Winter came and buried the mound in snow. Spring came with its winds and blew away what was left of the hat. Grass grew, then flowers. The mound of earth sank into anonymity, but there was always greenery there, and there were always flowers. And the sun always managed to find its way down to that one particular spot, no matter what the season.

And there ends the story of Jack the Hero.

* * * *

Where does a story end?

It's all very well to come in with a "happily ever after," but that doesn't mean it's over. The tyrant might be toppled, but who's going to make sure the kingdom keeps running? The prince and princess might wind up together, but will the relationship last past the ogre-rescue stage? The dragon may be slain, but who's going to clean up the mess?

Perhaps a story only truly ends when another one begins.

Perhaps...

Brother Conan lay the note on top of the book in his tent and did one last check. Gray robes neatly folded, check. The medallion identifying him as a member of the Withdrawn, check. The various tools and items that belonged not to him, but to the brotherhood, were all laid out, all accounted for.

There wasn't much left for himself but the clothes on his back and a few personal belongings, his old sword. Even the horse belonged to the librarians. Well, he'd get another soon enough.

It wasn't quite dawn as he crept out of the camp. Saying goodbye to everyone and trying to explain would have been awkward. Better this way. He'd had a taste of heroing, and looking after books just wasn't enough anymore. Somewhere out there, a future was waiting for him to carve his story into it.

Best get on with it, then.

He crept through the woods until he found a road. He headed west, toward the distant mountains. The morning sun bathed his muscled torso in golden light.

His story was about to begin.

* * * *

In another part of the Enchanted Forest, Mother Vieille felt a pricking of her thumbs. She looked around suspiciously, then stepped outside. She closed her eyes for a moment and let herself drift out into the world. There was something different out there, something she couldn't...

Ah, there it was. Balance. *Rightness.* A pain that had been around so long she'd got used to it had suddenly slipped away. She stood by the doorway, drumming her fingers against the jamb. Then, in the manner of someone testing a hypothesis, she pinched at a portion of the wall. The brown matter crumbled, and a small chunk came off in her hand. She brought it close, sniffed, rolled it in her fingers, then tried a careful bite.

Behind her, the wall healed itself as she chewed thoughtfully. After a moment, she nodded to herself. All was right with the world again, yes indeed.

Fresh gingerbread. You just couldn't beat it.

* * * *

On a road through the Enchanted Forest, a woman and a centauress strolled along in no particular hurry. Their conversation wandered almost as aimlessly as the trail which wound through the trees.

"All right. How about this...we have to have evil because it shows us what good is."

"I'm not at all sure that's true."

"Okay. Uhm, monsters are people too?"

"Ehhhh."

"Okay. Well, uhm...evil is...is...no wait. Um..."

"You know, Revka, maybe there isn't actually a moral. Have you thought of that?"

"Oh, there's got to be a moral. Big adventure like that, villains and things. Gotta be. Just wish I could suss it out, that's all."

"If you say so."

"Okay. How about this..."

The women walked along, leaving behind them only the sounds of the forest. All around, the woods teemed with life as nature went about her business. Ahead, there was nothing but the future.

Which, as endings go, ain't half bad.

THE END

(for real this time)

About K.L Mitchell

K.L. Mitchell was raised all over the south in a series of increasingly tiny towns until she finally joined the Air Force out of a desire for some Culture. She's spent most of her professional life working on computers in one capacity or another, and occasionally manages to get them to actually work.

She's been writing for fun most of her life, and for publication since about 2011. She's written for multiple websites and local publications, and in 2013 was a recurring columnist for the Kansas City Star. She lives with a gray cat named Molly and would like to be an astronaut when she grows up.

Connect with Kelly

Email: k_l_mitchell@mail.com

Facebook: https://www.facebook.com/KLMitchellHere/

Cover Design By : Rachel George
www.rachelgeorgeillustration.com

Note to Readers:

Thank you for reading a book from Desert Palm Press. We appreciate you as a reader and want to ensure you enjoy the reading process. We would like you to consider posting a review on your preferred media sites and/or your blog or website.

For more information on upcoming releases, author interviews, contest, giveaways and more, please sign up for our newsletter and visit us as at Desert Palm Press: www.desertpalmpress.com and "Like" us on Facebook: Desert Palm Press.

Bright Blessings

Made in the USA
Middletown, DE
17 September 2022